THE
FALL

An addictive crime thriller with a fiendish twist

D.E. WHITE

Detective Dove Milson Book 5

Joffe Books, London
www.joffebooks.com

First published in Great Britain in 2024

Cover art by Nebojša Zorić

ISBN: 978-1-83526-343-3

PROLOGUE

Witness Transcript: * * * * * * *A188360*

She was one of those people who could draw people in, you know? She used everyone, but because she made you feel special at the same time, like you were the only person who mattered, she got away with it. And she was gorgeous, sexy, and a little bit dangerous, yeah, that didn't do any harm, either.

She would come and go, never seemed to have a proper job, but always had some money. I never thought where it came from. We all knew she did drugs, pills mostly, and she drank too much, was a bit wild, but you only ever saw the glamour with her. Everyone always noticed her.

As we got older, it seemed harder for her to settle. The pills, I suppose, but she always told us she could take them or leave them. It was around that time, maybe a few months before, that it was really obvious she couldn't. Leave them, I mean. And I think that scared her. In the end, it was probably exactly what she needed, that scare, and it was pretty ironic that she was looking for a way out, a second chance when it happened.

I know what she did, because she told me outright, and I can kind of see why, but that doesn't stop it being tragic.

Looking back, the one and only time I saw the other side of her, perhaps the real her, was the night she died.

1

CHAPTER ONE

Detective Dove Milson was fiddling with the car radio when the three people plunged from the bridge.

By 8.35 p.m. the evening shadows had lengthened to darkness, and a light rain had started. Two hours ago, rush-hour traffic, full of tourists heading back from the coast, would have jostled with commuter traffic heading back home from London. But now the road was quiet, a great swathe of almost empty tarmac, lightly sprinkled with rain. After an unseasonably warm day, the clouds had rolled in from the sea, and the fog descended, reducing visibility to a few metres.

It was possible to make out the three huge concrete bridges which spanned the M27 motorway, only when you were almost underneath them. The wisps of sea fog dipped and swirled in the car headlights.

Dove's eyes were gritty and her shoulders aching after the long drive back from Cornwall in busy Friday night traffic. Trying to get comfortable in the passenger seat, her attention was on choosing a radio station when she heard her fiancé Quinn's sharp intake of breath, heard him swear and looked up. She gazed straight into the road ahead, just as they went under the first bridge. Something was falling from the bridge. *Someone* was falling. As Dove watched in horror and disbelief, she could see it wasn't just one person falling helplessly onto the deadly tarmac below, but several.

It seemed to take mere seconds for the first dark shape, silhouetted against the foggy, shadowed skyline, to hit the road. Seconds were all the nearest drivers had to swerve violently out of the way, to slam on their brakes.

"What the hell?" Quinn had stopped the car with a jolt, and was staring straight ahead. "Were those jumpers, or did something get chucked off the bridge?"

Brake lights flashed red as the final few vehicles ahead and around them ground to a halt. Vehicles were scattered across all three lanes, but at least they were stationary now. Those behind were now stopping too.

Her heart was pounding uncomfortably hard, and her breathing was fast. She still couldn't quite understand. How many people had fallen? Or was it an illusion — as Quinn suggested, debris and not bodies at all? There had recently been trouble with vandals chucking concrete blocks into the traffic from all three bridges. It was also a spot for suicide jumpers.

She shivered, straining her eyes upwards, trying to see if there was anyone on the bridge itself. But fresh tendrils of fog and the light rain on the windscreen blocked her view.

The three huge, arching bridges spanning the motorway were close together, concrete landmarks scarring the chalky, cliff-like boundaries of the motorway. From her position almost underneath them, they looked as tall as skyscrapers.

The road was flat here, right at the crest of the hill. Dove could see more vehicles were stopping behind them, and to their side. Ahead, in the gap between the scattered cars and a heavy goods vehicle, she could now spot something lying in the road. A dark shape sprawled on the darker tarmac.

Jumping from the fatally high bridge to the tarmac of the motorway below was never going to result in anything pretty. She could feel sweat start to prickle between her shoulder blades.

"It *is* jumpers. I can see someone in the road. What the hell is going on?" Dove snatched her phone out of her pocket, calling in the jumpers (or could they be fallers?) as a major incident.

Quinn carefully manoeuvred the car so they weren't blocking the route for the emergency vehicle. Then they were both out of the car, running towards the body Dove relaying information to the police call handler as she did so, phone clutched tightly in her sweaty palm.

She could hear her own voice, clear and calm, but it seemed to come from a long way away, lost in the clinging misty swathes of the sea fog. Her long dark hair flopped heavily across her shoulders as she ran towards the sprawled figure in the road.

CHAPTER TWO

In the aftermath of the incident, after that momentary eerie silence, the road now seemed to be filled with screams, crying, shouts. A smell of burnt rubber and metal emanated from some cars under the third bridge, where those behind had been unable to avoid those before them slamming on their brakes as they tried to avoid the fallers.

Quickly Dove counted — just seven vehicles involved. The fog seemed to be getting denser, shrouding the scene, creating an apocalyptic atmosphere of fear and disbelief.

Up ahead, almost right under the bridge, the huge HGV had stopped just in time, brakes still hissing with the strain. Its trailer was skewed across both carriageways, but amazingly still upright. The driver had jumped from his cab and was shouting something at another driver, who had left his car on the hard shoulder and was jogging towards the main crash site.

Dove was relieved. By some miracle, there appeared to be no serious injuries among the occupants of the vehicles. In rush hour, it would have been another story. She spoke quickly to the HGV driver, and he agreed to collect his hi-vis jacket and make sure the southbound traffic was stopped, well ahead of the incident, at least until the police arrived.

There wasn't anything else he could do to move his vehicle until the cars involved could move anyway.

"Get whoever is last in the queue to put their hazard lights on if they haven't already!" she called after the driver, as he jogged swiftly away. He turned briefly, gave her a thumbs-up and continued. Dove, satisfied the scene was as safe as she could make it, ran towards her fiancé, who was already bending over the first body sprawled on the road.

Dove slipped a little on the wet tarmac in her flip-flops. She wiped a hand across her eyes, her face damp with drizzle and the sweat of urgency and yanked a band out of her pocket, tying her hair out of the way. Ready for business. But the adrenaline was making her feel shaky. Her phone rang briefly as Control called back for an update, and Dove once more forced her voice to stay steady, clearly communicating what was happening. It was all about the facts and the numbers in her job, about staying focused on the task in hand.

She sounded professional. She knew she did . . . but standing in the middle of the motorway in denim shorts and flip-flops, fresh from a Cornwall heatwave, with a pool of blood inches from her bare toes, she felt anything but.

It took a while to adjust, to move her brain from holiday mode to work mode, but she found, to her relief, she was quickly taking in the vehicles, their positions, the people walking or standing helplessly under the vast bridge. With her photographic memory, she could recall so many useless facts, but also crime scenes down to the smallest detail. She glanced up again, narrowing her eyes against the shadows, trying to see movement, in fact, anything, but the top of the bridge was now cloaked in fog.

"Looks like we've got three jumpers," Quinn called out to her from his kneeling position. Bystanders gathered around, eager to help, or moved as far away as possibly, talking shrilly into mobile phones.

Dove looked down at the broken body of a woman. The long, curly dark hair was spread out on the road, the face mercifully hidden. There was a lot of blood, mainly around her head, and in a couple of places, Dove could see the pale sheen of bone. Open fractures on both forearms and her left leg made the scene particularly gruesome. But the worst thing was meeting Quinn's eyes, and seeing her question answered.

Quinn shook his head. "She's gone, I'm afraid. Possibly catastrophic bleeding from internal injuries, and she has massive trauma to her head." Shaking his own head, he muttered, "Shit" as he gently laid a hand on the dead woman's shoulder and reached down to close her eyes.

Dove moved with him to the next body, a young male. He had landed just a few feet from the first victim.

A bystander with grey hair and an umbrella, whose car door was still open, keys dangling from the ignition, glinting silver in the headlights of the vehicle behind, asked, "Is she dead, the first one? Are you police?"

"Paramedic and police. Yes, she's gone, I'm afraid," Quinn told her. "Emergency services are on the way, so it's just a question of seeing if we can do anything before they arrive." He added, grimly, "So sad. I still can't believe it."

As Dove and Quinn knelt either side of the second victim, she watched the bystander take off her coat and place it gently over the dead woman in the road.

"I'll look after her." The woman's voice shook, but she seemed steady enough, and Dove felt a raw pain in her own heart. She shut down hard on the emotion, focusing on Quinn, who was tending to the male victim.

A couple of teenagers were already bending over him as well. When Quinn introduced himself, they said they were both St John's Ambulance cadets, and had, like all the other drivers, swerved to avoid the three jumpers.

"We didn't move him. His neck is sort of twisted where he fell, but he's still breathing okay." Concerned expressions and breathless explanations.

"Good lads," Quinn said. He looked up at Dove, hope in his face. "They're right. He's still with us!" He turned to the cadets. "Keep him still as you can, and keep your hands where they are."

"Do you think he can hear us?" one of the boys asked anxiously. Dove caught sight of the new driver plates on a red BMW parked in the middle of the road.

"He might be able to. You can reassure him. Tell him not to move. Meanwhile, keep his head still, and monitor his breathing. Check he's maintaining an airway. The ambulance will be with us soon, okay?" Quinn was quickly, expertly checking the rest of the body.

The cadets nodded, heads bent, focused on their tasks, faces pale and set.

"His wallet must have fallen out of his pocket when he fell," one of them added. "I've got it safe. He had an ID card in the front and his name is Mark Davies."

Dove relayed this information to control, then put the phone on speaker so Quinn could also talk. The helicopter would be with them in twenty minutes and would transport the worst injured to hospital. The fog would make flying difficult, but they would try. The weather was still above minimal operating restrictions. She thanked God, not for the first time, that Quinn was a Critical Care Paramedic and, ironically, had recently been seconded to the air ambulance for six months.

Quinn looked up quickly from the boy. "Okay, let's move on to the next one."

Another woman bending over the third victim shouted at them, distraught, "Oh my God, do you know first aid? The woman over here, I think she might be alive."

"Hell," Dove muttered. "Come on, back up!"

Quinn and Dove moved immediately. To their relief, the wail of sirens could be heard, and the flash of blue lights pierced the muggy clouds. Dove felt like they had already been on scene for hours, but in reality — she glanced at her watch — it had been barely fifteen minutes. The rain was getting harder, washing the blood away in little streams. She once again wiped her wet face with her forearm, as she crouched with Quinn, ready to help the third victim.

The third jumper was another female. She was stirring, muttering, and combative, apparently unable to move much, but pushing away hands that tried to help her with surprising strength. Dove was pleased to see that, as usual in a crisis, members of the public had risen to the occasion, padding the patient's head carefully with a coat, as she thrashed around, laying a blanket over her broken body.

It never failed to warm Dove's heart how most people would try to save a life, and how much basic first aid was absorbed unconsciously from watching TV or reading books.

"We're trying to keep her still, but she's saying something, slurring her words. Do you think she's been drinking?" A tall man in a business suit was soaked from the rain, his hands shaking as he tried to gently restrain the injured patient.

Dove had already clocked the blood trickling from one of the woman's ears, and although Quinn spoke gently and clearly, asking her name, reassuring her, it was obvious from her blown pupil, and blood leaking from the ear that she had a potentially life-threatening head injury. Both arms also seemed to be comprehensively shattered, with open fractures to her radius and humerus.

The patient moaned again, and flailed an injured arm about, spraying blood onto the tarmac. She had fallen further away from the others, landing next to the central reservation, just missing the metal crash barriers.

Had they all jumped together as a suicide pact, or was this a terrible accident? Dove's mind was already spinning with potential motives, even while she gave her concentration to the patient lying between them. Quinn was again working quickly, trying to preserve another life, and she almost instinctively put her own hand onto one of the makeshift pads over the wounds, so he could tend the woman's head injury.

From experience of this kind of incident, Dove knew fractures to the spine and pelvis would also be likely. The relief as the emergency crews reached them, with the desperately needed equipment, medication and skills, was immense.

She moved away to allow the medics room to work, and watched Quinn greet his colleagues as the rest of the road crews started to arrive. Sadness caught in her chest, for the woman in front of them, who probably wasn't going to make it, for the other female already dead, and for the male victim, who lay so still.

Within minutes, it seemed, the scene was full of emergency responders, calmly, quickly, carrying out their tasks.

The helicopter, defying odds as the fog lifted but the rain intensified, successfully landed on the southbound carriageway, well clear of the telephone wires and the three bridges. With the two patients stabilised as best they could be, Dove was able to finally relinquish any first-aid duties.

She moved her hair out of her eyes, squared her shoulders and went to join her own colleagues. As she did so, she squinted upwards again. The weather made it impossible to be sure, but now the fog was lifting, it looked like one of the top railings that lined the bridge on either side was missing, creating a neat gap in the fence, directly above the fallers.

Walking further back to get a better view, she looked left and right. The broken portion of the railing was lying in the road, next to the red BMW. She studied it, as the rain trickled down her neck, and the steady, hypnotic flash of blue lights illuminated the scene.

It wasn't splintered or ragged. In fact, to her, each end looked like it had been neatly sawn.

CHAPTER THREE

Still pondering the railing, Dove gave her witness statement to a uniformed officer and waited for her own close-knit team to arrive. Quinn had gone with the second victim, the young male, to Abberley General. She wouldn't have expected anything less. The air ambulance doctors had taken the third woman in the helicopter.

Dove checked her phone, gratefully accepted a water bottle from the man in the suit, who had been helping with the third victim, and listened as the conversation flowed around her. From what she could hear, there seemed to be enough confusion between witness statements for there to be a very real possibility all three jumpers had not leapt to their deaths willingly. What had happened up on the bridge? She took another gulp of water, wiped rain and sweat out of her eyes, and walked back into the crowd of marooned drivers and their passengers.

The bystander who had laid a blanket over the deceased victim was clear she thought she had seen a group of people messing around on the bridge before the incident. The lorry driver, who had come onto the motorway via the slip road half a mile back, also thought he had spotted movement on the bridge before the incident.

Add this to the broken or cut railing, and it left three options: suicide, an accident, or murder. Dove shivered now as the rain soaked through her shirt.

The steady rain wasn't cold, but standing in shorts and a T-shirt wasn't much fun.

She fetched her raincoat from the car, sat briefly in the passenger seat, hidden from view by the general hustle and bustle, and dropped her head into her hands. Just for a moment, she felt her heartbeat, could hear her breathing. *Focus*, she told herself.

The Major Crimes Team were on the motorway as soon as the first responders had made the scene safe and the ambulances had departed. There had been a few walking wounded from those who had been involved in the minor pile-up under the bridge, but overall, they had been lucky, Dove thought, so incredibly lucky it hadn't been worse.

Now, harsh floodlights illuminated the tragic scenes, and white tents and yellow markers littered the road like forlorn Christmas decorations. Dove could see search teams up on the bridges, shining torches into the wooded area on the west side, towards the town, and onto the downland to the east.

"Bloody hell." DS Lindsey Alderton was one of the Major Crimes Team on call, and a particular friend of Dove's. "I heard you were on scene when it happened. That's what happens when you try and get away for a relaxing holiday." Her expression changed. "I also heard it's not a straight-cut suicide, or they wouldn't be dragging us out on a rainy night. You okay, mate?"

"Fine, thanks. I could do with a shot of coffee to keep me going. There are a couple of reports of a group messing around on the bridge before the victims jumped, and some of the other witness statements are now backing that up." Dove shrugged. "I didn't see anything apart from falling bodies."

She had found a packet of wet wipes in the car, wiped blood and dirt off her hands and forearms and pulled her hair into a long plait. She now felt ready for work, despite the emotions simmering underneath, despite tiredness and shock still making her shiver. As mentioned to Lindsey, she could do with some caffeine.

Quinn texted to say he would get a lift back and that both victims reached the hospital alive. She knew it could be hours before they both made it home. But that was their lives, saving others, solving crime, and it was a passion neither of them would be without. Their lazy holiday on the Cornish coast already seemed far away, the surf boards strapped to the roof rack on the car a distant reminder of the sun, salt and cans of beer on the beach.

An hour later, the last of the cars was being driven away, carefully navigating a path laid out towards the slipway on the middle bridge, which led towards the main roundabout and the main route into Abberley and Lymington-on-Sea. The HGV would remain in situ until a recovery service could right the trailer, though the driver had already hitched a ride with a fellow bystander.

Jess Meadow's van was pulling up near the first bridge, carefully avoiding the other emergency vehicles, and Dove waved to her. A Crime Scene Manager, and one of Dove's best friends, Jess was a no-nonsense woman, with a reputation for getting things done.

Jess responded to her greeting, but even as she got out of the vehicle, Dove could see concern on her face. Everyone was going to think it was too soon for Dove to return to active duty, especially with a major case like this one. There had been another reason for the time away: time to grieve and heal from her loss.

But not only did she feel a personal connection to this incident, having been one of the first on scene, this was exactly what she *did* need to distract her, to occupy her mind so she didn't spend every hour pondering what might have been. Her job had taught her *'what if'* was not a game to be playing, but it was hard not to dwell on what might have been.

DC Josh Conrad, his dark hair a mass of frizz and curls in the damp night, but radiating his usual interest and high energy, was greeting DI Blackman. He also waved at Dove, who waved back.

"Hi, boss." Dove walked across to the group, smiling at DI Jon Blackman as he stood, tall and lean with his long dark overcoat. He could have been a slightly detached bystander observing a distasteful scene. But Dove knew his thoughtful expression hid a sharp brain. His quick grey eyes were taking in the scene, and she could tell, under the outward appearance of calm authority, he was already making decisions, considering angles. He was a great boss and had helped make the team what it was today: close knit and extremely good at what they did.

"I understand you are one of our witnesses," he said now, to Dove, his expression registering a flicker of concern.

"I hardly saw anything. I was just saying to Lindsey, our car was a few metres back. I gave my statement, and Quinn did, too. He was helping with the second victim, and now he's gone on to the hospital with one of the road crews." Dove made a huge effort to sound brisk and impersonal. She appreciated everyone's concern, but she needed to get on with her job, had been looking forward to getting back on duty. It left less time to think about what might have been.

"A quick summary would be great, if you can manage it?" He glanced around as he spoke, taking in the orderly chaos, the downpour washing the blood-soaked tarmac, the debris of gloves and plastic wrapping left by the medics struggling to save the lives of the jumpers. A larger white tent had been erected over the deceased female.

Despite an unexpected wave of emotion, Dove managed to carefully stick to the bare facts, reiterating that two of the victims had still been alive when they were taken to Abberley General. She also pointed out the broken railing. Even as she mentioned this, DI Blackman's phone rang. He answered curtly, nodding.

"Okay, that was the hospital. The female went into cardiac arrest, but they got her back. She's gone straight down to theatre, and the male is still being assessed," he relayed.

Dove felt a wave of sadness, coupled with a spark of hope, remembering the woman's confused struggle as blood trickled from her ear, the warmth still in her body as Dove had held her hand briefly, trying to reassure and comfort. A connection had been made. She would find out what happened to this woman, to all three of them. If they needed justice to rest, if their families needed to know what had happened, she and the rest of the team would find the answers.

"Let's get cracking, then." Jess had her bag in her hand, as she approached the tented body, the hood of her jumpsuit zipped up under her chin. "We've got a team up on the bridge to see what we can get from the jump site. The site is sealed off and the roads crossing all three bridges are closed, with detours being put in place. The motorway is closed in both directions between Junction 8 and Junction 9 which obviously incorporates this area below the bridges and the slip road. Highways are sorting the necessary. Any news on the survivors?"

DI Blackman updated her, and she nodded. "We'll start on the deceased female." She gestured to the woman behind her, carrying camera equipment, to proceed. "And we'll get what we can, but this piss-awful weather isn't going to help anyone."

Dove watched Jess's eyes soften as they met her gaze, worry creasing her forehead. Jess waited until the others had moved out of earshot before speaking again. "Are you sure you . . . ?" She didn't finish the sentence, eyes widening, taking in Dove's shorts and beach shoes poking out from underneath her navy raincoat. "Shit, you were here already, weren't you? Jesus! What a way to end a holiday. You need to get back home and dry out."

"I will, as soon as Quinn gets back. I'm honestly fine, Jess." Dove smiled, forcing her stiff lips to move, injecting a confidence she didn't feel into her voice.

She glanced over as another car inched slowly down to the cordoned-off areas. The relief that ran through her body was as effective as a mug of coffee, as she saw Quinn climb out. The vehicle did a swift U-turn and vanished, most likely in the direction of Abberley General. He waved and started to walk through the rain, towards her.

As the team began to work through the crime scene, she took a quick moment to stand with her fiancé, who she knew would stay until she was ready to go home. But she hadn't been on call, and as a witness, had already made her contribution, so out of consideration for him, she suggested driving home now.

"I can't do anything else here, and I want to be in early in the morning," she told him. "How are the patients? The DI said the woman arrested?"

"She's in theatre, and to be honest, it'll be touch and go for both of them." His green eyes were shadowed with exhaustion, his black hair slicked back from the rain. "But at least they made it to hospital. They've got the best chance of making it, now."

Dove squeezed his hand before making her way over to the DI. "I'm going to head off, boss, if that's okay?"

He nodded slowly, eyes on Jess vanishing into the tent. "If you're sure."

She knew he wasn't really talking about going home now, but asking if she was sure she would be at work in the morning. "I am sure."

"Okay, then. This is already a bit of an odd one." He gazed thoughtfully up at the broken railing. "As far as I can see, in addition to the obvious conclusions, it could also be a rather public execution."

She felt a sudden coldness deep in her chest. Organized crime? It was true there had been trouble with the county lines drug dealers recently. Bigger trouble than they'd had on this area of the coast in years. Dove knew instantly which perpetrators he was thinking of: "The White Horses?"

It sounded so innocuous, which was probably the intention, but the White Horses had been warring over territory with another established organized crime gang, and it had already led to bloodshed.

"Maybe. Maybe not." He smiled at her. "All options are open at this point. See you in the morning, DC Milson."

She and Quinn walked slowly back to their car. They stood shoulder to shoulder for a moment, watching the scene. Her fiancé pulled her gently into a hug, and she leaned against him, careless for once if anyone observed this display of affection.

An illuminated pathway ran up the hill, spotlit like an airport runway, and there was a bustle of activity, but back here, in the shadows, she could lean her head on Quinn's shoulder, and close her eyes. Just for a moment.

Dove saw the falling figures again in her mind. It had been so quick, so shocking to see them tumble to their deaths. Perhaps one jumped and the others tried to save him or her? The strangeness of standing in the middle of a motorway, without any traffic, coupled with the eerie swirl of the sea fog, the patter of rain made the whole thing surreal . . . The slightest thing had affected her for the past few months. This was a *big* thing, but it was a chance to prove to herself she could do it, to see how far she had come.

She took a last look at the crime scene, at the huge concrete bridges arching above the road, before climbing wearily into the car. She and Quinn were both silent for the rest of the drive home.

Dove bit her lip as she stared out of the car window. Another reminder of how life could change in an instant. Had the fall seemed endless to the three, or had it come as a shock, a terrifying journey from life to death?

Three bodies in a matter of seconds. As DI Blackman had said, with many possibilities, just one speculation that would surely be raised by the press, given the current White Horses situation, was that this was a very public execution.

CHAPTER FOUR

By 6 a.m., the incident room was buzzing. The Major Incident teams were collating data with other emergency services, trawling the footage from the motorway traffic cams, exchanging views, scanning witness statements and drinking a lot of tea and coffee.

Dove, having grabbed a couple of hours restless sleep, now scanned quickly through social media, noting the press pictures of the incident site, as she waited for the briefing. Media speculation was wild. Given the unusual circumstances of the incident, it seemed everyone had their own personal view on what had really happened. As she had expected, the recent bout of organized crime was leading to speculation the deaths were linked to drugs.

She sighed. It was going to be a long day, and the sheer size and scope of the crime scene, plus the multiple bodies, was going to make this a tough one.

Emergency service colleagues were still working on scene, and roads would remain closed, along with large areas of the woodland and downland bordering the incident either side of the bridges. The weather was appalling, with the now heavy rain washing evidence away, making working conditions next to impossible for those combing the area for clues.

DI Jon Blackman and DI Lincoln were talking intently as the team finally assembled, all clutching steaming cups and iPads or notebooks.

DCI Franklin began. "Yesterday evening, three people apparently fell, were pushed, or jumped from the Saddle Bridge, which, as most of you know, is one of the three bridges spanning the motorway, located between junctions eight and nine. All three victims landed within metres of each other on the southbound carriageway."

Dove could feel the collective wince, closed her eyes briefly before opening them, pushing away the exhaustion, the vivid recollection of blood on the road, screaming, the smell of fuel, the sheer overwhelming size of the crime scene collectively. And the broken rail lying next to the red BMW.

She could feel the DCI glance over at her, knowing — as the whole room probably did by now — that she and Quinn had given witness statements, hours after it had happened, when they were still helping on scene, clothes smeared with blood and grit, faces dirty and sweaty.

Even this morning, as she looked in the mirror before she came to work, her amber eyes were shadowed with shock and exhaustion, her usually tanned and glowing skin sallow with lack of sleep and grief. Their time in Cornwall had kick-started the healing process. Last night's incident had set it back.

"The first 999 call came in at 20.39, followed by over twenty other calls. As you know, a Major Incident was declared by all three emergency services, and that stretch of motorway and associated roads will remain closed today, while colleagues investigate further." DCI Franklin turned to the screen behind him, and clicked the pointer in his hand. "All three bridges have traffic cam, and the Saddle Bridge cam picked up our victims as they fell. Unfortunately, only one, the main road bridge to Carlton Hill, has a camera actually up on the bridge. This structure, as you can see from the map, is the first bridge encountered by those travelling southbound on the motorway below."

DI Blackman picked up the thread at a nod from his boss. "Saddle Bridge is mainly used by farm vehicles and walkers heading for the Downs. It has access to the downland on the east side, and the woodland walks on the west side."

"You can also get access to the North Road from Saddle Bridge," DS Amin pointed out. "I've driven from Pengrove Road, and parked at the café further down when I walk my dogs. It's not a well-used route, but there is a cut-through." She pushed her short dark hair back, and stared at the map on screen.

The DCI nodded, added a detail to his notes and pointed to the screen as a photograph of a woman with short blonde hair and glasses appeared. "Victim one is thirty-eight-year-old Rebecca Hales, a single mum from Lymington-on-Sea. She is alive, but in critical condition. She told her family she was heading out to meet friends and would be home by eleven at the latest."

DS Steve Parker slipped into the room, muttered an apology and sat down next to Dove. A few senior members of the team shot him looks of disapproval, but Dove gave him a quick smile.

DI Lincoln took the next segment, as up on screen, the photograph of a smiling young man with curly brown hair appeared. "Victim number two is nineteen-year-old Mark Davies, from Lymington-on-Sea. Lives with his boyfriend, Lee Culvert, in Roedean House. His boyfriend says Mark told him he was out for a drink with a friend. Lee himself was out last night, visiting his mum, who lives in Brighton. No other family."

"Lucky there wasn't much traffic. It could have been so much worse," Steve commented. "He's still alive as well, isn't he, Mark Davies?"

"Incredibly, yes." DI Lincoln nodded. "He has extensive injuries, though, and is currently in ICU. We're unlikely to get a witness statement any time soon, poor lad."

"Victim number three is Amber Dionysus, twenty-seven, again from Lymington-on-Sea. She lived on her own, down near the old marina. Amber died at the scene." DI Martin, the newbie on the team, was looking as immaculate as usual, Dove noted. Her short red hair was spiked and glossy and she wore a crisp white shirt and dark trousers. "Next of kin, her mother, has been notified."

DCI Franklin took up the dialogue again, and clicked the pointer as he spoke. "This is the only footage we currently have, and it's from the Saddle Bridge traffic cameras. You can see that in addition to our fallers, the top rail from part of the protective barrier fence on the bridge also came down, which could suggest a number of things, including a deliberate attempt to kill."

The grainy video footage picked up the bodies around halfway through their fall towards the road. Dove could almost feel a collective wince from the entire room when the three hit the tarmac below.

The rail fell amid the bodies, which still suggested to her someone had perhaps leaned, or had been forced against it. She tapped her pen against her teeth, remembering the neatly sawn ends of the rail. A deliberate sabotage would mean a premeditated event. But what a way to kill three people. It was clumsy, unlikely . . .

"They don't all fall at exactly the same time," Lindsey commented, eyes narrowed, glasses pushed back over her forehead. A red scarf held her mass of brown curly hair away from her face, and her cheeks were pink from the warmth of the room. "Mark hits the ground first by a fraction of a second, and it looks like Amber, the deceased, was last. Hopefully we'll get some dash cam footage from drivers, particularly the HGV involved, but given the angle and height of the bridge, that might be a tad optimistic."

DI Blackman was scrolling on his iPad. "We have four witnesses stating they saw people, maybe a vehicle, on the bridge before the incident, but at this stage, it's impossible to say whether these people were our fallers, or whether others were involved."

"The weather was really bad," Dove pointed out. "The fog was coming in, and it was very quickly hard to see more than a few metres. You know what it's like. I'd be really surprised if anyone could spot much detail on a figure on any of the bridges, whether it was the victim or not, from the road." She paused, and frowned. "The lorry driver said it only caught his attention because fairly recently some kids had been chucking concrete blocks onto the road, and his windscreen had been shattered. I remember thinking the same thing and wondering for a moment if it was debris falling."

"Point taken. We'll get all of the footage from the traffic cameras cleaned up and check the before and after. It might be that the camera on Carlton bridge caught something — it depends how it's angled. I think there is another camera near the roundabout too. This is first impressions, people," the DCI said, looking up from his own device and removing his reading glasses to scan the room.

"Are we looking at a suicide pact, then?" DC Josh Conrad suggested. "Gang-related? Pretty unusual for round here, but it would make a big statement. Roedean House has seen a bit of dealing in the last year. And we've just moved Frankie Coote inside for a stretch. Maybe Big Dom is putting on a show of power for the White Horses? He's probably the only one stupid enough to do that."

DI Lincoln replied, "Could be, but let's keep an open mind. The woodland paths on the Abberley side of the bridge, the west side, are a common hangout for underage drinkers and drug users later in the evenings. This could be an accident, a bit of fun that went wrong. People spotted on the bridge could have been teenagers out for a laugh on a Friday night before they headed into town."

"But they haven't come forward, these teenagers?" Lindsey queried. "If it was some kind of dare, a game that turned nasty, or even a genuine accident, you would think the victims would fit the same rough demographic, but they are all different ages, and I'm guessing different social circles."

"Equally, if it was an accident, why didn't someone call 999?" Josh queried.

DI Blackman nodded. "Drugs don't discriminate, so it might explain a lot. Otherwise, why the hell would a twenty-seven-year-old, a thirty-eight-year-old and a nineteen-year-old be messing around on a bridge together on a Friday night?"

CHAPTER FIVE

It wasn't just the one incident that changed my life, and when you think of the chances of it happening again and again . . . I mean, hell, someone really doesn't like me, do they? It's almost like a game against an invisible opponent. An opponent who can do anything, move you around like a playing piece on a board, and laugh while they do it.

But people do like me. They always have. I'm funny, charming, caring and most of all, I listen with a sympathetic expression on my face. I don't care about their pathetic, boring little lives, but I realized early on, listening was all it took to get into their heads, and that's where the fun starts. Once you get into people's heads you can start to control them.

When I was ten, there was a girl at school who told me all about her fear of darkness, of being shut in. Her terror was electric, exciting, and I wanted to harness it. I asked her what her worst nightmare was, and she was crying when she told me. Why would you reveal your weakness like that? It took everything I had not to let my disdain show.

After I considered her predicament for a few weeks, opportunity quickly presented itself. It seemed like a logical step to lock her in the sports-equipment shed at the bottom of the playing field on Bonfire Night. She trusted me, and even when she was finally discovered, she never thought I would have been the one to lock her in. I flung myself into her arms when she was released, and held her as she cried, the staunch and loyal best friend. I even shed a few tears myself.

The Bonfire Night party at school had been loud, busy and thrumming with excited kids, stressed-out teachers and parents flocking to the candy floss and hot dog stands. The night was clear and bright, and my breath was smoky in the air, mirroring the towering bonfire. Safe in my little group of friends, I suggested a game, and that was how it all started.

It was only a couple of hours before she was discovered, after the party was over and the panic had set in. A missing child stirs up all sorts of emotions, and I watched with interest, my own parents too busy with the PTA tombola to do more than wave at me.

She was broken, terrified, when she emerged from her nightmare, but as I wrapped my treacherous arms around her shaking body, laid my warm cheek next to her cold one, I could feel the fizz of triumph, of a new kind of excitement. I knew, even at that young age, that she was still a follower.

You believe what you want to believe, don't you? Aged ten, she believed I was her best friend, and aged eighteen, she probably still thought the same thing. But that doesn't mean any of it was true. I don't believe in friends. The concept leaves you open to being screwed over.

CHAPTER SIX

Dove bit her thumbnail to stop herself yawning. Tiredness was coming in waves, and she really needed a bacon sandwich with brown sauce. And another coffee. But now more than ever, she needed to give the appearance of being on top of things, being 'fully functional', as the bereavement counsellor had said.

Dove had told her exactly what she could do with her 'fully functional', which had made her feel better for a while. Then she felt guilty for being rude to a woman who was, after all, a professional just doing her job. She went back in to apologize.

The DI was speaking again. ". . . if there were other people involved, or anyone who witnessed the incident up on the bridge, they have not yet come forward. As we have already ascertained, the visibility was poor, so let's keep an open mind."

Dove nodded briskly, as though the comment was aimed in her direction, aware some heads had turned, aware most of the team already knew she'd been a witness.

They would be watching her too, she thought, but in a different way. They would be waiting to catch her if she fell. She cleared her throat and reiterated her earlier statement.

"Like I said, I would be surprised if any of the drivers were able to see what was happening on the bridges. You know what these sudden coastal fogs are like. But if any of the witnesses were driving up on the bridges, or even the slip road to the second bridge, they might have seen something."

"Yeah, sea fog is great. Clear and bright one minute, total obliteration the next," DC Josh Conrad said, running a hand through his thick, curly hair, and leaning thoughtfully back in his chair. "I wonder if our victims checked the weather forecast."

"Something to consider," DI Blackman nodded.

Dove listened as DCI Franklin, who would operate as Senior Investigating Officer during the case, holding the reins, taking on overall management, began to assign initial leads. Dove and Steve were last to be assigned. "DS Parker and DC Milson, you make a start on the deceased, Amber. According to her mother, she was staying at the George pub for a weekend break. You know the one. It's right in the centre of town." He pushed his reading glasses down over his nose, and glanced at his notes. "She checked in on Friday afternoon. Her mother has already been informed and we've sent Bernie over as Family Liaison Officer. Amber lived a few miles down the road from her mother, had a rented place near the port. Forensics should be there about eleven."

"Yes, boss." Dove chucked her empty coffee cup in the bin and followed her partner out into the open-plan office area.

Steve still walked with a slight limp, a constant reminder of the attack they had both survived last time they tangled with an organized crime gang. He followed Dove as she headed for the stairs, pausing by the coffee machine. "Let's get something in town," he said. "I can tell you're desperate for another caffeine fix, and I'm craving some of Eden's iced doughnuts. You know, I really hope this case isn't drug-related, because I've sort of had enough of the local gangs. Whitehorse Estate is worse than the Seaview just now."

Dove smiled at him, feeling as always, a trace of guilt that her partner had been left with the visible limp, and months of painful physiotherapy, while her own injuries had healed to neat scars across her ribs. The scars matched the one across her abdomen, older, but also inflicted by an organized crime gang.

She shook memories away. "I'm right with you on that one. Anyway, let's get that coffee." Dove's sister, Ren, and niece ran a coffee shop and bakery in town, and Steve was a devoted customer. He and his wife had even ordered a christening cake from Eden, who was branching out into sugar craft. "Why were you so late, anyway?"

He pulled a face. "Bad night with the baby. He's fine, just teething, but I overslept big time. Might have been easier if I'd been on call last night. I could have just slept here on the sofa, and would probably have got more sleep."

Steve already had two children, and his wife was now unexpectedly pregnant with a third. Dove was about to sympathise, and suggest she drove while he grabbed five minutes shuteye, when she heard her name called from back in the briefing room.

"Detective Milson?" It was DCI Franklin, his massive frame filling the doorway. "Can I have a quick word?"

"Bugger," said Dove under her breath as she retraced her steps. "See you in the car, and yes to the doughnuts." She looked away quickly from Steve's expression of concern. She didn't want concern and kindness. She needed to get her teeth stuck firmly into this weird case, so she didn't break down.

The DCI's office was claustrophobic, and her head spun briefly, heat rising up in a wash of colour across her cheeks. She bit her lip and squared her shoulders. DI Blackman was there too, leaning against the wall, studying her face, his phone in his hand.

It had been a tough couple of months, and she wasn't sure if she would really ever be whole again. A piece had been torn away from her heart, and every day she thought about what had happened, going over and over, obsessively trying to find a reason, someone to blame.

She drew a blank. *Nothing about death makes sense*, Quinn had told her, as shocked and devastated as she was, but calmer and more accepting. They had postponed the wedding, unable to face looking at the space where Gaia should have sat.

"It must have been extremely traumatic witnessing the incident last night, and we were wondering if you might feel better on another case. We have the stabbing in St Leonards to follow up. DI Colban is going to lead on that one, and hopefully get it wrapped up fairly quickly. That's a smaller team, but almost certain to be gang-related, and you do have experience in that area."

Not the kind of experience that needed to be brought to the surface at this moment in time. In fact, it was the last thing she needed. Dove took a long calming breath, and smiled. "Thanks, but I'm happy where I am, and happy working with Steve."

Her partner was what she needed, too. They knew each other inside-out, knew when to offer reassurance, when to administer a kick up the backside. She felt sick at the thought of losing her work support system. It wasn't just Steve, her whole team were working on this case, and if she was going to be able to function normally, she needed to get stuck in.

Plus, DI Colban was a gloomy bastard. Rumoured to only ever be fully awake during the hours of darkness, and similar in temperament to DI Lincoln, he wasn't someone she wanted to be working with just now.

"We're just concerned, after your sister's death, that this may be too much, too soon, especially given you witnessed this event."

He was a good DCI, Franklin. Dove had a lot of respect for the grey-haired veteran officer standing in front of her, but she needed to work so hard her bones ached and thoughts were driven away through sheer exhaustion. Only then would she stop trying to make sense of something that might never make sense. Gaia was dead. It was horrifying, heartbreaking and very final.

"I appreciate your concern, but I am honestly okay to work. I'm . . ." She mentally crossed her fingers. "I'm still going to counselling sessions, and if I start to feel in any way that this is not the case for me, or that I need more leave, I will let you know." Dove was pleased to hear herself sounding so clear and calm. A contrast to the turmoil in her mind.

DI Blackman nodded. "Being a witness to something like this is tough on anyone, but especially after what you have been through in the last few months, you and your family. Just take it easy, Dove. We're all here for you."

She nodded, hoping she wouldn't burst into tears. Instead, she swallowed hard and smiled briskly at both of them. "I'm fine, honestly. Very ready to crack on with the case."

"Just so you know, stepping away from this one will not affect your chances of promotion. Your record with us is excellent." DCI Franklin smiled suddenly. "I'd like to see you move up a rank, and I think you would like it too, but remember if you need time out, just let us know and take it. No fuck-ups."

This made the corners of her mouth rise. In a way the sympathy, and welfare checks, genuine though they were, just made her sore and defensive.

After another couple of minutes chit-chat, she signed the paperwork, and determinedly made sure her hand didn't shake. They looked unconvinced by what she felt was a fairly stellar performance, but had to let her go anyway. Mainly, Dove thought, as she hurried downstairs, because they were short-staffed. They always were.

Steve was waiting by the car with a coffee in a real mug.

"How the hell did you manage that?" She smiled in appreciation. "Are you my actual guardian angel or what?"

"I sneaked into the custody suite when they weren't looking. They have a nice kitchen set-up, *and* an upgraded coffee machine that works without being kicked. Smug bastards." Steve was grinning with triumph. "I feel better already about today."

Dove wrapped her cold hands around the mug for comfort as he started the car, and took a big swig of the hot liquid.

"I might put in for a transfer to Custody, if they have coffee this good on tap."

"That's what I thought. I might come with you. I'd wait until you've got that promotion, though. Did they say anything about it just now?" Steve frowned at the sat nav, tapping buttons.

"No . . . Well, only to say if I needed some time out, it wouldn't affect my chances. You do know that works better if you use a touch screen?"

"That's good to know. You okay to go, or do you need to drink a bit more of that?"

Dove gulped another few mouthfuls, scalding her mouth but lowering the liquid level to a safe height, and laughed. "Let's get going before anyone realizes we've pinched a mug."

"What else did the DCI say?"

"Checking I'm not going crazy. No, he's a good bloke. I told him I was fine."

"Well, if you need anything at all, just say." He indicated right and headed along the coast road towards the George pub, where Amber had spent her last afternoon alive.

CHAPTER SEVEN

Steve stopped the car outside Boots the chemist, and Dove ran into her sister Ren's coffee shop to pick up their usual order. To her relief, Ren was serving behind the counter and greeted her with her usual bright smile. Only someone who knew her well could have seen behind the brightness to the shadows and sadness in her eyes.

"You okay, love?" Ren asked. "I got your text, but I was worried about you. Must have been hell on that road last night. Those poor people. I can't imagine . . ." Her voice trailed off, and she gave a shrug.

"Yeah, it wasn't good," Dove admitted. "Got to grab and run, because Steve's in the car. Are you all right?" In an unusual display of affection, Dove reached over and squeezed her sister's hand over the counter before she took her cardboard tray of coffees and the bag of warm sugary cinnamon doughnuts. They stood for a second, hands clasped, eyes locked, each drawing comfort from the other, before Dove pulled quickly away. "Text me if you need me," she told her sister, and waved briskly to Eden, whose face could just be seen through the steamy window of the kitchen door.

"Same. Stay safe, love."

Ren had lost a lot of weight, Dove thought. She had become pale and subdued since Gaia's death. Being self-employed, she had hardly taken any time off, except for the funeral, but had confided that, in a strange way, her little business had saved her. She had few staff, but they were a close-knit bunch, and she was able to lean on them when she needed to.

Everyone processes their grief in a different way, Dove reminded herself, but she still felt responsible for Ren. In a funny way, she hadn't ever felt responsible for Gaia, because she had been so tough, so dismissive of any affection, and so successful in everything she did.

It was just an accident, she repeated inside her head. *Just a stupid accident.*

* * *

The George public house was a rundown, red-brick building wedged between a betting shop and a Chinese takeaway. A 'Rooms Available' sign swung gently in the wind, its rusty chains attached to a drooping metal pole above the door.

"DS Steve Parker and DC Dove Milson. Can we have a word with the owner, please?" Steve smiled pleasantly at the elderly man behind the reception desk, chattering non-stop on a mobile phone.

The receptionist glanced up from his phone, scowled at them, and jerked a thumb towards the room to the right of the reception desk, before continuing what appeared to be an argument with a family member. ". . . *she* told him, because *his* niece was her ex-husband's girlfriend, so don't get so fired up about everything. It was Sarah's new employee's uncle's cousin who . . ."

Amused rather than annoyed by his rudeness, Dove knocked on and pushed the grubby, white-painted door the receptionist had indicated. The rusty plaque, swinging from one screw, announced it to be the Manager's Office.

"Mr Grenold?"

The man behind the desk in the overcrowded office space was wearing a navy knitted vest top and neon-orange tracksuit trousers. His greying chest hair peeked through the fabric of his top and his large belly rested comfortably on his thighs.

At least he was more accommodating than his receptionist, Dove thought, as Mr Grenold beamed at them. "You're the police, aren't you? Such a tragedy, what happened. I saw it on the news, and of course, I was expecting you to come round. I made sure everything was left just how it was when she went out, and I've got the CCTV recordings for you."

He was so keen to help, and so anxious to make sure he had done the right thing. Dove felt herself warming to him, but wondering why the hell he had such a grumpy receptionist. She noticed a copy of *True Crime* magazine under a pile of papers on his desk.

"It would be great to have a quick look at the CCTV, and then if you can download it onto a memory stick for us to take now, we can avoid troubling you later," Steve told him politely.

Mr Grenold had already pressed a few keyboard buttons and spun the screen around to show them the footage.

Dove leaned close to watch, studying every movement of the surprisingly good quality recordings. The CCTV showed Amber arriving at the George on foot at 1.55 p.m., and leaving at 6.30 p.m., walking swiftly up the road towards the busy junction. Where did she go between that time and landing in the road under Saddle Bridge at 8.35 p.m.?

Amber was tall and slim, walking confidently, chin up, but not hurrying. She had a gym holdall and a small shoulder bag with her as she entered the hotel. Her long dark hair was up in a sleek ponytail, a few curls escaping to frame her face.

"Did Amber bring a car with her?" Dove asked, as she glanced at the almost empty car park visible through the net-lined windows. She was still struggling to see why Amber would have booked a night here. It wasn't the nicest place in town, but she must have had a reason. Was she supposed to meet Mark and Rebecca here? Tapping her fingers against her thigh in frustration, she realized Mr Grenold was answering her question.

He was shaking his head. "No, or if she did, she didn't park here. All guests have to register their vehicles." He smiled and shrugged. "But I charge on a daily rate, so I know guests often leave their cars a few blocks down on the residential streets." He tutted in disapproval. "Do you want me to take you up to the room she stayed in, then? I checked her in, you know. She seemed very normal. Pretty girl and very polite." His eager expression faltered a bit, as he added, "I can't believe she was dead a few hours later. She was so . . . alive."

Steve agreed that it would be useful to see the room and thanked him for the memory stick he'd provided. Apparently cheered by this, Mr Grenold beamed at them again. He ponderously led the way across the sticky carpet towards the stairs.

Passing reception, Dove met Steve's eyes and bit her lip as the man behind the desk, who was now bright red in the face, yelled, "*She's your mother's lover, so you sort it out!*"

Serenely ignoring the disturbance, bombarding them with more questions about Amber, Mr Grenold led them up to the first floor, pulled a key from his pocket and opened the door of room 19. "The woman that called earlier said you might be sending a Forensics team down to check this place out. Anything I can do to help, just let me know. Such a shame, that poor girl."

He showed every sign of wanting to stay in the room while they looked around, but Dove finally managed to send him gently back downstairs, promising to let him know when they were leaving, and to return the key.

"Nice friendly bloke," Dove said, closing the bedroom door firmly, and Steve rolled his eyes. She breathed in the stale air of the room, the faint hint of perfume and hairspray. Mr Grenold had said Amber Dionysus had seemed 'normal'. *Everyone was* normal *until something happened*, she thought bitterly.

"So . . . she checks in yesterday afternoon, earlyish," Steve said slowly, slipping on a pair of gloves as he began looking around the room. "And she leaves yesterday evening at 6.30 p.m. but wasn't supposed to check out until this morning. Funny destination for a weekend break, this place."

"That's what I was thinking." Dove smiled, amused that he was looking at the smears on the furniture, and shifting his feet on the tacky brown carpet. "It's a good forty-minute walk to Saddle Bridge from here, if she walked all the way. Maybe she took the bus, or got a lift? We need to check and see if she had a car, and as Mr G said, ditched it nearby rather than pay parking fees. But even if she walked all the way, that is quite a time gap between leaving here and falling off the bridge. What else was she doing that afternoon?"

"Hopefully, we'll find that out fairly soon," Steve said, continuing his search.

The Forensics team would be in later, but there was a chance this could be a murder case, so time was of the essence. Any evidence would need to be fast-tracked straight to the labs. The first twenty-four hours after an incident were critical.

"And with a bit of luck, she left us some clues right here." Dove added optimistically, as she too donned gloves.

As they continued their search, there was a tap on the door, and a young girl in a maroon housekeeping tabard peered round. "Sorry to bother you, but you're here about the woman who died, aren't you? Amber. Can I . . . Can I talk to you?"

Dove, who had been checking the clothes in the wardrobe, fully turned and smiled at the girl. The names of the victims had only just been released, but — and this was partly due to the large number of witnesses at the scene — word travelled fast. "Sure. Did you see her when she stayed here?"

"Yeah, she was nice. I couldn't believe it when I saw she'd died last night. And by suicide too. That's horrible."

Steve raised his eyebrows at Dove and spoke gently to the girl. "Did you talk to Amber? Come in and sit down."

CHAPTER EIGHT

The girl perched nervously on a chair by the table and fiddled
with the lead on the kettle. Her short hair was dyed blue and
purple ombre, and her eyes were heavy with dark make-up.
"She gave me a fiver for bringing her a McDonald's yesterday afternoon. We don't have room service, but she got here
yesterday afternoon a bit early, and I was just finishing getting the rooms ready. Said she had some work to do, and as
the bar wasn't serving food until six, would I mind popping
across the road and getting her a takeout." She shrugged. "I
finished the last two rooms and did it."

"How did she seem?" Steve asked.

"Fine. Not like she was thinking about taking her own
life, if that's what you mean. But it must have been like a
suicide pact, mustn't it? Like they all jumped together, like it
was a cult or something." She visibly shivered. "Why would
anyone do that?"

It always shocked Dove, how quickly news travelled
since everyone was glued to social media, and how quickly
theories gained credence. While the investigating team were
still keeping an open mind, considering at least three possibilities, others had already decided they knew exactly what
happened last night.

"I don't understand why anyone would do that," the girl repeated, her gaze going from Dove to Steve as though she expected an answer. "I saw the video on social media. It freaked me out."

Dove smiled reassuringly at her. There was a video of at least one of the victims hurtling to their death doing the rounds on the socials. While it could be useful to have footage from the public, it also often made the pain for grieving families a hell of a lot worse.

The girl sitting in front of them swallowed hard, twisting her leather bracelets around and around on her tanned wrist. She looked to be in her late teens or early twenties. Dove felt a painful jolt somewhere deep in her chest, and instinctively her fingers went to her own wrist, hidden by her shirt cuff, touching the leather and beads close to her own skin. It had been one of Gaia's, and she and Ren had each taken one. A little physical part of their sister to carry around each day. She blinked, forcing herself to listen to the conversation.

"We are keeping an open mind," Steve said blandly. "When did you last see Amber?"

"Friday evening, about 5 p.m. Maybe a bit later. I finish the rooms and then quite often do a shift at the bar. She said hi when she went past in the corridor. She seemed like . . . normal, you know. I asked if she needed anything, and she said she was happy as she was. She was working on a laptop when I brought her takeaway up."

"Did you see what she was working on?" Steve asked thoughtfully.

"Not really." The girl's eyes slid sideways as she contemplated. "I did notice she was looking at something on YouTube, but I didn't really see what that was about."

"Did she have a car here?" Dove was looking out the window, which faced the car park. The weed-matted concrete square was almost empty.

"Don't think so. You can check with Mr G. Unless she took it with her when she left."

"You've been very helpful. Would you mind signing a witness statement?"

The CCTV had shown Amber leaving on foot, walking swiftly up the road towards the busy junction and the centre of town.

The girl nodded. "Don't mind. I can't believe it. Why would she jump off the bridge? I mean, she was just here, alive and talking, and now she's . . . not."

"That's what we're trying to find out," Steve said. "Thank you for your time."

Dismissed, the girl left, still visibly distressed. Dove heard the trolley creak as she started towards the next room.

Amber's room was tidy, with nothing hanging in the wardrobe, or in the drawers. The gym bag was still half-packed, and there were only a small number of toiletries in the tiny bathroom.

"MacBook," Dove said, leaning into the bag, and gently pulling it out. "And a few receipts for groceries, petrol . . . One for some stationery from the WHSmith's in Pengrove Road. It's bugging me why, if she was living just half an hour down the coast, why she would book into this place for the night? I know her mum apparently said she was having a weekend break, but this is not, and no offence to Mr Grenold, somewhere your average twenty-seven-year-old would come for some chill time."

"Maybe she was with a new boyfriend? Married new boyfriend? Or perhaps it was a group meet-up, between our three victims? Perhaps it was with someone she didn't want to know where she lived." He frowned as he dismissed this. "But then, she would surely have just met them out at a bar or somewhere. No need to invite them to her home."

Dove felt in the side pockets of the bag and pulled out a few leaflets. "Natural health remedies, yoga classes." She was trying to get a sense of who Amber had been, and most importantly, why she might have chosen to end her life. Or more importantly, if she hadn't made a choice, who had made it for her. She couldn't explain it, but she wanted to believe this wasn't a suicide pact. She wanted someone to blame.

At the bottom of the bag was a notebook, the pages still crisp and new. Under her gloved fingers, a card fell out. Curious, she flipped it over and studied it carefully. The image showed a bleak desolate moorland landscape, with a single white flower in the foreground. It looked like a sympathy card, the photograph speaking of grief and loneliness. The wording inside was simple, and handwritten in neat, black capital letters:

> DEAREST AMBER,
>   VISIT US ANY TIME, AND WE ARE ALWAYS HERE FOR YOU.
>   LOUISE, AND ALL YOUR FRIENDS AT THE RETREAT.

CHAPTER NINE

"Any date on that?" Steve was reading over her shoulder.

"No." Dove flipped the card over again, re-checking the back. "Nothing. It's not exactly the cheeriest card to send to someone though, is it?"

"Not really. More depressing than condoling really. If someone sent that to me, it would go straight in the bin. Anything else?"

"An envelope, paracetamol, an energy drink . . ." Dove, with trepidation, opened the pink envelope addressed to 'Mum' and was relieved to discover it was just a birthday card.

Steve was looking at his phone now. "There's a note on the file, updated from the initial visit, saying that according to the Family Liaison Officer, the mother is adamant she won't talk to anyone else as part of the investigation." he said, scanning through the documents on his phone.

"Who is the FLO again?" Dove was trying to keep her mind off the card. Gaia's apartment had been filled with the same kind of sympathy cards, white roses, lilies, and sadness. She and Ren had arranged a celebration of Gaia's life after the funeral, held at California Dreams. This had raised some eyebrows, but the remaining siblings felt it was right. Even their parents, flying back briefly from their world travels, agreed it was the kind of thing Gaia would have wanted.

"Bernie Collins . . . Dove? Are you okay?"

"Sorry. What?" She realized then that Steve must have answered her question and had to give herself a mental shake and refocus.

"Bernie Collins. The FLO."

"Yes. Do you know him?"

Steve nodded approvingly. "Yeah. Bernie's a top bloke. So anyway, this card. Bloody depressing, if you ask me. But maybe that's a thing, this yoga on a bleak moorland. Fitness freaks would love it, don't you think?"

Despite her pain, Dove felt her mouth twitch. Steve had this way of making everything seem better.

"What?" he demanded, pulling off his gloves and peering out of the window.

"Yoga on a bleak moorland. Hardly." She grinned, relieved to be feeling amusement, relieved to be feeling anything but the rawness of grief. Yoga had been part of her life for a few years now, and she loved it just as much as her surfing. "How would you know what fitness freaks like?"

"Just because I don't treat my own body as a temple, doesn't mean I don't know how these people think," he informed her.

"It's a sympathy card, rather than just a business follow-up, like she was going through something when she was staying at the Retreat." Dove frowned. "Maybe she had a recent bereavement?"

"Maybe. Wonder why she kept it. More to the point, I wonder if they all have one of these cards. It would lend weight to the cult theory, even though I can't believe right now that we could have a cult in Abberley or Lymington. People are way too nosy!" He was watching her carefully now. "Bag it and let's get going."

Dove followed him back down the stairs. Did Amber always keep it there, the card? Or had she thrust it into the zip pocket and forgotten about it? Maybe she'd kept it intentionally, as a treasured memory, and it was important to her.

All these tiny details would go into building the picture they had of Amber, and hopefully lead to understanding exactly what had happened last night, and why.

The receptionist barely looked up as they exited the building. He was texting furiously, head down, ignoring a hovering guest. Mr Grenold was waiting next to the front door, sipping delicately from a coffee cup. He beamed at them again, as Steve handed the key back and promised they would be in touch.

Dove got busy on her phone as soon as they were back in the car. "There are so many retreats around here, assuming it is around here, but the only one I can find just called the Retreat is at Saddleworth Farm." She traced the Google maps route with a finger on the screen. "That's just the other side of Saddle Bridge, isn't it?" An update pinged on her phone. "We might as well check it out, because Forensics are at Amber's place now, and as you say, her mother is still refusing to talk to anyone but Bernie."

* * *

The long way through Lymington-on-Sea was choked with traffic, and the roadworks next to the mortuary kept them trapped for ten minutes. Dove avoided looking at the ugly concrete building, instead diving back into the case file, checking information as various specialist teams submitted their reports. With three victims, it was going to be a tough process isolating all the relevant information from the dross, she thought wearily.

At least the rain had stopped, and a thread of pale blue was winding like a ribbon across the sky. "Jess will be fuming after all this rain. It'll take even longer to process everything. Are you sure you don't want me to drive?" Dove had noted he was wincing from the stop-start progress through town.

"I'm good, thanks. I could do with a bit of a walk, just to stretch the knee a bit, though."

Saddleworth Farm was hard to access, buried in a beautiful position in a cleft of the Downs, encircled by woods on two sides and approached by a narrow, winding lane full of potholes. The quickest way would have been to access via one of the two road bridges which spanned the motorway, but these were still cordoned off, along with Saddle Bridge.

Taking the longer, scenic route, Steve eventually turned off a narrow lane, eased the car over a speed bump, and emerged from the woods into a gravel car park at the front of a long, narrow farmhouse. Surrounding the farmhouse were various wooden buildings, a neat garden and what looked like an orchard.

Although the main road was just a couple of fields away, the noise was buried by the gentle folds of the Downs. Sheep grazed the ancient turf, undisturbed, and seagulls and hawks soared high about, circling on lazy wings. The steep slope next to the driveway was crowded with autumnal trees, and Dove glimpsed the dark sheen of water down below, and what looked to be a wooden lodge and platform at the edge of a lake.

Steve stretched his knee gratefully. "Well, it's just the place I can imagine people chilling out in. Back to nature and all that."

"Yeah, it's nice." Dove knocked on the front door and introduced herself and Steve.

"Oh. You're with the police? Is it about that terrible accident on the motorway last night?" A smiling young woman in expensive-looking loungewear showed them into a living room that managed to be minimalistic despite the structure of the old farmhouse. White and oatmeal.

"It does relate to the incident last night, yes," Steve said. "How did you hear about it?"

"Oh, everyone knows those three people fell off the bridges." Her smile was just a little too determined. "An accident, maybe from messing around, but still a tragedy." Her pale, shiny hair was pinned up in a wooden clip and her green eyes seemed to linger just a little too long on the wall behind them. "You'll want to speak to Louise, I expect. She runs the Retreat. The rest of us are just freelancers. But we're very much one happy family here at the Retreat." The last sentence was said defensively.

"What do you teach?" Dove asked, watching her carefully.

"Pilates. Sorry, I didn't even tell you my name." A nervous giggle and a quick hand over her mouth confirmed she wasn't quite as serene as she had first appeared. "I'm Kirstie. Louise is at the sound bath, but she'll be finished in five minutes. I'll get you a drink and you can wait in here." Without letting them answer, she disappeared, sandals slapping on the wooden floorboards.

Dove immediately moved towards the wall behind them. It was covered with photographs. Happy groups of guests doing yoga, swimming in the lake down by the woods, hiking across the rugged downland. Everyone was smiling, linking arms, hugging each other.

"Can't see Amber in any of those," Dove murmured to Steve, as she moved back to the sofa. "One very happy family indeed though, judging by the pictures."

"Very professional." he replied, and showed her his phone, which was displaying the Retreat's website. "Must have cost a bit to pull together."

Kirstie returned with a jug of water and glasses on a wooden tray, long blonde hair escaping from the clip, flopping over one slender shoulder as she put the refreshments on the table. "Can I help at all, while you're waiting?" She seemed completely composed now.

"Do you work here often?" Steve asked.

"A couple of times a week. More in the high seasons. But as I said, I'm freelance, so I'm not here all the time. I teach at the gym in Abberley as well. Louise has turned the old dairy into bedrooms, so if we're doing a five-day retreat or something, the instructors can stay over."

"Do you recognize this woman?" Steve showed a photo on his iPad.

The woman studied Amber's serious face and shook her head. "Sorry, doesn't ring any bells. Was she a guest? Oh!" Her hand went back to her mouth, eyes wide. "I've just realized . . . her name. She was one of *them*, wasn't she?"

"Amber Dionysus was one of the victims of yesterday's incident, yes." Steve said.

Dove had snapped a photo of the card from Amber's bag, and she showed this to Kirstie. "This was found among Amber's possessions." She wondered if Kirstie was as ditzy as she seemed, or if that was unfair, and it was just shock.

"Oh, I see. You think she *was* a guest. Oh my God! You really need to talk to Louise, because she knows everyone, and she remembers everyone. She was devastated to hear about the bridge accidents, especially when it was so close to us. Louise likes to help everyone, and she gets upset when she can't." The woman smiled shakily at them, her face pale and drawn suddenly. "She's got the biggest heart, and she's the best teacher. I'll go and see if I can find her. She should be finished by now." She almost ran from the room, and Dove heard the front door bang, followed by the scurry of hurried feet on gravel.

"Interesting. She's pretty in love with Louise, isn't she? Unless it's just for show." Dove said, going back to the photos. Why *was* Kirstie so on edge? Or was it just realising she might have come into contact with Amber before she died? The pale room, the calm blandness and the peace were setting her on edge. It was almost soporific.

Steve's phone rang as they waited, and, as they were the only people in the room, he put DI Blackman on speakerphone with the volume low, so they could both hear, but the conversation remained private.

"We have confirmation that both Rebecca Hales and Mark Davies have also stayed at the Retreat within the last year." Dove could hear bustle and voices in the background as DI Blackman paused. "As you're already on scene, can you get any dates, and as much information as you can about guests and staff, sent over? Oh, and Lindsey has just rung from the hospital. Mark's boyfriend, Lee, has stated Mark recently received a card similar to the one in the photograph you sent over. He can't remember what happened to the card, but he does remember Mark seemed pretty freaked out about it."

CHAPTER TEN

Dove frowned, thinking hard, as Steve ended the call. "I guess it's not so much of a coincidence if you think about it, all three being guests here. A well-being weekend might attract you if you wanted to escape from real life, but just as much as if you fancied a nice chilled-out time on the Downs. And they had to meet somewhere and have some kind of common ground. Perhaps this was it?"

Steve looked around the room. "If all three victims had been going through some kind of crisis, they might have booked in to heal — maybe giving weight to the suicide-pact theory?" He shrugged then indicated his phone. "The website is filled with glowing testimonials and happy, serious-looking people in no end of yoga positions." He snorted with sudden amusement.

"Mmm . . . not necessarily the crisis bit," Dove said. "I mean, you don't always come to a retreat because you have something major to sort out, do you? I sense that aversion to yoga coming through again, DS Parker."

"I don't get it, just like I don't get the whole healthy living thing. It brings me out in a rash. I bet you don't get chips and a burger at mealtimes here. In fact, you probably have to drink green juice all day. It's like a spa. But each to their own. Let's see what the owner has to say."

Dove could hear footsteps outside and experienced a pang of frustration. This was shaping up to be a slow-moving case, with no answers yet forthcoming. She reminded herself this was only the start of the investigation — not even a day old. Her patience had been another thing to go following Gaia's death, and she needed to keep that very much to herself at work.

"I am so shocked by what happened. We all are." Louise Grayson, the owner of the Retreat, was tall and bony with short grey hair, cut in layers around her face, and tinted rose pink around her fringe and neck. Her dark eyes were framed with wrinkles, and when she smiled, her teeth were perfect and very white against her tanned skin. She wore an armful of leather bracelets, and her nose stud was a tiny silver feather.

The overall effect was fierce, Dove thought approvingly, watching the other woman take a seat opposite. There was a little twist of pain in her chest, because something about the woman reminded her of Gaia, in both appearance and in her general demeanour. That had happened a lot since Gaia's death. Suddenly every street, every TV programme, and every magazine seemed to be full of women who reminded her in some small way of her sister.

"What do you remember about the three victims?" Steve asked, after the introductions. He indicated the iPad that he'd placed on the small table between them.

Louise tapped all three photographs showing on the screen, her manicured purple fingernail clicking sharply on its surface. "Yes, I recognize all of them. Mark, Amber and Rebecca." She looked up. "It was only Amber and Rebecca's names mentioned in the press this morning. And Rebecca and Mark are still alive, aren't they?"

"Right. But you recognized them. Were they here together?" Dove asked.

"Yes, and fairly recently, if I remember correctly. We can look on the computer. Come into the office." She led the way briskly into another near all-white room and pulled up some spreadsheets. "Amber was here in August . . . I suppose you

48

will want access to all her notes?" A crease of worry appeared on her forehead. "The guest records are confidential, but I . . ."

"We understand that, but as you must see, this is a major investigation," Dove pointed out.

"I know. I'm really just devastated, and I know she's dead, but apart from the legal stuff, it feels like betraying a confidence . . ." She was scrolling down the lists again. "Mark Davies was here in August on the same retreat as Amber. Oh, the August retreat was Amber's second visit. She had already been for a one-night stay back in June."

"Is that usual, for guests to come back again?" Steve queried.

Louise smiled, amusement warming her rather cool expression. "Yes, we often have repeat guests. We have a few who come every month, and of course, we have a daily class schedule." She laughed. "I always say they're like my little army, my regulars."

Steve nodded. "So Mark Davies?"

Louise clicked and checked the screen, "Regarding Mark, he was . . . fragile. Not physically, but he was on a pathway scheme. His visit was funded by the community trust, and I remember his partner came to join him for an evening yoga session. Well, you will see in the notes."

"And Rebecca Hales?" Dove asked.

"She came to a weekend retreat in August as well. All seemed to get on very well." Louise smiled again. "I try to make sure nobody feels like they have to be sociable if they don't want to, and many guests do come for the solitude and escape, but equally, some come to join up with like-minded people. It certainly seemed to be the case with these three guests."

"And was there anything that linked these three especially? The reason they were here, maybe?" Steve suggested.

"Well, they didn't know each other before their retreat, because I remember asking. Amber was a teaching assistant at a primary school, I think, and a very private person. She didn't open up about any special reason she was here. I would say . . . I would say she seemed to be reassessing her life on her latest visit. She seemed to enjoy herself." Louise leaned back in her chair, eyes still on the screen, fingers steepled as she talked. "Mark, he had suffered immense childhood trauma and was very damaged. He talked about it quite openly and was having professional therapy. He told me he saw a counsellor once a month."

"And Rebecca?"

Louise looked at the details on her screen. "Rebecca . . . I don't remember her as well. She was sent a gift voucher for her weekend, as I recall, and was just taking a break from work and family commitments. She had older teenage children, I think. And she had lost her husband . . . something about a car wreck, I think?"

Dove glanced at Steve. Three very different people, but all linked by the Retreat. "Do you know who gave Rebecca the gift voucher?"

"Not without delving into the financial spreadsheets, which I am happy to do, but it will take time. It might be possible to find out." Louise spoke crisply. "We have records of every transaction, but we also ask a couple of optional questions, for marketing. Things like, 'How did you hear about the Retreat?', and, 'Would you like to join our newsletter?'" She glanced at the clock on the wall as her watch beeped. "Sorry, I need to take a class in ten minutes, and I must set up. You're welcome to stay, have some green tea, some iced coffee, but it's forty minutes long, and I'm sure you probably have other places to be."

Dove looked at her sharply, but the words were said without an edge, in the same brisk businesslike tone. She gave the appearance of someone very in control, and also someone you could trust with secrets. Well, that was her business, wasn't it?

"That's fine, and you're correct, we need to get going. I just need to ask where you were yesterday evening?" Steve said.

"You mean, do I have an alibi?" She smiled. "I was right here filling out paperwork."

"Was anyone else with you?"

"No, but there were other instructors around, and we have eight guests staying with us, plus two more arriving later today." She looked at them, some of the coolness returning to her expression. "I had nothing to do with any of their deaths. My community will be in mourning after this tragedy. We're a very close-knit group, and what we have here is very special."

"These are just routine questions, for the process of elimination," Dove told her. She was unable to resist adding, just to see Louise's reaction: "And only one victim has died so far."

"Of course." The other woman met her eyes.

For a moment, Dove thought she did see sadness, but wondered uneasily if it was her own, echoed in Louise's eyes.

Louise leaned down to switch off the computer. "Forgive me, I really must go."

"Thanks very much for your time, and if you could send over the relevant files as soon as possible?" Steve passed her his card. "Oh, just one last thing. Do you recognize this?"

Dove leaned over and showed Louise the photograph of the sombre-looking card she had removed from Amber's bag. It was safe and sealed in plastic, waiting until they headed back to the station and Dove could sign it in as evidence. Yet another thing for Forensics to add to their mountains of paperwork and exhibits. But as Jess always said, "Even the smallest, most inconspicuous piece of evidence can turn out to be that golden nugget we need to move forward."

Louise's forehead creased again, as she frowned, eyes down, staring at the card. "No. Absolutely not. This isn't something we would send out." She turned and rummaged in a drawer, producing a plastic folder. "These are our compliment slips, hard copy vouchers and other stationery. As you can see, it's all branded with the blue sky, and the sheep. It's . . . well, it sets a very different tone for our followers, don't you think?"

"Any idea who might have sent this?" Steve asked.

"That will be for you to find out," she told him firmly. "But I will also ask questions. I don't like it at all that someone might have been impersonating me or my business." Her

51

eyes were angry now, and her mouth, tight. "Now if you will excuse me . . ."

A smiling, still slightly vacant Kirstie showed them out, this time through the back door, which led onto a neat lawn and the vegetable garden. She pointed back at a window. "One of our guest rooms. Isn't it pretty?"

Dove peered in at the window. It was a small, plain room with the familiar neutral décor, but the bed had a faux fur throw and cushions, and a window seat looking out onto views of the Downs. The only splash of colour was a vase of yellow chrysanthemums standing on the white-painted side table, and a blue-striped biscuit tin on the dressing table.

It was still bland, despite the colour. Still had such a strange feeling of enforced tranquillity, but also maybe of somewhere you wouldn't want to leave. Dove told herself she was being stupid, but the feeling persisted. It was all too perfect. The gardens with cookie-cutter lawn edges, the bursts of wildflowers along the immaculate gravel walkways. The buildings were so pristine, so *Instagrammable*, as her nieces would have said. Was that even a word? She crunched along the white gravel behind Steve and wondered with a wry twist of amusement what her nieces Delta and Eden would think of this place. Neither of them shared her love of yoga.

"We have a couple of guests arriving later today, so it's all ready for them," Kirstie explained. She fidgeted with her hair as she led them round the house to the car park, her leather sandals flip-flapping as they left gravel and walked over slate paving stones edged with herbs.

As they were leaving, she suddenly laid a hand on Dove's arm, and her eyes almost pleaded. "You know, lots of people come here who aren't in trouble. This is a well-being centre, not somewhere for those considering ending their lives. We run a full programme of yoga classes, guided walks, PT sessions, and we offer massages and acupuncture. It's a *family*."

The sunny expression had vanished now, words tripping over one another as though she was desperate to make them understand, to absolve herself and the Retreat from blame.

"If anyone does show signs of serious mental health or medical concerns, we wouldn't hesitate to refer them, because we are not medically qualified, that isn't what we do . . . Sorry, I'm just . . . *It isn't our fault.*"

"It's okay." Dove smiled at her, while she considered her reaction. Did Kirstie *feel* like she had played a part in this, and was concerned about being blamed? Or was the guilt stemming from the fact that she actually *had* played a part? "It is daunting when the police show up on your doorstep, and a case like this is particularly harrowing, especially for relatives and friends left behind."

Kirstie winced at this, but Dove continued kindly, "We're just trying to find out what happened, not singling anyone out for blame. If there is anything you remember, or want to tell us in confidence, you can call us."

"I know, I do know, it's just . . . we aren't some kind of weird cult, and as I say, if I felt any of the guests were on the verge of, well, suicide, I would reach out, confidential or not. And I know Louise and the other instructors and staff would do the same. The press . . . We've already had a couple of journalists round even before you arrived, and they weren't very kind. It was almost like they'd made up their minds before they even spoke to us."

"We understand, and we don't make assumptions, we gather evidence," Steve reassured her. "As DC Milson says, you've got our cards, so if you do remember anything that might be useful, just give us a call."

His phone buzzed and he glanced down at the same time as Dove glanced at hers. It was a message to the investigating team.

Dove spoke to Kirstie over her shoulder as she got into the car. "You know, you don't have to talk to the press. Just tell them 'no comment'. It's an ongoing investigation, and you are cooperating fully with the police." Her mind, though, had already switched to processing the latest update.

"Thanks, I'll tell Louise," Kirstie called after them, turning quickly and heading off down a side path.

Dove glanced in the rear-view mirror, watching the woman vanish down the hill, into the woods, then turned back to her phone. The text to the team had been brief: Rebecca Hales had died without regaining consciousness.

"So that just leaves us with Mark," Dove said softly, glancing at the sweep of pine woods circling the farm, the sunlit plateau dropping into shadows and darkness. "And I wonder if someone out there is just as interested as we are in whether he regains consciousness?"

CHAPTER ELEVEN

By the time Dove and Steve returned to the police station, it was 3.30 p.m. and for those members of the team present, there was a quick regroup. This was essential with such a large case, and so many officers working on discovering what had happened to the three different victims. With reinforcements, the team now numbered twenty, and many, many more were working behind the scenes.

"Okay, let's find out where we are on this." DI Blackman nodded at DI Waters, the most recent member of the team.

She said briskly, "Thanks, Jon. All three victims stayed at the Retreat, at Saddleworth Farm, located three miles north of the scene, in August. We have the victims' files from the owner, Louise Grayson, and these have been added to your Workspace for the case, along with current last known movements leading up to the incident."

Dove was downing another coffee, and Steve eating a Mars bar, while they added notes on their own screens. She twisted a strand of hair in her fingers as she worked, trying to force connections, her gaze occasionally landing on the incident board with its three photographs of smiling faces. Two people who would now never smile again, and one with his life hanging in the balance.

DI Waters was quickly adding details to the already crowded board with a blue marker pen. "You will all know by now that, very sadly, Rebecca Hales died in surgery. She had a ruptured spleen, amongst other extensive injuries. Her family was with her."

"I think we're wasting our time chasing other possibilities. This reads like a suicide pact," DS Pete Wyndham said suddenly, dismissively, as he bit into a bacon roll. Ketchup oozed onto the desk, and Dove saw DI Waters wince and a few others turn to stare at Pete.

"The victims didn't appear to be in any kind of crisis," Steve pointed out. "It's far too early to rule anything out yet. And the broken rail could suggest some kind of accident, or even a deliberate killing."

"So? The cameras show nobody else was near them when they jumped, okay? This has all the red flags of a pact." Pete held up a hand. "Not conclusively, but I'm just saying we can wrap this up pretty quickly and move on to the Wakefield stabbing. That's two stabbings in twenty-four hours. We're stretched enough as it is, without wasting time on people who choose to die."

Dove was watching Pete's face as he finally realized he had said way too much. He went quiet, making a big deal of finishing his bacon roll and slurping coffee. Straight-talking, abrasive DS Pete 'Donkey' Wyndham was now attempting to bluster it out. It was always interesting to get glimpses of the real person behind the detective, as, in general, they were damn good at not wearing their hearts on their shirtsleeves.

But suicide was a contentious issue. And an emotive one. Dove's own strong opinion, both professional and personal, was that you should never judge. How could anyone else possibly know what went on in another's head? Everyone was different, felt things differently, reacted differently. It never hurt to be kind, to show a little empathy and compassion. Whatever was driving Pete Wyndham, she was pretty sure it was neither of those things.

Dove hastily swallowed the last of her coffee and turned back to DI Waters, who, despite the fact it was now past 4 p.m., was still looking cool and crisp, the white shirt still immaculately ironed, the hair still perfectly in place. She was frowning at Pete, but seemed a little unsure of her comeback.

"Thank you for your insight, DS Wyndham," DI Blackman cut in coolly. "We are all aware the force is over-stretched, but if we could just take each investigation one stage at a time, to ensure nothing is missed?"

Pete ignored him, head down in his iPad. Definitely a raw nerve touched, Dove concluded, as the briefing finished.

Back at her desk, Dove began to sort through the files from the Retreat, trawling through spreadsheets and trying to match dates. So far there was no evidence that Amber, Rebecca and Mark had ever crossed paths before the weekend retreat in August. They lived in different parts of town, had different family situations, were at different stages of life.

She tapped a pen against the desk, thinking hard. A headache was niggling away at the base of her skull, and she popped a couple of paracetamols, washing them down with half a bottle of water. She couldn't afford to fall apart on the first day, and she had learned the hard way to take care of herself.

They really needed the data from the three phones but, as usual, Jess, her team, and the labs, were all stacking work. It had been a busy week for the team, what with Dove only just coming back from leave, and as DS Wyndham correctly pointed out, they were short-staffed. The tech data, specifically communications between the three victims, had been flagged, and would jump to the top of the pile, but even so, it was a time-consuming and intensive job, combing hundreds of phone records.

After an hour, Lindsey stopped by her desk, delivering a bumper pack of jelly sweets. "On sale at the garage. Just in case you need a sugar fix."

Dove spun her chair round and looked up at her colleague. Lindsey had never even brought her a coffee before.

"Thanks, I think I'm going cross-eyed. A sugar high is exactly what I need." She stretched her arms above her head and yawned. "What have you got on Mark Davies?"

Lindsey sat on the edge of the desk, causing Steve, who was on the phone, to shift his paperwork with a muffled curse. "A damaged kid, looked for help but didn't get anything from the usual routes. He was in and out of care when he was younger, social services waiting lists and all the usual stuff." She waited until Dove tore open the packet of sweets before nicking a few. "But he seemed to be turning his life around. New boyfriend who adores him, says he was going to get a dog. They were planning a holiday to the Lake District for next spring. All good stuff."

"Job?" Dove let the sugar fizz on her tongue.

"He was working part-time for a gardener. She says he was a nice lad, always on time and had a good attitude."

"Not having any kind of mental health crisis, then?" Dove queried, thinking back to DS Wyndham's dismissive comments.

"No. Previously, yes, but he's moving on. Or if he was having some kind of breakdown, he was keeping it well hidden. He's local, Roedean House, and the last sighting was a street cam near the car park down by the pier at 7. p.m. His boyfriend is absolutely devastated, more so thinking that it was a suicide attempt and he failed to appreciate Mark was getting depressed again. Bloody rumour mill churning out all this 'bridge jumper suicide pact' bollocks." She rolled her eyes. "The poor kid's sitting down at the hospital at his bedside right now praying for him to wake up."

"Doesn't help, does it, all this social media shit?" Dove agreed, tipping another trickle of sweets into her hand, as Lindsey headed back to her desk, playfully whacking her partner, Josh, on the back of the head as she sat down. "Got anything new?"

DC Josh Conrad glanced round with a look of the long-suffering: "You do realize you just assaulted me?"

"Get over it, pretty boy, and let's get moving. We're off to Roedean House."

Dove grinned at the pair. Lindsey was extremely brisk, blunt and impatient, but she had a big heart. Who else had said that recently? Kirstie at the Retreat. She had described Louise, the owner, in the same way.

"Amber's car is in the garage for repairs. She hired a vehicle on Friday morning from Pink Lady Car Rental," Steve announced from his desk. "She was meant to drop it off at 1 p.m. today, but of course, she didn't."

"The car rental place is near the industrial estates." Dove peered at his screen. "So where is the car now? She left the George pub on foot last night."

"The owner of the rental place just called it in as stolen. It doesn't look like they've connected it to last night's incident." Steve walked across to DI Blackman to update him.

"Let's go and check it out then," Dove said, as he returned. "I'll drive, and we can grab some food after we do the interview."

"On it. The DI's going to put a BOLO out."

* * *

Her adrenaline crackling at a possible new lead, mixed with her recent sugar hit, Dove wove through the traffic to the car rental depot. Having parked up, they took in the Portakabin office, and on entry found it to be inexplicably filled to bursting with fleshy-leaved tropical house plants. After fighting their way through the jungle, they discovered a petite girl with a tangled mane of fiery red hair, shouting into her mobile phone.

She looked an apology at Dove and Steve and finished her call, before chucking her mobile phone down on the desk. "Wankers! Sorry, bloody local garage thinking they can piss around with bill payments." She flashed a smile. "What can I do for you?"

"Are you Terri Sealey?" Dove asked, wondering if it was something in the air, that everyone was yelling into their mobiles today.

"Yes. You must be police. You look like police." Her smile dimmed a notch. "Are you here about the stolen car?" She looked expectantly from one to the other. "Did you find it yet?"

"No, sorry." Steve filled her in on the case and she swore again.

"I saw that on Twitter this morning. Horrible. I've been so busy with other shit all day, that it didn't click." She rummaged on her desk, long pink nails clicking as she flicked through her paperwork, finally extracting a printout. "This is Amber Dionysus' driver's licence, insurance details and a copy of her signed contract."

Dove took the documents, neatly held together by a pink paper clip and flipped through. Standard documents and a scan of the driver's licence. The address was the same one they had on file for Amber. The same address Forensics would have now vacated, as they moved onto their next job. She hoped to God they had found something.

"The customer picked up from our Southford office on Wednesday and was due to deliver back by 1 p.m. today. But if she's dead, then what the hell has she done with my car?" Terri lit a cigarette. She moved her chair back from the desk, and crossed her legs, skin-tight stretch blue jeans and white tank top, showing off her muscular physique.

"You don't have trackers on your vehicles?" Steve asked.

She rolled her eyes. "Too expensive. And they're rental cars, not security vans."

"Right. Can you put us in touch with the person who dealt with Amber when she picked up her car?" Steve asked.

"Neil Barnes. You gonna drive over and talk to him? He won't like that. He hates coppers." She paused. "He's not great at answering the phone, either. I tried to ring him about the missing car, but his mobile is going straight to answerphone. Kevin's there, though. He's Neil's assistant.

But he doesn't know anything else about Amber Dionysus. I already spoke to him."

"I'm sure Neil will be happy to help with the investigation when he finds out he isn't the one being investigated," Steve told her, with a big smile.

She nodded slowly, eyes narrowing, assessing, before she passed a pink business card over to Steve. The logo was a pair of shiny pink lips kissing a shiny pink car, with two addresses typed below. "Phone numbers are on there. We close at six at both depots, so you'd better get a move on. Neil never stays late, so he'll be locking up on the dot."

The dense, earthy smell of the plant jungle, combined with the cigarette smoke, was making Dove feel sick, and she was pleased to get outside in the fresh air. The air was still muggy, but the warmth of the late afternoon September sun was already drying puddles from the earlier downpour.

CHAPTER TWELVE

"Do you want me to drive?" Dove asked, noting Steve was limping again.

"Nope. I'm good. Let's get going before the car rental place closes."

Back in the car, Dove pulled out her phone and tried to trace the route Amber might have taken the night she died. "Southford is only twenty minutes down the coast. I don't get why Amber would rent a car at all. Unless she originally planned to use the vehicle in a suicide attempt?" She leaned back against her seat, briefly closing her eyes against the sunlight, trying to put Amber's movements into the timeline in her head. "It's just as weird as trying to untangle why the hell she booked in at the George, when she lives practically just down the road."

"Not quite, but I know what you mean. It doesn't add up. It doesn't tie in with the other victims' movements either. As far as we know, they all had separate routes to Saddle Bridge, all made their own way up there. And you're right: if she rented a car on Friday morning, and needed to get up to Saddle Bridge, why not use it to drive up there?"

"Do you know this Neil Barnes, the car rental bloke in Southford?" Dove twisted a strand of hair in her fingers, staring unseeingly at the road ahead. "I got the impression you might have history, from the face you pulled when his name came up?"

"Did I? My mistake." He grinned as he pulled out onto the main road. "We've crossed paths. He's done time years ago, for burglary and assault, I think, but he's an okay bloke. Not many brains, and he seems to get dragged into scams. Usually get-rich-quick ones." Steve had a lot of local knowledge, having spent years in uniform before he joined the MCT. He pulled into a lay-by. "Actually, let's think about this logically, get a route Amber might have taken from the Southford depot and drive it now, albeit in reverse. Hell, we might find she ditched the car soon after she picked it up. It won't take us any longer than going along the Coast Road, not at this time of the afternoon."

"We could drive across Chanton Way and down North Street," Dove suggested thoughtfully, studying the map on the sat nav. "No cameras on any of the back roads, but it might be worth a look. She could have parked it in any of a hundred residential areas, though."

Dove sent the details of Neil at Pink Lady Cars to the DI, while Steve set the sat nav and pulled out. A motorcycle courier flashed past, nearly taking their wing mirror off. He swerved and gave them a V-sign as he continued.

"Pretty sure you indicated there," Dove commented, mildly annoyed.

"Pretty sure I did, too. Let's find Mr Barnes via the scenic route."

* * *

With no sign of the missing Pink Lady rental car on their route east, Steve eventually drove into a rundown car yard, which sat between two near-derelict buildings. The Southford depot of Pink Lady Cars was almost deserted apart from three lines of cars. Another makeshift office was housed in a Portakabin. Tracking down Kevin, who was washing two Renault Clios, Dove enquired after Neil Barnes.

The boy, who Dove thought was probably not more than seventeen or eighteen, shrugged. "Dunno where he is. I opened up this morning and he wasn't here. Sometimes he's late on a Saturday, because it's never that busy. I gave out a set of keys, took back two more sets and logged all the vehicles in and out. That was when I noticed the missing one. I gave it a couple of hours, figured she might just be late." He shrugged again. "I covered for him when the boss rang, because Neil gives me a bit of extra cash, when I do."

"Does Neil often just disappear when he's supposed to be working?" Dove asked.

Another shrug. "Sometimes. I don't care. He's a good bloke, but if he's not here I can easily handle stuff on my own."

"Did you see the woman who rented the missing car?" Steve asked.

"Oh yeah. She turned up and asked to see Neil. I thought she was maybe one of his girlfriends. He's had a few . . . I mean, as well as Tanya." The kid's cheeks flushed red as he glanced down at his sponge and bucket. "When Neil came out and saw her, this Amber woman, he looked really freaked out, so I thought I had been right, and maybe he'd been caught cheating."

"Has Neil seemed to be behaving any differently over the past week or so?" Dove put in. "Has he vanished more often, or confided in you, maybe?"

"Yeah, he has been really stressed out, but he wouldn't tell me what was going on. No kidding, he went absolutely white when he saw Amber, like he was seeing a ghost. He took her into the office. They had a row."

"Did you hear what they were arguing about?" Dove asked.

Kevin shook his head and chucked the dirty soapy water down the drain. "Didn't hear much, but it seemed like she was trying to get him to do something, like meet her on a date, and he wouldn't. She mentioned a video, so maybe she's got something on him. Anyway, she came out after about an hour, really calm and not bothered at all, and I sorted her out with keys and that, but Neil stayed in there for ages with the blinds drawn."

Steve showed Kevin the photos on his iPad and the kid positively identified Amber as the woman who rented the car, but didn't know either Mark or Rebecca. "Can you let us know if Neil does get in touch?"

"Is he in trouble?"

"No, we just need to speak to him. He could help us to find out what happened to Amber," Dove explained. She could tell Kevin wasn't buying it, and wondered if he had secrets of his own.

But he seemed cooperative enough, walking briskly into the office and coming out with a bit of paper. "I've written Tanya's number down . . . like, his main girlfriend he lives with." His light grey eyes were thoughtful, contemplative. "She called this morning looking for him, too. She was in a right state."

"Thanks, that's really helpful." Steve smiled at the boy.

As they walked away, the kid called after them, "Neil's all right, you know, so I hope he really isn't in trouble. He's got kids, and he's a good dad, so whatever else he does in his spare time . . . I mean, it can't be that bad, right?"

"What do you think of that?" Dove asked, as they got back into the car, and she slid the key into the ignition.

"I think Neil Barnes suddenly got really interesting." Steve took out his phone and, looking at the scrap of paper the kid had given them, tapped out a number. "If he was having an affair with Amber, and now he's done a vanishing act . . ."

"And the car she rented is missing." Dove finished his sentence as she started their own car, picked a different route back into town, and joined the queue of traffic inching past Sainsbury's. She hadn't asked Steve if he wanted her to drive, but had simply put her hand in his pocket and pulled out the car keys, taking his amused and resigned reaction as agreement.

After a while, Steve put his phone down. "No answer from Neil's phone and the voicemail is full. The girlfriend's phone goes straight to voicemail. Let's get back for the briefing and then chase them up."

* * *

By 7 p.m., the room was packed, the incident board had been extended by another metre, and three boxes of doughnuts were doing the rounds. Dove selected one and sank her teeth into it as she listened to the DCI give an up-to-date recap, before giving the nod to DS Amin, who, partnered with DS Wyndham, had been allocated Rebecca Hales to investigate.

"Rebecca Hales. Friends and family say she wasn't depressed and would never have left her kids. Her ex, the kids' dad, died in 2019. Apparently, she had a tough time then, but is now running her own business. Her mum gave her a weekend at the Retreat for her birthday in January, but she only got around to using the voucher in August." DS Amin pushed her hair back wearily. "The search team did find prescription anti-depressants at her home, and in the purse she was carrying at the time of the incident. Prozac, or Fluoxetine. But they found nothing that pointed to suicide."

"Anything of interest on the timeline?" DI Blackman was leaning against the wall, updating notes on his iPad. He glanced up at DS Amin, and she replied quickly.

"She lives near the station, and the kids were having a sleepover with their friends. Last sighting is 7.20 p.m., when she was waiting at the bus stop on North Shore Road. She gets on the 404, which would take her up towards the motorway bridges."

DS Wyndham was also reading from notes, and he added, "One of her kids told the FLO she had been staying up late recently, looking at videos. He said it was out of character because she always needs to be up early for work. She is . . . *was* . . . a florist."

"Neil Barnes was looking at a video with Amber when she rented the car," Steve said. "According to the kid who works there, they had a row, and today he's a no-show at the depot."

"And Amber was looking at videos in her room at the George. One of the young housekeepers mentioned she was watching a video on her laptop. She suggested it might be YouTube." Dove made some doodles on her notepad. "Maybe they were all involved in some kind of emotional blackmail attempt. What if Amber had an affair with Neil, and she confided in Mark and Rebecca when she met them at the Retreat?" But it sounded off, even as she spoke the words aloud. There had to be a connection, but surely Amber wouldn't have confided in people she had just met?

"What would they get out of it, though?" Lindsey asked. "Can't be money, because Neil doesn't appear to be flush with cash. Emotional blackmail . . . mmm." Lindsey looked doubtful. "Maybe Amber wanted Neil to leave his girlfriend for her? A love triangle? But I'm not getting it, to be honest."

"We'll see what comes back from the lab on the victims' tech devices," DCI Franklin said. "Anything else for background? Have we eliminated any drugs links yet? We need to narrow this down, people. I don't need to tell you this, but the press are watching every move, and we're under pressure to get answers and fast."

DI Blackman was looking at the incident boards. "There isn't any link to the White Horses, or any other indication this is drugs-related at the moment. But we're still waiting on Amber's post-mortem, and the lab tox screens."

"I'll chase them now," the DCI promised, picking up his phone and leaving the room, muttering, "I know we're short-staffed, but this is ridiculous!"

Lindsey provided an update on Mark Davies, finishing with, "He may have had a rough time previously, but there is nothing to show he was suicidal at any point. Concerns were mainly for his personal welfare, which is why he was in temp sheltered accommodation." She glanced at her notes. "He was doing an access learning course in horticulture. His boyfriend is adamant Mark was in no way suicidal, but he did say he could be far too trusting and innocent. He seemed to feel he had failed Mark by not looking after him."

"And the update from the hospital an hour ago says he is still in critical condition," Josh added, yawning. He had a mug of tea on the table in front of him, and an energy drink in his hand.

Dove studied the timelines, the different possible routes each had taken to supposedly end their lives. There was no common denominator so far. Different modes of transport, different backgrounds and demographics, and yet somehow, they had been at the bridge at the same time. What videos had they all been watching? Had it been through a platform like YouTube? TikTok? One video, specifically?

DCI Franklin returned from his call. "A few answers, and the rest of the specifics are being fast-tracked." He looked down at the notepad in his hand. "We do have a red flag on the tox screens for Mark. He had diazepam in his blood. Not a high dosage, but given his size and weight, it would certainly have affected his physical actions and thought processes." He paused to allow this to sink in.

"They were all members of the Retreat online chat group, and we have isolated their messages, but there doesn't appear to have been any talk of suicide, no arguments, just normal chat. What time is the next yoga class, I'm walking at 10 a.m., does anyone want to join me, blah, blah. Lots of talk about how the Retreat changed their lives, how the teaching is so special. Again, blah, blah." DCI Franklin was skimming the notes again, highlighting key points as he came to them. "Admins on the chat group are the owner Louise, then Meredith and Tina, who are both freelance teachers attached to the retreat. Finally, the lab is working on triangulation of phones and is going to zero in on videos and search histories from all other tech devices."

With it clear DCI Franklin had finished his update, DI Waters added further information. "The news on the broken railing is that section of the bridge was replaced two weeks ago, so it could be faulty work on the original structure, whereby whoever built it simply put the rail in place and forgot the securing screws. The second option is that it was deliberately unscrewed in anticipation of three people jumping or falling through it."

Lastly, Steve updated them on Amber. Neil Barnes was quickly highlighted as a person of interest.

"Can you two get over to Neil's girlfriend now and see if she knows anything?" DI Blackman asked. He glanced at his watch. "I don't want to lose this Neil Barnes thread if we can help it. Bernie says Martha Dionysus, Amber's mother, is still refusing to cooperate in so far as speaking to us further." He ran his eyes down a document. "Amber's best friend, Elise, is on holiday in Spain, but she contacted us and asked to speak to the investigating team. She hasn't seen her for nearly five days, but she is adamant Amber was fine, happy and loving her job as a teaching assistant at a local primary school. She was the one who told us Amber's car was in the garage for repairs."

"I wonder which garage Amber's car is being repaired at," Dove said. "I'll ring Elise back and see if she knows."

CHAPTER THIRTEEN

My first boyfriend is probably the only one who ever saw the real me. At thirteen, I was starting to realize most people can't distance their emotions, can't control their feelings and just don't have the extra imagination or inclination to want to control others.

I did feel anger. That was real. Sadness? Well, I could cry. I continued to watch a lot of movies, TV, social media, soaking up the facial expressions, the reactions. At home, nobody really cared what I did, and it was always so busy I could just blend in with the background noise. Which was perfect, because I could, and did, invent a whole new life for myself.

My boyfriend was called Tom, and we dated for a couple of months, as young teens do. We went to the fair on the seafront, a few McDonald's, nothing much. Mostly we just hung out round school. It was just before I found my crowd, my wild friends, who I fooled myself into thinking were a lot like me. Really, they were just an early example of my followers.

But at thirteen, I was still perfecting my acting, changing myself into whoever I thought I might want to be on a daily basis. But more, it was becoming about who they wanted me to be. I realized I didn't have to be just the one person. I could play a different part for everyone. That way, nobody ever really knew who I was deep down.

Tom wasn't as easy to read as most people are, and I was intrigued, wanting a challenge, I suppose. He liked football, played on the school team, the local youth team, and seemed outwardly confident, with no flaws, no chinks in his armour. Until, finally, he confided his cousin had died falling off the cliffs over near Claw Beach and he had a fear of heights.

So that was it. I needed to get him somewhere high up to test my theory. Eventually, I managed to convince him to go to the Lighthouse Café. The café is in a room at the bottom, but after Cokes and a burger, I used all my powers of persuasion to get him to climb to the top with me.

I saw it as me winning. He saw it as him winning, because he was facing his fear.

At the top, he was terrified. There were a couple of tourists taking photos, but they soon vanished back down the winding stairs.

I walked to the balcony guard rail and leaned back, tilting my face upwards to the sun, just to see what he would do. I could feel my long hair fanning out in the breeze, the slight dizziness that comes with being high up. He came straight over and pulled me roughly away.

"Don't be so bloody stupid. Why would you do that?" His voice was rough, angry. And afraid.

"Chill. Why not? The rail's safe. I'm just having fun."

This clearly annoyed him, but I moved slightly, shifting our positions, so he could appreciate the true danger, the true exhilaration. We had our backs to the railings, and behind us, the whole world was spread sparkling at our feet, hundreds of feet down as we clung together.

I gave him a push in the chest, just a little one.

CHAPTER FOURTEEN

It was a warm evening, all trace of rain gone, the sky washed pale blue and blush pink. The sun was low over the sea, making the wet roads shimmer. Dove looked longingly at the sea, rippling with idle waves.

It was a perfect time of day for some paddle boarding, or for heading further up the coast and catching some waves at Claw Beach or West Point, where the winds and rocks made for some good surfing in the right conditions.

But instead of heading home, she was driving towards the eastern side of Lymington-on-Sea, past the betting shops, the clubs and the souvenir kiosks, and out onto another concrete estate, and Steve was on the phone to his wife, explaining he would be late. The rain had washed litter to the side of the roads, clogging the storm drains with takeaway cartons and broken bottles.

As she drove, using her hands-free system, Dove drew a blank with Elise, Amber's best friend, but left a voicemail asking for a call back asap, before pulling up outside Neil's address.

Neil Barnes' girlfriend, Tanya, answered the door to their flat on this Saturday evening, with a toddler on each hip, and a perfect face of make-up. Dove, an experienced aunt and godmother, looked at her with respect.

Steve did the introductions, and Tanya looked puzzled. "You said on the phone, you're working on this three bridges case, but I don't see what that's got to do with Neil. He isn't one of the ones who jumped off the bridge, is he?"

"We're just following up leads. There's a chance Neil might be able to help us with the investigation."

"Okay . . ." The two children were soon seated, watching *Peppa Pig* on TV in the living area, and Tanya took them into the kitchen.

"I don't know where Neil has gone, or what you think he might know, but he's done it this time." She slicked a stray piece of platinum blonde hair back behind her ear. Tiny gold earrings glinted in the late evening sunlight pouring in at the window. She leaned against the sink while the kettle boiled, arms folded. "He doesn't get that you can't just disappear without any message, leave your kids and do whatever the hell you want."

"Has Neil disappeared before?" Steve queried.

"Oh, yes. Right after Millie was born. I was studying to be a midwife then, so it was tough juggling everything." She smiled, with a touch of steel. "But it was okay, you know? I had a goal, and I knew what I wanted. Neil buggered off to stay with that idiot, Max, and his stupid girlfriend. I can't remember what her name was."

"Is Max a friend?" Steve asked.

Tanya grabbed some mugs from the cupboard and made tea while she answered. "Max Carter is a friend of Neil's. They go way back, and they used to share a flat. I rang him, but he says he hasn't seen Neil, either. Not that he wouldn't tell me lies if it suited him, the sly bastard." She frowned. "But it's true Neil hasn't seen much of Max for a year or so now. The girlfriend was Kerrie or Karon or something. I never met her, but occasionally Neil would bang on about what a pain she was and how she was always dragging Max down. I'll tell you for nothing, Max didn't need anyone to drag him down, because he was doing a great job of that all by himself."

"Has Neil been acting normally in the last week? Anything different, especially yesterday, that might help us to find him," Dove said gently. The clock on the kitchen wall read a quarter past seven, but she had almost forgotten her exhaustion in the thrill of actually chasing down a decent lead.

"Well, he's been pretty stressed all week, but I've been working twelve-hour shifts, so I haven't seen him that much . . . um . . . he did get a call really late on maybe Wednesday...? I was annoyed because it woke me up, and I had to get up for an early shift. It was about 2 a.m., and he got out of bed and went into the kitchen, shut the door." Tanya dumped hot drinks on the small island table in the middle of the kitchen, peered round the doorway to check on the kids, and then scribbled on a bit of paper. "Max's number. He works at a garage, but I can't remember which one . . . Sorry, like I said, we don't exactly socialize."

Dove exchanged glances with Steve. "Did he say what the call was about?"

"No, and I didn't ask. I thought it might be one of his girlfriends." She sighed, sadness in her eyes and weariness in her expression. "I'm going to leave him as soon as the girls start school. It's not far off, and he's had enough chances."

"Did he know that?"

"I didn't tell him, because I wanted to be organized with childcare and that, when I booted him out. I almost always pay the rent on this place, and it's in my name."

Steve brought out the photos, and Tanya pointed at the one of Amber. "That looks like Max's ex, I think. They split up ages ago, but Neil has some photos of them on his phone. I can't be absolutely sure, but it could be her. Sorry, I don't know the others." She tapped the pictures of Rebecca and Mark.

"You think this one is Max's girlfriend?" Steve asked carefully.

Dove caught his glance and felt her own heart jump a little. Finally, this all seemed to be unravelling a little. It was like picking at a knot: once a little bit came loose, you could start to undo the threads one at a time.

"Yes. I mean, no. His ex. I never met her. But I told you, she hasn't been on the scene for years now. Neil said Max would never have kept his job if she was still around. She was wild, always wanting to go out partying, even now they're grown-ups." Tanya considered. "It was recent. Neil was looking at the old photos. Like, last week or something, because I remember joking that he was getting old and grey now."

"So, she was a long-term girlfriend, maybe?" Dove was trying to picture it in her head. Had Amber Dionysus been Max Carter's girlfriend, not Neil's? The description Tanya gave certainly didn't seem to fit with what other witnesses had said about Amber.

"And you last saw Neil when?"

"When I got back from work, at 5 p.m., my mum said he dropped the girls off as usual that morning and went to work, but when I got home, he was — well, he was stressing about something." She stopped and leaned against the counter, thinking. "I got the shopping on the way home, and I started getting dinner ready, when he said he needed to go out."

"Did he seem upset?" Steve asked.

"Angry, maybe. I asked if he was okay, and told him to get back for dinner, but—" she sighed — "I was trying to get organized for work the next morning, sort the girls out, and he just went in the bedroom, came out with his gym bag and said he was going for a workout."

"Did he have a car?"

"Yes, but he didn't take it. Someone must have picked him up, because by the time I settled Anna and went to the door, he was gone, and the car was still outside." A tear slid down her cheek, and she brushed it impatiently away. "I know he's left us properly this time, and we'll be okay, but what a shit. My sisters said he was a loser, and they were right."

Dove comforted her awkwardly. "I'm really sorry. Did he leave a phone or laptop or anything?"

"No, after he didn't get back for dinner, I saw he'd taken everything with him, even a few clothes. I've been ringing and texting his number, but get nothing." She sniffed. "I thought he'd be back, but when there was just nothing . . . that's why I even rang Max, because I figured if he was in trouble, that's where he would go." Tanya's eyes were shining with tears. "This isn't about some stupid affair, is it? He's done something badly wrong this time. I can tell you wouldn't be here unless he was in real trouble."

CHAPTER FIFTEEN

There was no answer from Max Carter's mobile. Dove, leaning against the car door in the darkness, enjoying the sweetness of the evening air, letting the gentle breeze fan her hair, debated their next move.

"Let's call it a night," Steve said, yawning. "We can pick up in the morning, and we've got a good lead, even if we've no clue where we're going with it!"

"Okay," Dove agreed, slightly reluctantly. "If Neil and Max have something to do with Amber, and Neil is now missing, it does point towards both of them somehow being involved in her death last night, doesn't it? Perhaps the involvement of the other two victims was coincidental. You're right. I'll send this intel in now, and we'll pick it up tomorrow."

She didn't want to leave it, but knew she needed a break to recharge. Besides, most of the day team would have already gone home, leaving the skeleton night shift to carry on sifting information in the incident room. And in this case, there was already a hell of a lot of information to sift through.

Dove shook her hair out of her eyes and left the window open as she drove them back into town. The Coast Road led them back through to Lymington-on-Sea towards quaint and pretty Abberley, and was crammed with partygoers heading for the bars and clubs on the promenade. Dove braked sharply to avoid a group of men clutching beer bottles, staggering across the road.

"Bit early to be that drunk," Steve observed, with some amusement.

"You're getting old, DS Parker," Dove informed him. "I bet you had the wildest Saturday nights when you were younger."

Her partner laughed. "I did, but my idea of a great night out is more gastropub than clubs these days. Actually, scrap that. I'm quite fond of a pizza on the sofa and an uninterrupted night's sleep."

Dove dropped him off and drove towards home. As usual her quiet street soothed her, as did the scents of salt and unseasonal but welcome warm weather mingling with the waft of a BBQ two doors along. It was familiar and she felt safe here, shrugging off the day for a while as she enjoyed her homecoming. Little things she had learned to appreciate since Gaia died, that she had barely taken time to notice before.

Layla purred around her ankles, demanding attention, before disappearing into the back garden on silent paws to hunt. Dove poured a glass of wine, kicked off her shoes and sank down onto the sofa, closing her eyes for a few minutes. But her brain was still working, refusing to quit for the night.

She knew she was exhausted. But, still wired, she pulled her laptop down onto the sofa, tore open a packet of crisps, and opened some files. She went back to the list of the Retreat's guests, highlighting when each of the three victims had stayed. Neither Neil nor Max were on the list, not that she thought they would be. A search for Max Carter and garages in the local area drew a blank.

Her phone pinged with a text. Quinn would be home by midnight, and she answered his text quickly before she got lost in her research. Her head was spinning. She knew she should get out her yoga mat, and plug into her meditation app, but she couldn't let it go.

She logged into her work account and cross-checked her notes against the information logged in the police database, HOLMES for Amber, her mother and then variations of all three victims, and came up with zero. Max Carter and Neil Barnes both had criminal records. Petty stuff, but Max had gone inside for a stretch back in 2017 for dealing.

Feeling like she was onto a losing streak, Dove went back to the extensive guest list for the Retreat. As she scanned the names, she reached for another glass of wine to boost her flagging energy levels, and suddenly froze. One of the names on the list was Gaia Smith-Minton.

Her sister had stayed at the Retreat. Dove put her glass down with an unsteady hand, her heart racing. What the hell? Twice. She had been there in 2019 and once more this year, just two months before she died.

Why would her tough-talking, borderline gangster sister want to stay at Saddleworth Farm to do yoga? She hated things like that, and was always taking the piss out of Dove, who loved yoga. Dove dropped her head into her hands briefly, her mind whirling in confusion.

Quinn wasn't home, and rather than face a lonely hour staring at the TV trying to take her mind off Gaia, Dove scooped up Layla and went into the spare room. The cat purred her approval and immediately began slinking between the boxes.

Gaia's things. She and Ren had divided up the boxes from Gaia's apartment, promising each other they would go through them 'at some point'. Tonight, wanting to feel near to her sister, and curious about the Retreat, Dove started to open the cardboard lids.

Dove opened the first box, carefully taking out Gaia's belongings, forcing herself to remember the best and worst things about her sister, forcing herself not to scream and sob.

There was a lot of paperwork, old mobiles, an old laptop. She knew her sister had been a meticulous creature, street smart and nobody's fool, so she wasn't surprised she had left behind an orderly life.

Some old birthday cards from Eden and Delta. She half-smiled. A few photos in a silver envelope. Old, childhood memories. That was surprising, as Gaia had been the one who professed hatred of the hippy lifestyle.

A slip of paper with her name on.

Dove felt her heart give an uncomfortable stutter for a moment and took a long deep breath. The first time this had happened she had freaked out, but after investigation it had turned out to be an arrhythmia linked to stress. If she got too tired, emotional, angry, it was triggered.

Automatically, she breathed deeply several more times before she felt her heart settle back into a normal rhythm. God, surely she was too young to have bloody heart problems! But her breath was shortening as she picked up the blue and gold slip. It was a voucher. She turned it over in her hands, feeling the expensive rustle of silky paper, taking in the now familiar logo, sky-blue with a sheep motif. Her name at the top, Gaia's at the bottom.

Gaia had bought her a voucher for the Retreat at Saddleworth Farm. But she had never given it to her . . . Puzzled, Dove looked for the date. November last year. A Christmas gift she had decided against? A purchase forgotten in the chaos of running her business empire, stashed away in haste and lost amongst the paperwork?

Dove reached for her phone and pulled up the website. Yes, gift vouchers could be purchased to order. She flipped back to hers. It lasted for a year, and was for a weekend retreat. Had Gaia enjoyed hers so much she wanted to gift her sister the experience, too? But then, wouldn't she have also explained she had been a guest?

She rang Ren. "You all right, lovely?" Her sister's voice was sharp with worry. "Did you just get home?"

"Yes, I'm fine. Sorry to disturb you this late, I just wanted to ask you something . . . Ren, did Gaia ever mention buying me a gift voucher to the Retreat for last Christmas? Or for my birthday or something?"

There was silence as Ren considered the question, before she answered with certainty. "No, absolutely not. She got you that silver necklace with the amber pendant for a Christmas present, didn't she?"

"Hmm . . . I know, it's just . . ." She told her sister about the voucher.

"I can't think why she didn't give it to you, but I suppose she must have forgotten about it. Or perhaps she was saving it for your birthday?"

"The weekend retreats aren't cheap, though. It costs five hundred pounds for a guest pass and accommodation."

"Love, think about how much Gaia was making from the business. I doubt five hundred would have seemed like much to her, and she was so astute with money. She was always the one who saved her pocket money, wasn't she?" There was a smile in Ren's voice.

Despite herself, Dove felt herself relax a little, shoulders drooping, tension draining away. "True. I suppose you're right, and she just forgot about it. I just wonder why she wanted me to go?"

Silence again, this time for longer, before Ren said surprisingly, "You're thinking of using the voucher, aren't you?"

"Yes." Dove bit her thumbnail, staring into the darkness outside. The window was open just a crack, and a breath of salty air caressed her face, drying the tears on her cheeks. In her mind, she could see ten-year-old Gaia stashing all her pocket money in an old tobacco tin she had kept in her sock drawer. God knows where she had found it, but every note or coin was listed on a notepad and accounted for.

"If you want to, if it helps even the tiniest bit with your grief, you should do it. You love yoga and meditation and all that. Gaia knew that." Ren's voice was gentle.

"I think you're right." Dove cleared her throat, trying to push the emotions away. "It's worse at night, isn't it?"

"Yes, yes, it is." They were both silent for a while, and Dove listened to her sister breathing softly at the other end of the phone before she spoke again. "Do you want to come over?"

"No, thanks, Ren. I'm okay, really. Quinn's back soon."

"Ah, good." She could hear the relief in Ren's voice. "Now, are you sure you're okay about this voucher?"

"Yes, thanks, Ren. I'll try and come over tomorrow after work, shall I? Sleep well." She ended her call and went back into the kitchen just as the front door banged, and Quinn walked in, face pale with exhaustion.

CHAPTER SIXTEEN

He threw his bags and jacket into the pile in the tiny hallway. "Hi, babe, how's it going?"

"Busy." Dove passed him a glass of wine, glancing at her watch. "I ordered a curry in. It should be here in fifteen minutes. I know it's late, but I thought we could do with a treat after last night."

"You star! I'll just grab a shower, and you can tell me how the investigation is going." He kissed her as he passed, heading for the stairs.

The house still smelled faintly of new paint and new carpets. An arson attack had devastated the building just a few months ago. It was a Victorian, brick-built end of terrace, and luckily the fire hadn't spread any further along the row or caused any loss of life. The arsonist had been a woman who had become obsessed with Quinn. Although he spent a long time denying it, her fiancé had got himself a stalker. And one obsessed enough to eventually follow him home from work and throw a Molotov Cocktail through his window in a jealous rage.

Dove sipped her wine as she kept an eye on the road, waiting for her food delivery, trying to keep her mind off the case. Quinn had recently been involved in a court case, against the woman who not only stalked him, but also eventually tried to kill them both. The case had attracted local media interest, and Quinn had become very withdrawn, even once the guilty verdict had been given and the woman had been sentenced, he was still struggling to deal with the light-hearted banter at work.

She thought part of the reason was his insistence people were laughing at him, that it wasn't okay to complain, as a man, about being stalked by a woman. He had admitted he felt stupid, and in some way, he also felt he was to blame. In addition to the case, Gaia's sudden death had devastated the whole family. A tough load to carry, but at least they had each other.

Twenty minutes later, Quinn was back downstairs, pouring another glass of wine and sinking gratefully onto the sofa. His hair was wet, framing his face, and he had pulled on a white T-shirt and grey joggers. Still tanned from the hot summer, she noted nonetheless the purple shadows under his eyes, and the lines across his forehead. But then he smiled, and she felt her heart give that stupid little flutter, as it always did. And this flutter had nothing to do with stress. Whatever happened, whatever life threw at them — and with their jobs, it threw plenty of heavy obstacles into their paths — they were on the same team.

"How was your shift?" She leaned in and kissed him before answering the doorbell and divvying up the takeaway onto various dishes on the coffee table. Finally, she settled back beside him, a bowl of saag aloo and a handful of naan bread balanced on her lap.

"Yeah, not bad. Just a few shouts, including a kid who had fallen from a treehouse. It could have been bad, but he only had a broken wrist." He grinned. "His mum said he was like a rubber ball, always falling and bouncing up again." Quinn tore a piece of naan and loaded it with delicious-smelling tikka masala as he spoke. "How about you? Anything new on the jumpers?"

His secondment to the regional air ambulance had given him a chance to experience a different side to his job, and although Dove still worried the court case had taken such a toll on his mental health, she was pleased he seemed upbeat tonight. Especially after yesterday's trauma. The challenges he faced as a Critical Care Paramedic were immense, but he did generally thrive on his job, as she did on hers.

"Mark Davies still hasn't regained consciousness, but his doctors say he's doing well," she reported.

"Amazing, considering the height he jumped from, and where he landed," Quinn observed. "I'm really glad. With a bit of luck, he should pull through." He sighed. "I heard about the other woman, Rebecca."

"I know. It's crap, isn't it?"

She told him a bit about the investigation, and he responded with some of his gossip from the ambulance service. It was an easy, comfortable way of offloading without burdening the other person, without betraying professional confidences, and Dove enjoyed the routine. It made her feel safe, anchored. The healing that had begun in Cornwall was still in the background of her heart and mind. She just needed to get over the shock of last night.

The healing for her wasn't about forgetting, of course not — just a slight easing of the pain, allowing the memories to reform, to become more precious than ever before.

They finished their meal and cleared up. Layla, who had slipped back inside the house on silent velvet paws, also liked curry and was busy finishing the remains of the chicken korma when Dove discovered her on the worktop. Her long grey tail was curling upwards like a resting chameleon, her purr indicating her satisfaction at the unexpected treat. "Bad cat," Dove told her. "Go and catch a mouse or something."

Layla looked at her thoughtfully, licking sauce from her whiskers before exiting swiftly through the kitchen window Dove had opened. The night air was cool and damp now, bringing the taste of the sea and the smell of autumn.

"Have you thought any more about the wedding?" Quinn came up behind her and put his arms around her. His voice was tentative.

She closed the window and laid her head against his solid chest, feeling his steady heartbeat, his warmth. "Yes. I think you're right and we should do it next month."

"Only if you're sure? October isn't exactly prime wedding month, but it's a warm autumn, isn't it? I'm sure we can still get everyone outside if that's what you want."

"I never thought we'd have a wedding later in the year, because of having it on the beach, but we don't need loads of people. We never did," she said. "I checked the long-range weather forecast, and it looks okay. Even the shipping forecast isn't predicting imminent snowstorms or anything."

"It won't take long to sort out. Do you want me to book the hotel? Or actually, why don't you let Ren take over?" He was smiling, she could tell, even though she couldn't see him. She could feel it.

"She was doing a pretty good job before . . . before Gaia died." Dove swallowed hard. "At least we all chose the dress together. That makes it even more special, you know?"

He kissed her cheek, and stayed close, arms wrapped around her, his breath warm on her cheek. "Oh, babe, it's never going to seem right with Gaia gone, is it?"

"No, but she would be furious if she thought we weren't getting on with our lives, and she said a party on the beach was the only way to tie the knot, didn't she?" Dove was attempting to be stoic. "We never wanted a big do, just the wedding bit and a small beach party. If we stick to that, we can just look forward to it and not stress about wedding planning stuff." Changing the subject abruptly, as the pain in her chest stabbed at her consciousness, she asked, "Quinn, did Gaia ever mention the Retreat to you?"

"The Retreat you're investigating? No, that wouldn't be her thing, would it? She used to take the piss out of your yoga and meditation."

Dove turned round to face him. "She bought me a voucher for the Retreat, for a weekend. I found it in her things when I was sorting them out. She bought it last year, right after she stayed at the same place for a three-day Relaxation and Discovery Retreat."

"Shit." Quinn's green eyes sparkled with interest. "Well, she was a dark horse. I never would have thought she was into that. Wonder why she didn't give you the voucher for Christmas, though?"

"I suppose she forgot. Ren thought it might have been a birthday gift, but again, why didn't she give it to me? It was expensive. Too expensive to waste."

"Expensive to us, or to Gaia? Because we have very different standards of living," Quinn pointed out.

"That's exactly what Ren said." Dove was silent for a moment, her mind going over the case, seeing the victims, all the paths that had led to the Retreat. But where did their paths lead when they left Saddleworth Farm?

"Maybe she tried it, but didn't like it? Or perhaps she went with someone?" Quinn suggested. "I'm sure it doesn't matter in the grand scheme of things."

"No. I suppose . . ." She turned away. "I've just got a couple of emails to do before I come to bed."

He nodded, understanding she needed her space. "I'm going to watch the football, then. I'm on nights from tomorrow, so I might as well get into the sleep pattern."

She kissed him and padded towards the office. Logically, she knew there was no connection between her case and her sister. She had been seeing connections everywhere since Gaia died, and each new discovery created fresh grief, deep in her chest. Gaia's death had been an accident.

On impulse, making certain Quinn was distracted by his home team scoring, she went back into the spare room, and very gently, quietly pulled out the rest of the contents of the box where she had discovered the gift voucher. Right at the bottom, tucked under a paper diary from last year, she found it. A card with the same desolate moorland scene, the white lily. She flipped it open with shaking fingers:

Dearest Gaia,
Visit us any time, and we are always here for you.
Louise, and all your friends at the Retreat.

CHAPTER SEVENTEEN

Despite the late night, Dove woke at 5.30 a.m. and crept downstairs without disturbing Quinn. Layla was extremely vocal in the mornings, weaving around her cold bare legs, demanding breakfast.

Wrapping her hands around a cup of coffee, Dove watched the clouds moving in from the sea from her kitchen window. The few patches of faded orange and gold in the early morning sky were rapidly obliterated by the huge grey thunderclouds. She thought about her wedding, now next month, and realized again that she didn't care what the weather was like. If it was snowing or sleeting, she would still be there, dancing on the beach with her family, enjoying hers and Quinn's day and enjoying being alive. It was what Gaia would have wanted. It was what *she* wanted.

She went through to the office and picked up the gift voucher for the Retreat. It was actually Ren who had given her the idea. *You're thinking of using the voucher, aren't you?* Picking up her phone, Dove clicked on the Retreat bookings page, and ascertained it was perfectly possible to swap a whole weekend for an evening. If she booked for an evening, as soon as the case was wrapped up, it might give her some closure. But first, they would need to wrap the case, and after yesterday, it seemed as though that might take months.

Dove stood watching the clouds massing over the sea. She could hardly take time out when they were in the middle of an investigation, and especially not when the Retreat had already come up as part of it. But it would soon be six months since Gaia had died, and she felt she was discovering a part of her sister she hadn't previously known.

If the Retreat suddenly became the centre of the case, she would have to scrap the idea, but it did seem like a good way of honouring Gaia's memory, spending peaceful time with her dead sister before her wedding.

The voucher was dated until November this year, so there was no hurry. She and Quinn wouldn't be able to book any leave for a honeymoon at such short notice, and she didn't really feel the need to take another holiday, when they had just come back from Cornwall. Also, she admitted to herself, she was curious. She wanted to be where her sister had been, to walk in her footsteps, wonder what she had been feeling, especially now.

The case had hooked her as usual, but she could feel she was less focused on her work this time. Dove sighed softly. She would have to be extremely careful not to let this show, but in her heart, she was struggling. It wasn't that the case was less personal, that she was any less desperate to find out what had really happened to Rebecca, Mark and Amber, especially as she had been present at the scene when the incident occurred.

It was more that she felt she had been ripped apart in the last six months, and instead of plunging straight into a case with her emotions ready to engage, she had created subconscious barriers in her mind, in a feeble effort to protect herself.

It was strange to be able to admit this, but the holiday in Cornwall and the counselling had helped. She glanced at the clock and put down her mug. There was just time to try and take care of herself. With renewed optimism, she pulled out her yoga mat and started her morning stretches.

* * *

The morning briefing was complex, and the incident boards were filling up to the extent that they now covered the entire wall. Lines of blue, green and red marker pen indicated last movements, rows of photographs showed last contacts, witnesses, snapshots of forensics information, and evidence.

Dove studied Amber's post-mortem results, which had been uploaded to the file by the pathologists; expedited as a favour by her now favourite pathologist friend. She had died of extensive head injuries and had numerous other fractures and internal bleeds. Nothing on the report was red-flagged as abnormal or requiring further investigation.

"Mark had a neighbour who died in the motorway crash in 2019. It was that horrific major incident right under the three bridges, and the press dubbed it 'The Three Bridges Crash'," Lindsey was reporting. "Mark's neighbour was called Edna Coving. She was eighty-one and she was a widow. One of the other neighbours said she used to look after Mark, and they had a strong relationship. Edna took an interest in all of the kids at Roedean House, and was a volunteer for years before she retired, the warden said."

"And Mark's boyfriend says he has been mentioning her recently?" DI Lincoln, returning briefly from a recent stabbing case, had slid unnoticed into the room. As usual when there was a major case, he seemed to live at the police station.

"Right. Three months after the three bridges crash, Mark was offered the chance to apply for this weekend at the Retreat as part of a local authority rehabilitation fund. The funding only came through this year," Lindsey explained.

"Rebecca lost her ex-husband in the same crash," DS Amin added, glancing down at her notes. "They divorced in 2018, but according to family and friends, remained on good terms and shared childcare. The family and friends we've spoken to say she really struggled to move on, even though she had another boyfriend. She was diagnosed with depression in January this year, and has taken prescription medication for that."

"And Amber?" The DI looked at Steve and Dove, raising an eyebrow. The atmosphere was charged again — new information and the crackle of a chance at unpicking the investigation.

"No connection to the three bridges crash that we know of, but she seems to have been a very private person. Her mum is the only relative, and she's refusing to talk to us at the moment. Bernie, as the FLO, says she basically threw him out and refuses to admit her daughter is dead."

Steve shifted on his seat, and Dove, sitting next to him, could see him flexing his injured knee as though it was bothering him.

Dove said, "We have found a connection between Amber and the rental car manager, Neil Barnes. According to Neil's girlfriend, Amber was in a long-term relationship with a Max Carter until a couple of years ago. Could be again, possibly."

Steve followed up with an update from last night, to add that he had now discovered Max Carter worked at Benson's Garage & MOT Centre. "We'll head straight over there after the brief."

Impressed, Dove winked at him, and he grinned back triumphantly, before finishing his coffee.

DI Blackman continued, "We finally have preliminary reports on all three victims' tech devices. They show that they were all recently checking out websites and social media connected to the 2019 three bridges crash." He glanced at his notes. "Amber's search history indicates she watched one particular video over fifty times within the last six weeks."

"What's the date of the first search?" DI Lincoln asked.

"August the fourteenth this year. They all have data showing searches from then, which was when they were all at the Retreat, increasing in frequency right up until Friday night. Here's the clip from a dash cam . . ." DI Blackman clicked, and the screen on the back wall of the briefing room flickered to life. "This particular car was around six vehicles back from the main crash, so it gives a good perspective on what happened . . . This was also used in the inquest, but it seems pirated copies have made their way into the public domain. It features on numerous social media sites."

Dove studied the clip carefully. It showed a white Ford Escort weaving in and out of the traffic, dodging between the fast and middle lanes of the motorway, finally careering in front of the lorry just as the traffic flowed under the first bridge.

"It was never traced, was it? The car, or the driver," Steve said. "I remember the media appeals."

"It wasn't, despite extensive searches and repeated calls for information. As you can see the numberplate is filthy, and unreadable." DI Martin was spinning a pen in her fingers, staring at the now-frozen video clip. "We need to find out if Amber has any connection to the three bridges crash. It happened in the exact spot they all jumped, and for any of those present who were on duty, you will remember it was one of the worst pile-ups we've seen on that road." DI Martin took a swig of tea, and Dove noticed her hand shook slightly, before she continued. "Eighteen vehicles involved. Seven people died."

CHAPTER EIGHTEEN

"There's a Facebook page for the crash victims. It was set up in their memory and it had a GoFundMe link for the families . . ." DS Amin was reading off her iPad, glasses pushed back on her head, frowning intently at her screen. "Not sure if it's still active, but I can check it out."

DI Blackman made a note. "On the subject of videos, you will have all seen the clip of what appears to be a group messing around on the bridge before the incident. This does corroborate the statement from the driver who thought he saw people up there before our third jumper landed. But he did add the fog was bad, he was distracted by what he could see in his rear-view mirror, and it was raining."

DI Waters clicked the screen to show the video of the group of people on the bridge. "The content creator has now admitted faking this. It was taken some time last year, when he and some others were filming some YouTube videos for his channel. He heard a rumour that this might be a gang-related execution, and saw all the media fuss, decided to put himself bang in the middle of it. The entire clip was edited and time-stamped to make it look like a group facing off against our three victims. Stupid attention-seeking bastard," she added, with a flash of annoyance.

"What about the witness statement from the driver who also thought she saw other people on the bridge?" DS Wyndham asked.

"She now thinks she was mistaken. She says with the fog and everything, she must have been confused. She's retracted her original statement," DI Waters said.

"Right, so we have no reliable witnesses from those who originally said they thought they saw other people on any of the bridges?" DCI Franklin frowned.

"Correct."

"We have a number of conversations between Mark, Rebecca and Amber. There are also a number of calls made from Amber's phone to an unlisted number. This was a sample text conversation between Mark and Rebecca at 4.32 p.m. on Friday."

R u sure you still want to go thru with this? You don't have to!

Why? Do u want to pull out?

No! But it's different for you. I need to do this.

See u later.

DCI Franklin said, "None of the highlighted conversations reveal anything about what they were planning, and having looked at them, I would say they are deliberately vague, suggesting they were being careful, and probably discussed logistics either face-to-face or during calls. Between August fourteenth, when the retreat weekend finished, and Friday night, there are well over fifty conversations between Mark, Rebecca, and Amber. Many of these lasted well over an hour."

"We still haven't found Amber's phone." DI Blackman scrolled through his notes thoughtfully.

"There is a report from a witness who responded to our request for information. The witness was driving past the woodland walk parking area near the east side of Saddle Bridge. We have a dash cam showing a woman resembling Rebecca walking along the footpath next to the nature reserve. The driver was stuck in the queue at the roadworks and has a couple of minutes of footage before Rebecca disappears into the trees. She was wearing that distinctive red raincoat, so she wasn't exactly creeping around."

DI Lincoln finished up, "There are no witness statements that have been corroborated for Rebecca or Mark, apart from a cyclist on the roundabout who thinks he saw Mark walking up to the town side of the bridge. He is reluctant to commit though, says it was filthy weather and he can't be sure. But that would place Mark on the route we think he took. As in, he came from this side of the bridge, not the downland side."

"As did Amber, if she was walking through the woods at 7.15 p.m.," Steve pointed out. "We are still looking for her rental car, and we already checked the car parks on both sides of Saddle Bridge. Regarding the rental car, her own car is being fixed at Benson's, and she was due to return the hire car yesterday morning and pick up her own car yesterday afternoon."

"Benson's is on the main bus route. Maybe she was going to pick up her car that way," Dove suggested. "Rebecca's car was found in the car park off Pengrove Road, which makes sense if she was then seen walking into the woodland. There are only a few spaces at the entrance, and there's an hourly parking charge."

DI Waters added, "Plus, Pengrove Road is more anonymous? We'll put out a second appeal for information, for anyone who was in the vicinity of all three bridges during the relevant time period."

After the briefing, Dove took the card Gaia had received into the DI's office and explained where she had found it.

He gave her a hard look, before nodding. "Interesting, especially as Louise denies it was sent by her, or any of her staff. She seems extremely keen to help in any way she can, and at this stage, I do believe her."

"Someone masquerading as the Retreat?" Dove suggested. "I don't imagine there can be any others that both

Gaia, Mark and Amber have attended run by a woman called Louise. And although we don't know if Rebecca had a card, I'd say it was highly likely."

DI Blackman cracked a smile. "True. Okay, I'll put a note on the file for forensics to look out for these cards and see if we can get anything from Amber's one."

"It's okay, you can take Gaia's too." Dove handed it over. "She would have wanted this case solved, if it has anything to do with her. Although her card seems to be the anomaly at the moment. She wasn't on the August retreat and, as far as I know, she didn't know Amber, Mark or Rebecca."

In her heart, she felt that Gaia wasn't involved in this mess, whatever it turned out to be, even though she still got that nagging anxiety her sister might have got into trouble. Those days were well over, and despite her former wayward tendencies, Gaia had always been one to fight injustice. She would never have picked a fight with someone in trouble — she would have tried to help.

Steve called out as she walked across the busy room.

"Bernie just rang."

"Amber's FLO?" Dove was picking up her bag and car keys, ready for the trip to Benson's Garage.

"Right. He says Amber's mum, Martha, called him this morning and told him Amber must have been murdered by a cult, namely the Retreat, and she would talk to the investigating team later, but not to him. And no, she says she doesn't have any evidence, she just knows." He rolled his eyes. "I thought we were the only ones allowed to go off on a tangent because we 'just know'."

"She's playing games, do you think?" Dove was intrigued, and a bit annoyed. "Although maybe it's genuine confusion. I suppose grief gets people in different ways."

He shrugged. "Denial, wants someone to blame. Or she really does know something we don't. She has a rock-solid alibi, so we can't insist she speak to us. Bernie will hopefully be able to talk her around, make her see she could know something that might help us find out what really happened to her daughter." Steve looked at his watch. "Anyway, let's go and find Max Carter. I feel like we've been in the office all morning."

Dove waved an expansive arm, taking in the extra officers in the rooms. There was a sense of energy in the air, the hustle of her colleagues, and the smell of stale coffee. "Big case. You know what that means."

"Lots of briefings, so we don't screw it up." Steve grinned and led the way out of the room.

CHAPTER NINETEEN

On the way out, having punched the vending machine in the corridor into submission, Dove balanced her coffee and her phone. An idea was lodged in her brain. She replayed the grainy camera footage from Saddle Bridge, focusing on the initial frames, watching the bodies falling. Before she could change her mind, she punched out a number.

"I just want to make a call," she said to Steve, as they got into the car.

Dove's call connected, and to her surprise, she got through to the person she needed to speak to immediately.

She introduced herself quickly, and added, "I'm working on the Saddle Bridge investigation from Friday night, Dr Francis. Sorry to bother you. I can only imagine how busy you are, but I have a couple of questions about Amber Dionysus's injuries."

Next to her, she could see Steve digging into a packet of crisps as he drove, and listening intently to the call on speakerphone.

The pathologist paused so long before answering, she wondered if there was a problem, but then his voice came through sharp and confident. "Of course. You will have seen the PM results on the file? How can I help?"

"It's a bit of a wild card, but would you say Amber's injuries are consistent with someone *jumping* from a height?" She held her breath, very aware how ambiguous her question was, and hoping he wouldn't be offended. The pathologist often lectured that the field of forensics dealt with evidence, and facts, not magic or wild hunches. This was definitely the latter.

"What are you implying?" His voice was still sharp.

She had only met George Francis once, but he was young and smart. Jess called him posh, which was an actual sin in Jess's rulebook, but even Jess admitted he was pretty damn good at his job. "I mean, would there be any injuries you would expect to see in someone jumping from a height, as opposed to someone who was pushed, or fell?"

"I see what you're getting at . . . And your other victim, Rebecca Hales, is on the PM list, but we haven't got to her yet. Disappointing she didn't make it. One always hopes . . . In answer to your question, it is possible to speculate, based on injuries, but there are so many factors which can affect the victim, including trajectory of the fall or jump. For Amber Dionysus . . ." He paused again. "If I were to go out on a limb, and this is just supposition, I would have expected more injuries to the lower part of her body if she had landed feet first, as from a jump. Her left femur was fractured, pelvis, left clavicle, three ribs, both forearms comprehensively shattered. She also presented with severe trauma to the head, which was ultimately the cause of death."

Dove took a deep breath. "Thank you, that's very helpful."

"You suspect she was pushed?" Dr Francis asked bluntly.

"Not really, and there is no evidence to support it at the moment," Dove said honestly. "It was just a thought. Sorry to have wasted your time."

"I understand. Unfortunately, whatever the start of the incident, the end result was injuries severe enough to kill. I know Rebecca Hales was fast-tracked, and she's actually on the table now, so you might have her results by this afternoon. Her medical notes are already available."

"Thank you. And yes, I've seen the hospital notes."

She ended the call and tapped the dashboard thoughtfully with a fingernail. What if . . . It was always *what if,* until you had stone cold evidence right in front of you, but instead of the three victims jumping of their own free will, she was seeing shadowy figures on the bridge. Perhaps Neil or Max. But why?

"Nice idea, but it is just supposition," Steve informed her, as he overtook a slow-moving van. "From what we already have, there is a whole lot going on under the surface of our three victims' lives. We're already got the link to the Retreat, and now for Amber, we have tenuous connections to our friendly locals, Neil and Max."

"You think they were murdered?" Dove queried. "I'm still not sold. There's a fair bit of evidence for some kind of well-being cult, I suppose?" she added doubtfully.

He popped some chewing gum in his mouth, and shook his head. "I wouldn't go that far, but I think something weird went down on the bridge on Friday night. What made you think of calling Dr Francis?"

"The angles of their falls on the videos. Earlier, when I was waiting for the briefing, I checked on the PM for Amber, and then accessed Rebecca's and Mark's medical records from Abberley General." She caught his expression. "I got it signed off!"

"Didn't say you didn't." Steve took a gulp of coffee while the car was stationary at the traffic lights. The thunderclouds of early morning had given way to dull, dense cloud and a few light spatters of rain.

"Well, Rebecca had lots of lower-limb injuries," Dove explained. "She had fractured thoracic and lumbar vertebrae, and a broken pelvis, which caused internal bleeding. Mark has similar injuries, but he also had two broken ribs, leading to a pneumothorax, and a head injury," Dove explained.

"And Amber died of her head injuries?" Steve's voice was still sceptical.

They were passing the Tesco roundabout, and she waited while Steve paused to navigate the traffic lights over the bridge, before she answered. "It doesn't fly, does it? I mean, Dr Francis said any number of factors can influence the injury pattern. Was she pushed?"

"I can see where you're coming from, but surely it must vary. I mean, I've been to jumpers who have plunged head-first by choice, or their body has changed position on the way down," Steve pointed out.

"I know, and I don't think there is a pattern." She yawned, and massaged her forehead with her thumb and forefinger. "Which means I just wasted an hour this morning gathering useless data."

"Data is never useless. I mean, the injury pattern is inter-esting." Steve scrunched his lunch wrappers into a ball. "And you're forgetting trend analysis."

"True," Dove agreed reluctantly, seeing it in her mind, replaying the events like a film reel. Maybe two had jumped, and one had dithered, changing their mind, seeing their friends leap towards certain death. But why jump in the first place? "I hope Mark regains consciousness. Chances are, he could bust this whole case wide open just by opening his mouth."

"If he wants to," Steve said, as they arrived at their des-tination. "I'd say it depends on exactly what the agenda was for all three of them. And what happens next will also depend on our next interview. I'm pretty interested to hear what Max Carter has to say about his ex-girlfriend's death and his best friend's apparent disappearance."

CHAPTER TWENTY

Witness Transcript: * * * * * * B188361

I've lived with this for years now. I know what happened that night, and I still can't believe it. Yes, it was stupid, and yes, we should have known better than to make promises. But what do you do when someone comes to you for help? Someone you are close to, maybe even a little bit in love with . . .

Do I feel guilty? No. It wasn't my fault, and at the time, I did what I thought was right. You can't change what happened, and this was a way of moving forward.

CHAPTER TWENTY-ONE

Benson's Garage & MOT Centre was a grubby back street affair, and the man signing MOT certificates in the cluttered office at first denied all knowledge of Max Carter and Neil Barnes.

"The manager's around. You can talk to them. I don't know any of those names, and none of them work here. We don't need police hanging around the garage scaring off customers."

"How about one of your customers? Amber Dionysus brought her car to be repaired on Tuesday last week. I assume it's still here?" Dove said pleasantly. Most people were happy to try and help with investigations, but equally, there were a lot who — whether from bad experiences or general opinions — hated any police officers on sight.

The man waved a hand at the blank computer screen. "It's been down since last night. Bloody thing's broken, and we can't access the files."

"We can always chat down at the station," Steve pointed out, clearly annoyed and making a show of looking at his watch.

"I don't see why you're interested, that's all. You said you're looking into the Saddle Bridge thing from Friday night. Well, those idiots jumped off it. End of. There's no big mystery, and it's nobody's fault." The man scowled at them, his big square face ruddy with exertion and anger.

"Thanks for your insight, but if you could just answer the questions, we'll be out of here super fast," Dove told him. "Or, as DS Parker suggested, we can get a uniform car to come and pick you up for that chat, if that would be easier?"

He swore under his breath, wiped his hands on oil-streaked navy overalls and indicated the bay on the left, where a car was up on the ramp. A man was busy with tools under-neath the exhaust area, his navy overalled legs and boots just visible.

"Max! Coppers want a word." He turned back to Dove and Steve. "And before you start asking me shit, the only things I know about Max are that he lives above the garage, and has done for years now. He had a girlfriend a while back, and she lived with him, but she was trouble, so Max booted her out. I've never seen her. End of story and no comment." He walked off, viciously punched out a number on his mobile and jammed it against his ear, while he threw a last comment at them. "That what you wanted?"

Dove shrugged, raised an amused eyebrow at Steve's smile, and turned her attention towards the mechanic, as Max Carter emerged slowly from underneath the car. His skin was pock-marked and spotted, his hair greasy and lank. He sported an oil-stained white T-shirt, and his beer belly hung over the rolled-down blue overalls. His expression was sour.

"What have I done now?" he asked. "Tanya rang and said you were looking for Neil, but I don't know where he is." His gaze darted from one to the other of them, and he was breathing fast, fists clenched. "I don't need any hassle from the police, so whatever Neil's done, it's down to him and Tanya."

Dove introduced herself and Steve, and explained they were investigating the Saddle Bridge incident, gauging his reaction.

Weirdly, he seemed to relax slightly, she noted. Did he expect something else? He was still peering defensively through his greasy fringe, but the fists loosened, and his hands hung limply by his sides. He could only be late thirties, maximum. The years had not been kind to this man.

"Why would you think Neil has done something wrong?" Steve asked.

He shrugged. "He always turns up, every few days. My best mate, but he's a loser. Anyway, it's about time he pitched up asking for money or some smack." He laughed, a harsh guttural sound. "And don't look at me like it was my fault. Neil always knows exactly what he's doing, despite his lovey-dovey relationship with Tanya. She's a fool not to see what he's really like."

"When did you last hear from him?"

"Dunno. Maybe Friday. We don't keep in touch, really." His words were coming fast, and he didn't seem to realise he was contradicting himself.

"So, you don't know where he is now?"

"I said not, didn't I?" Max snapped.

Dove, watching him carefully, thought he was telling the truth, but she could discern something else behind his defensiveness. Anxiety. He was worried about either his friend, or the situation. Interesting.

"Tanya mentioned you knew Amber Dionysus, that you dated?" Steve asked.

Max's expression changed, and he seemed to be reassessing, eyes darting from one officer to the other. Max Carter would have been a rubbish poker player, Dove concluded. Everything was reflected on his face. Was he shocked that they knew already about his link to Amber?

"Yeah, a long time ago. I suppose you want Amber's car." He jerked a thumb towards the back of the shed, where rows of vehicles were parked outside on the concrete yard. "I saw on the news she was one of the jumpers. Can't say I'm surprised."

"Surprised that she's dead?" Steve raised an eyebrow.

"Surprised she killed herself! She was the do-gooder one in that family. Her mum put her up on a pedestal, and bloody Amber was the angel girl, trying to live up to her mum's expectations. It must have been a strain, because underneath, she wasn't like that really, I reckon. Probably couldn't take the strain any longer." His tone was dismissive, but Dove could see he was working hard at nonchalance.

"We are keeping an open mind," Steve said pleasantly.

His expression sharpened. "I bet you are, but I read it in the paper. She and those others jumped off the fucking bridge. What are you trying to say? That she's still alive?" He laughed again. "Maybe you lot need the overtime money, because this one is an open-and-shut case. Three people jumped off a bridge and killed themselves."

"How do you know Neil Barnes?"

"We shared the flat for a few years, known each other since we were teenagers." His face softened a bit and he pulled a vape from his pocket. "Neil always kept trying to be something he wasn't, a bit like Amber. When he met Tanya, he thought he could go straight, keep off the drugs, and hold down a proper job, but he kept falling off the wagon."

Steve made a few notes. "Did Neil seem especially worried about anything lately?"

"Told you, I haven't seen him for a while. He works for Pink Lady Cars in Southford. He lives Elmside way, with Tanya and the kids." Max scowled again, but Dove noted something else in his expression; concern, and very possibly fear. "Don't try and drag him into whatever mess Amber got herself into. He's a pain in the arse, but he doesn't deserve any more shit."

"When did you last see Neil?"

"Maybe last month. He dropped by for a chat, bunked off work. He likes to keep that boss of his on her toes. Can't remember what we talked about. Just, you know, stuff."

"And when did you last see Amber? If you didn't keep in touch, you must have been surprised when she brought her car in for repairs," Dove asked, eyeing him with interest. Did he know where Neil was? He kept wiping his nose, and a sheen of sweat had appeared on his forehead that had nothing to do with the manual work he'd just been doing. He was extremely defensive of his friend, but equally, seemed very critical of Amber. Was it genuine, though?

"No, she dropped her car in and that was it. No hard feelings. We split ages ago, anyway." He stopped and his eyes went wide, unfocused, for a second. "Am I right, then? Is Amber alive, really? Are you faking it?" He was getting agitated suddenly, and his face was reddening, huge oily fists clenched. "I want to know if she's dead. Is she dead?"

"What? Of course she isn't still alive. Calm down, Mr Carter. Is there somewhere more private we can talk?" Steve asked, his tone even, but his eyes watchful.

Far from calming the man, Steve's words seemed to make him angry, and he started balling one fist, then the other. His eyes flicked from Dove to Steve and back again, before he addressed the space over their heads: "*Is* she dead, though? Did you see her body?"

What had he taken? Dove wondered as she and her partner both took a step back, and adrenaline crackled. Was he about to take a swing at them? He seemed to have lost all sense of reason, and was now muttering to himself, barely focusing on them at all.

"*Max?*"

There was a clang from the ramp further along the bays, and a woman walked briskly towards them. She was tall, with dark glasses pushed onto the top of her head, and curly chestnut hair. "Sorry to interrupt, Max, I need the ramp in twenty for the Mini. Can you shift it in five?" The woman nodded at Dove and Steve, wiped her hands on her greasy overalls and continued quickly towards the office.

Max hadn't spoken again, and from his vacant expression, Dove wondered if he had even registered the woman's request. Whatever artificial stimulant he had taken before they arrived still seemed to be lingering, and not in a good way. His face remained flushed, shoulders squared, and fists clenched as though he was headed for a fight.

107

Dove spoke clearly, calmly, trying to engage the man in front of them. "Max, listen to me." She waited a second until he made eye contact. "Amber is dead. She died from injuries sustained from the fall from the bridge. We are trying to find out what happened to her and the other two people who were hurt on Friday night."

At last, the words seemed to penetrate his brain, and he blew out a long breath of apparent relief, scowling at them, but relaxing his aggressive physical stance. "Well, okay then, but I haven't seen Amber for over a year, until she showed up last week wanting her car fixed."

"Can you tell us about Neil?"

Max nodded. "Christmas 2019, I threw Neil out of the flat because he was messing with my head and my business. I'm straight now, but he and Amber always wanted money for this and money for that. It gives business a bad rep to have people like that around."

"Where were you on Friday night between seven and nine p.m., Mr Carter?" Dove asked. She was beginning to think Max Carter would be worth bringing in for a formal interview. He had already contradicted himself several times over Neil, and there was clearly something going on that would be worth further questioning.

"Fuck off! I was at home, in front of the TV with a few cans and a ham and mushroom pizza." His eyes widened, colour rising again as he wiped a sleeve across his sweaty face.

"Max! Hurry up with the bloody car!" the woman shouted from the office.

"Look, I just need to shift this car . . . We can talk in the office after, all right? And you can check our CCTV. That's a good idea, isn't it? Me and Amber were fine when she brought the car in, just fine." He was babbling now, turning towards the ramp.

It happened so quickly that Dove, Steve, and a mechanic pushing a trolley loaded with tyres across the concrete had to jump back. The ramp dropped like a stone, with a heavy creaking and banging of metal on metal. Chips of rust, metal shards and dirt spattered, and the car bounced on its suspension as it landed.

Dove wiped grime from her face and tried to see where Max was.

The female mechanic rushed back towards the bay and yelled, "Max! What the fuck are you doing?"

A door slammed as Dove started towards the ramp, but Max had vanished. Running footsteps could be heard drumming along the concrete path outside the garage.

Swearing, Dove dived past the ramp, wrenched open the fire door and followed. Outside, she paused, checking for danger, checking for signs of bloody Max Carter. Her breathing was fast, and the fresh air made her gasp.

Where the hell had he gone? The large expanse of concrete was crowded with vehicles and bordered by scrubland. She jogged a little way along to her left, glancing to either side.

A slight noise made her turn as she was passing a row of recycling skips, and she dodged out the way as a load of wooden crates came tumbling down from above. One glanced off her shoulder and she winced. *"Max!"*

CHAPTER TWENTY-TWO

A few quick strides and she was over the obstruction, running into the tripwire of dying brambles and weeds. She was making enough noise to cover any Max might have been making and he launched himself from some rusting machinery, landing squarely on top of her.

She landed on her back. Pain. In her back. In her head as it struck concrete. She struggled frantically to escape, sweat pouring from her body, making her eyes sting. Several of Max's punches landed, and she felt her shoulder burn, and blood seep into her mouth from a harsh jab.

"Max, stop!" She tried to yell at him, but her chest was constricted, and the words came out in a strangled croak. His red, sweaty face was right above hers, his eyes glazed and burning as he lifted a brick in his left hand.

Dove jack-knifed her body, feeling his weight slip a little, dodging the blow as the brick came crashing down, missing her cheek by inches. She blinked hard to clear brick dust from her eyes as his hands fastened on her throat.

"*Max!*" One final effort, frantic struggle, and she felt his hand slip from its grip on her right wrist.

"You need to leave this alone, okay? You just... need to leave it!" he croaked out. The glazed and furious eyes held hers for a further fraction of a second, before he landed one last punch, which made her head spin, rolled off and started to run.

Coughing, staggering to her feet, Dove went to follow. Where the hell was Steve? Pain in every part of her body, but she followed, gradually regaining her balance. She licked blood from the corner of her mouth and wiped it from above her left eye.

She was as fast as she could possibly be, given the circumstances, but then her ankle caught fast in a mat of weeds, she fell onto her knees, and knew she was done.

Struggling free, swearing, Dove climbed wearily to her feet just as she heard the sound of a motorbike screaming off down the main road. There were too many high-sided vehicles parked in the way to see if it was Max, but she couldn't hear him running any more.

"*Shit.*" Dove bent double to catch her breath, hands on hips, fuming he had got away. In a straight run, she would have caught him up easily, but on this kind of territory, he had known exactly where to go. She kicked at the weeds that had tripped her as she made her way back to the garage, hobbling as the full extent of her beating began to make itself known.

Steve called out from a few yards away. "Has he gone? I called it in and said I'd get back with details. Dove?" He rounded a row of vans, moving slowly, but limping slightly, and saw her for the first time. "Bloody hell, Dove, do you need an ambulance?"

"No, just a first-aid kit maybe. I heard a motorbike take off towards town," she said with disgust.

Steve was examining her injuries, anger and concern in his face. He was clearly fuming that he had taken so long to get to her, but Dove knew better than to mention it. "He beat you up? Why?"

"Whatever he had been taking made him just lose it. You know that look, when they're past all reasoning and don't know what the hell they're doing?"

He nodded. "Yeah, I do know. Shit, though, do you think anything's broken? He's a big bloke."

"I'm not exactly tiny myself." Dove straightened up, pulled her shoulders back and winced as she touched her face. "Hopefully, it's just bruising."

"Well, you don't look very pretty, so it's a good thing you aren't getting married tomorrow. Are you sure you don't need the medics?"

"Don't fuss. I'm fine. It'll hurt more tomorrow. Looks worse than it is." She wasn't sure about that, but was unreasonably furious they had lost Max Carter. Dove also knew she would have to take herself down to A&E for a check-up when her fiancé saw the state she was in. But not now, not when they finally had a decent lead.

"If you're sure." He was holding her right arm, gently turning it over, studying the livid red marks on skin that would surely turn to a rainbow of bruising over the next twenty-four hours.

They surveyed the area for a moment. The train line ran along one side of the concrete, and to the right was a long line of parked HGVs at the driving school, and a towering mass of factories. A huge area, with plenty of places to hide, even if he hadn't already done a runner.

"I can't believe we lost him, the sneaky little bastard," Dove said furiously, trying to push her anger down, to focus.

"I think we can take it that Mr Carter is somehow involved in this, and knows more than he wanted to share with us." Steve was making the call to control with an update. As he was waiting for the phone to be answered, he added, "You'd better see if they've got a first-aid kit here, and a decent sink, or I will personally be driving you to the hospital."

Dove ignored this, and waited until he'd finished the call before she continued the conversation. "He seemed to get freaked out when we pushed about Neil and Amber, and he went into far too much detail about where he supposedly was on Friday night."

Steve was still limping as he followed her back into the garage area. "He did, didn't he? Bloody ham and mushroom pizza . . . I'll ring the DI, too."

Dove left him on the phone, updating the DI on the situation, and went back into the office to speak to the manager, who turned out to be the woman who had shouted at Max.

"Jesus, love, look at you. You run into a wall, or what?"

"Yeah. Can I have your first-aid kit to clean myself up a bit?"

The manager passed her a big green box. "Help yourself. There's a washroom back there. Did Max do that?"

"He did."

"I'm shocked. Seriously, he never seemed like a violent guy, even when he was on the gear. In fact, I would have said he was a good bloke in general, and I get all sorts wanting jobs down here."

"Well, he was on the gear today, and I don't think he likes me very much." Dove flicked open the box and headed for the washroom.

Although not the cleanest, the room was big enough for her to strip off her shirt and inspect the damage in the dusty mirror. There were antiseptic wipes in the kit, and she ripped them open with her teeth, wincing as she dabbed at the cuts on her face.

When she'd finished, she considered her reflection. Battered and soon to be extremely bruised, but she didn't think stitches were needed on the cuts, which had stopped bleeding. Her ribs were tender, but she could breathe without too much pain.

Dove cleared up, chucked the waste in the swing bin, snapped the case shut and headed back to the office, where Steve was waiting.

The manager glanced at Dove, sensibly said nothing, and continued talking to Steve. "Max still lives above the garage. I've got a spare set of keys, if you want to have a look? I've got nothing to hide and if he's in trouble, I'm not helping him out. He's a grotty little bastard, but he's quite good at his job when he bothers to get out of bed." She pointed out the door to a spiral metal staircase. "To be honest, I'm not exactly overwhelmed with applicants for a mechanic job on this side of town."

Dove quickly showed her the photos of the three victims and Neil Barnes, but she shook her head.

"Oh, wait a minute, this woman looks familiar." She paused. "I know, she brought her car in here, didn't she?"

"Yes, Max said it's parked out the back, but she's now deceased, so I'm sure her family will be in touch to make arrangements in due course. If we could have a look at the CCTV from Tuesday, when Amber brought her car, that might be useful."

The woman drew a sharp breath, still looking at Amber's photo. "Got it. I suppose you want to take a look inside the car now?"

"Please," Dove replied.

A quick search revealed nothing of interest inside the vehicle, and CCTV confirmed the car had been parked in the same space since Tuesday when Amber dropped it off. Nobody had been near it since, and the manager told them they were waiting for the new brake pads to arrive.

"Nobody else has been near it," she added as Dove handed back the key fob. "Do you think Max is somehow involved in her death? That's why he just took off?"

"We're just eliminating people from our enquiries," Steve told her.

She nodded slowly, as if drawing her own conclusions, and reached into her desk. "Keys to Flat B. Watch the stairs, they can be slippery."

Steve caught the thrown ring of keys deftly, and he and Dove headed out of the garage.

"Do you want to wait down here?" Dove asked, concerned for Steve's knee as she eyed the spiral staircase.

"I'm okay, honestly, just pissed off we lost him," Steve said. "Although I'm still not seeing exactly what part he and

Neil might have played in our bridge jumper deaths, they both just made it to the top of the list in terms of interest."

Dove agreed, but added, "I can't see it either, but we have links to drugs — okay, minor ones — and possibly a messy kind of love triangle?"

Steve opened the door, and Dove slipped her gloves on, taking in the space. Max's flat was a decent size, but in poor repair and strewn with chaos of messy living. Empty takeaway cartons, drug paraphernalia, and a few really expensive pieces of tech, including a massive wide screen TV and gaming equipment. The stink was worse in the kitchenette area, where it didn't look like any washing of clothes or crockery had been done for weeks.

"I wonder if he ever cleans anything. This place is a health hazard." Dove wrinkled her nose and struggled to speak between her coughing. "Disgusting." She moved towards the coffee table, which had a laptop and piles of paperwork on its stained surface. Careful to avoid the silver foil, dirt and scattered sharps, she started to leaf through the documents one at a time.

Bank statements, an arrears demand for an unpaid mobile phone bill, TV licence and council tax. She paused as she reached the bottom of the untidy heap.

"Anything?" Steve called out, as he returned from the bedroom area.

Dove said nothing, but held up a single card, with the now familiar scene of desolate moorland and the poignant lily in the foreground.

Dear Max,
You are welcome to visit us any time.
Louise and all your friends at the Retreat.

"You have got to be fucking kidding me. No way was he ever a guest at the Retreat!" Steve was incredulous.

"His name wasn't on the guest lists," Dove said, thankful once again for her photographic memory. "But we only went back two years, because that covered the relevant time period of our victims. He might not have used a real name. You're right, though. He doesn't seem the type for meditation. But you can't ever assume, can you? It might be a secret passion, or he might even have done some mechanic work on their farm vehicles, or been dating someone who works there."

Steve was looking out of the window now, parting the dirty net curtains with a gloved fingertip. "He was shitting himself the whole time we talked to him. What if he wasn't freaking out because he's guilty, but because he's scared. What if the cards are a warning?"

Dove stared at him, considering, remembering with a catch of fear in her heart that Gaia had also received a card. "You mean he might be scared of Neil Barnes? That Neil is sending the cards?"

"Well, whoever. Maybe he ran because he was afraid someone would come after him, not because we rattled him. If he knows what really happened on Friday night, and someone, maybe Neil, is putting pressure on him, it could be a reason to get out."

Dove's phone rang as they walked back across the road to their car, stepping over the rusty fallen sign proclaiming Benson's Garage & MOT Centre. It was Dr Francis from the mortuary.

"DC Milson? I've sent the information through to your DI, but as you were asking about injuries earlier, I wanted to let you know the team has already flagged a couple of anomalies. I know how important these early indications can be."

Dove waved to Steve to stop walking, and put her phone on speaker. "Go on."

"Rebecca Hales's injuries are consistent with a fall from a height, but we also discovered what we would call classic crush injuries — bruising to her left side, by shape and pattern. The bruising on her back forms a distinctive pattern of two long bars, which are the approximate size and width of the railings along the side of the bridge."

Dove caught her breath. "So she was, what, forced against the railings by someone?"

"Rather more force than that. There are traces of paint and metal under her nails, which we are currently running tests on. It looks like she was crushed against the railings by a vehicle." Dr Francis paused. "You will see on the file the same paint traces have been logged from the bridge, and the guard rail."

"But Amber didn't show any of the same injuries?" Dove checked.

"No crush injuries, but if you check the file, you will see she has fibres from Rebecca Hales's clothing, which were collected from her chest and torso area." A spark of something in his voice: "Jess said you would be interested in anything unusual."

"Jess was right," Dove said, "Thank you for letting me know."

"That's okay. I understand you were also on the Glass Dolls case. It's one of my favourites in recent years."

Unable to even think how to respond to this, but aware Jess must have put in a good word for her, she found herself muttering thanks and ending the call.

"Well, that was weird. Pretty damn sure the pathologist doesn't normally call a random DC with information." Dove shrugged. "I didn't think he and Jess got on very well, but she must have said something in my favour recently."

"Friends in high places." Steve winked at her. "No prizes for guessing Amber's rental car was involved in the incident, and that's why it's been ditched." His face was alight with interest. "Shit, though, what the hell happened on that bridge? And if there was a car involved, why didn't it go over the edge, too?"

CHAPTER TWENTY-THREE

Steve checked in with DI Blackman, and leaned back in the passenger seat, to study the notes from the pathologist on file. "You know, what I still can't see is why the hell they were all on the bridge in the first place? I mean, granted there was some kind of rendezvous, but there are plenty of places nearby they could have used."

"Emotional significance? It is accessible, but also pretty remote, I guess. Easy to make a quick getaway?" Dove slowed the car to make a left turn into Stone Lane. "You okay if we stop for a coffee?"

"Fine by me." He shot her a concerned look. "Does it hurt?"

Dove made a face, glanced in the mirror, and then nodded. "A bit. I need some food and caffeine and then I'll be fine."

She pulled in at Salty's Burger Van, which served most of the industrial estates this side of town.

The lay-by was quiet, with just a couple of HGVs and a dirty blue van parked up. A few men sat on white plastic chairs, lingering over tea and a cigarette, despite the inclement weather.

"Dove, mate, what the fuck have you been doing?" Salty leaned over the counter of his van to study her face, his jowls wobbling, beady black eyes fixed on her injuries.

"Hi, Salty. Just a minor accident. Can we get coffees and a cheesy chips, please?"

"Sure." He busied himself at the hot water urn, calling over his shoulder, "I had some journalist bloke here this morning. He said he was working on the bridge deaths, said he thought there was a connection with the Retreat."

Dove said nothing, and when Salty turned he winked, placing steaming mugs of coffee in front of them. "Go and sit down and I'll bring your chips."

Despite sitting down exceptionally carefully, Dove winced as various painful places made contact with the hard plastic chair.

Salty bustled over, a large newspaper wrap of chips in his hands, a bottle of brown sauce in the other. "Here you go. Make yourselves comfortable."

* * *

On the way back to the station, Dove slowed the car to pass a struggling line of runners, staggering up East Hill. The last three had stopped running altogether and were peering into the dense trees at the side of the road, pointing. One was already on his phone, and Dove could see their reaction to whatever was in the woodland was one of urgency or shock.

Steve was reading the pathologist's report out loud, adding his own thoughts and scribbling notes on a pad with his free hand. "The rental car was a black BMW 4 Series, which makes the grill height and bonnet width correspond with Rebecca's injuries. I wonder if Mark and Amber saw what happened, tried to pull her out the way . . . Dove?"

Dove was pulling up next to the runners. "Police. You guys all right?"

"There's a car down there." He pointed into the steep drop and the woodland that bordered the road along this stretch. "We weren't sure whether to call 999, but it looks like it might have been there a while, so we don't want to waste anyone's time. The airbag has blown. You can kind of just see it — where the leaves are off those trees."

"But you can't see where it went off the road, so it's not like it's just happened," his friend pointed out. "Even so, we wanted to let someone know, just in case nobody else spotted it."

"We'll take a look and do what needs to be done," Dove reassured him.

Dove edged the car into the next lay-by, which was helpfully only a couple of metres further on.

Standing on the muddy strip of grass verge, squinting through the trees. Dove could clearly see the car, and the registration plate. She didn't even have to check.

"What do you think?" Steve asked. He was still sitting in the passenger seat, sore leg stretched out, phone clamped to his ear. "The runners are right, there's no sign it just went off the road."

"It's the missing rental from Pink Lady Cars," Dove stated.

"Shit. What were the chances?" Steve relayed the information into his phone, his voice alight with excitement, and then ended the call. He winced as he manoeuvred himself out of the vehicle and joined Dove on the muddy grass strip bordering the lay-by.

The car was nose-down, and had come to rest in the steepest part of the old quarry area. "I can't see any way it could have gone off this road, but there looks like a path through the undergrowth over there, on the other side." Steve pondered. "No way I'm getting down there with this dodgy knee. Let's wait for the recovery team. There's probably an easier way in from North Road."

"There's another way down to the bottom of the quarry. It's right where the old quarry track runs down almost parallel with the woodland walks, plus it's accessible from Pengrove Road and Saddle Bridge. I'll go down this way and have a quick look, though," Dove told him briskly, elated at the chance find. Sometimes, although it was a rare occurrence, life gave you a handout on a plate. "It's worth finding out if there's anything useful in there as soon as possible. The whole access area to the old quarry has been cordoned off still, hasn't it? Which means this vehicle must have been ditched on the Friday night after the incident."

"I guess whoever left it here, only had to give it a push in the right direction if they pinched the keys, especially if they thought it might be evidence that leads directly to them."

Dove, preparing to navigate the slope downwards, nodded as she passed her jacket to Steve. "Right, I'm ready to go."

"It's going to do wonders for your bruises."

High on adrenaline, she shrugged, and turned back to the task in hand. Using a mixture of sliding and climbing, she got to the bottom, following some kind of wild animal path. The yellowing autumn ferns and dying undergrowth closed softly behind her, and although the going was soft and slippery, the drop wasn't as steep as it had looked from the road.

Dove gave Steve a thumbs-up and approached the car. On the opposite side of the ravine, she could clearly see the scar through the undergrowth the vehicle had made on its journey from the old quarry track to its current position.

It was very wet and boggy at the bottom of the quarry, and she splashed through a couple of unexpected boggy places, breathing in the dense, cloying smell of fallen leaves, rotting wood, and mud. She proceeded with caution as she caught the waft of another scent, a familiar one which made her stomach clench and her heart race.

The paintwork was scratched and dented, and the car was lying rear end up, slightly tilted onto one side. The windows and the windscreen were cracked, and the airbags had deployed. She remembered what Terri Sealey from the car rental said about safety. The woman would be furious, and rightly so. But her attention was on the driver's seat. "Hello? Can you hear me?"

It was a standard approach, but she was already pretty sure the shadowy figure she could see would not be answering any questions. Automatically, she pulled out a pair of gloves and slipped them on.

The stench of death and rotten food made her gag. As she got closer, she could see blood on the glass of the shattered driver's window. She slipped once in her haste, as a patch of thick mud caught her unawares. *Shit!* There was definitely a body inside the car.

Dove inched round until she could see properly and came face-to-face with Neil Barnes. His pupils were fixed and dilated, and his skin was colourless. With a gloved hand, she pressed gently. Rigor had set in, and he was stiff and lifeless. ROLE: the one acronym she always remembered from the training course. Recognition Of Life Extinct.

Stepping carefully back the way she had come, aware of the need to preserve evidence, Dove pulled out her phone and called Steve to report her findings. It was too far to shout, and she didn't want to broadcast the news of a dead body.

"Bloody hell," her partner said. "You come back up, and I'll call it in."

"There is something a bit strange on first impressions," Dove told him, aware of her breath coming fast, sounding very loud in the green and silent ravine. "He's in the driver's seat, and his head is resting against the steering wheel and airbag. There's blood all over the place . . . on the windscreen and the side window and the headrest, but as far as I can see, his primary injury is to the back of his head. He looks like he's been hit hard from behind with a blunt object, the size of a brick or large stone, maybe. Whatever was used, the force of the blow was enough to cave half his skull in."

There was silence on the phone for a heartbeat, and she could almost hear Steve's brain ticking over. "I'll call it in right now. Looks like that's another one for your new best friend, Dr Francis. I wonder if Max is responsible?"

"And then sent the car down into the quarry to delay us finding the evidence? I wondered that, too. I'm coming back up." Dove zipped her phone securely back into her pocket and took a last quick look around what was now a potential crime scene.

There was a small handbag in the passenger seat, along with a water bottle with the logo of a local gym chain, and a carrier bag from a local food chain. That explained the nauseous smell of rotting food emanating from the car, mixed with the odour of death.

Amber hadn't been carrying any ID, and there had been no purse or bag on her body when it was discovered, so perhaps this was hers. And even more hopefully, her phone might be inside.

While this was a lucky break for the investigating team, although apparently not for Neil Barnes, it was one that seemed sure as hell to bring up as many questions as answers.

* * *

It took three hours for the car to be recovered, after a full scene search by Jess's team. The general early opinion was that Dove was correct. Neil Barnes had died from a blow to the head. Evidence showed this had been *before* he had been placed in the car, and the vehicle then sent over the edge of the old quarry.

Questions had been asked about Dove's battered face, but she had deflected them, aware she was going to look worse tomorrow, and keen to get on with the matter in hand.

"If I had to guess at this stage, I'd say the chances of his surviving that blow, without medical treatment within the hour, would be minimal," Jess said, as she carried a box back to her van, stepping carefully on the plates along the quarry track. "It must have been some force. The trauma would certainly have caused a massive cerebral haemorrhage."

CHAPTER TWENTY-FOUR

"Time of death?" DI Blackman queried tentatively, as they stood later, surveying the scene.

Dove sipped from a water bottle. His eyes rested on her face for a moment, before meeting her eyes, but he made no further comment on her appearance, merely waited politely for Jess's answer. She already knew how much paperwork would be involved when she got back to the station, and mentally cursed Max Carter to hell and back.

It was warm and humid now, and the mosquitoes and tiny flies in the woods were hovering in a cloud.

"He's been dead at least thirty-six hours, judging by the stage of rigor and temperature of the body," Jess told them, batting off the midges with an impatient hand. "The car went off the edge just there." She pointed to muddy, chalk-streaked wheel tracks above the tree line. "I can't be sure, but it is entirely probable, given our other evidence at this stage, that this victim died the same night as the three who came off the bridge."

Dove waited until the DI and Steve turned back towards the cars, parked carefully away from the scene, before lowering her voice and murmuring to Jess, "Exactly what did you say to Dr Francis about me?"

Jess's eyes widened, and she grinned. "Oh, nothing much. I just mentioned you in passing, said you had been personally and professionally involved in the Glass Dolls case, and had a keen interest in pathology."

"Which is true, but he called me earlier to tell me about Rebecca Hales's crush injuries," Dove told her. "And I thought you two didn't get on?"

Her friend loaded a box containing carefully bagged samples into the van. "He's very good, and I didn't say we don't get on. I just said we come from different worlds. He's a massive true crime fan, and he's put the Glass Dolls case in his thesis or whatever he's doing for a master's degree at university." She snorted. "Academics! But I can just see him bashing away on his computer in the evenings. From what I've heard, he has zero social life and is married to the job."

"Wow." Dove was impressed, if still uncertain exactly why Dr Francis seemed to now view her as someone of interest. "Well, thanks anyway. It's always good to have a mate on the pathology team."

"Try not to get beaten up by any crazies this afternoon," Jess told her sternly. "Have you had painkillers?"

"Paracetamol, and I'm fine, Jess."

Jess shot her a disbelieving look and turned back to her iPad.

Back at the station, Dove let Steve go ahead while she grabbed burgers and fries from the catering van in the car park. Waiting in the queue, she checked her texts, always lingering over Gaia's last message.

She indulged herself, smoothing her finger across the screen tenderly as she reread her sister's words. It was stupid. She knew she should delete the text, but she couldn't. It was like carrying a tiny part of Gaia around with her. A part that couldn't be taken away.

See you at Ren's tomorrow. G

Gaia had never been one for emojis and kisses in messages. she thought, with a wry smile, but it still hurt so much that there had never been another tomorrow for her sister.

Mentally hauling herself away from that headspace, Dove collected and delivered her partner's lunch as he sat at his computer. She narrowly avoided dropping it in his lap as she tried to answer a text from Ren at the same time.

"Thanks for that. Stop trying to multi-task because we know you can't do it . . . Look, I've got something juicy." He pointed at the screen, to an online chat group. "According to this online forum, in 2017 Amber was suspected of being part of a scam, taking money from a donation page set up by a local charity. It links to an online article in a local newspaper."

Dove clicked send on her text, leaned closer, brushing her long dark hair out of her eyes, and read the article. According to the post, Amber had been working at the charity shop and used her connections to steal money from the charity via their social media donation page. Others had commented and agreed, before the thread was locked after a hundred posts. "What chat room are you in?"

"Just a random local page off social media. As I said, that was 2017, so a while ago, but it never went any further because she has no criminal convictions, of fraud or otherwise. The chat room doesn't look well-used after 2020, but there are over four hundred threads prior to that."

"The postings are pretty blatant," Dove said. "I'm surprised they got away with that, if she wasn't charged in the end. It should have been taken down. And the actual article doesn't mention her name, it just says the charity has had some money scammed off them."

"It's possible the chat forum became defunct and the admins left it up but un-moderated. Look, there's over six pages for local posts in other threads, all on Abberley and Lymington-on-Sea, and these are all recently updated."

Dove emptied a packet of ketchup and munched her burger while she considered the possibilities. The sauce stung the cut on one side of her mouth. "Maybe Amber made a fresh start after that? Max and Tanya gave the impression she was a bit wild when she was younger. The whole thing about being Max's girlfriend, but also maybe having a fling with Neil, is a bit odd. Oh, I checked, and Rebecca and Mark have zero connections so far to Neil or Max, so it all comes back to Amber for the time being."

DI Blackman approached them, waving a bit of paper. "Jess is a miracle. A match to prints on the car, plus the paint samples, height and logistics. It looks like we do have ourselves the car that was involved in crushing Rebecca Hales against the bridge prior to her fall."

"What about the other prints?" DS Amin peered over, on her way back to her desk with two cups of coffee.

"Neil Barnes, and Max Carter's inside the car," the DI continued. "Amber, Rebecca and Mark's fingerprints from the bonnet area and door. It's a treasure trove of evidence."

"I wonder why whoever disposed of Neil and the car didn't just burn it off?" Steve wondered aloud.

"We were on scene very quickly," DS Amin suggested. "If they wanted to dispose of it quickly, but not to draw attention to it, that was a quick and easy route. And it must have been quick, because the whole area around all three bridges was sealed off by 10 p.m. The old quarry was just out of range of the main search area, but easily accessible for our perpetrator."

"Are we looking at Max Carter as our main suspect now?" DCI Franklin came out of his office and walked towards them, carrying a pile of paperwork.

"Yes," DI Blackman told him. "To summarize the current evidence: Rebecca Hales was hit with the car Amber Dionysus rented, which seems to have been instrumental in causing the rail to loosen, and all three of our bridge victims to fall to their deaths. I would say it does rule out a suicide pact, but it's wide open whether we are looking at four murders, or a mix of accidental death and murder."

"Neil Barnes was murdered," added DI Waters thoughtfully. "I wonder how premeditated all this was. I mean, I really don't think even the stupidest perpetrator would lay odds on crushing three people with a car on the bridge. There are much easier and sure-fire ways to kill. This feels like a spur-of-the-moment incident, or possibly a genuine accident, perhaps triggered by anger from whoever was in the driver's seat?"

DI Blackman agreed. "Exactly. To add to that, I am relieved to say, a potential significant witness has come forward to say she heard two women arguing at 7.50 p.m. She was walking her dog on the lower of the two paths on the woodland walks that run alongside Saddle Bridge, and she heard the argument, which escalated as a man also became involved. She was concerned, but too far away to consider intervening. The voices seemed to move further away, and quieten down, so she assumed everything was okay."

"Why hasn't she come forward until now?" the DCI queried, a note of annoyance creeping into his normally calm tone. His grey hair was rumpled and his eyes bloodshot.

DI Waters explained, "She went up to Scotland to visit a sick relative that evening, and she's only just got back. Says she didn't see how it could be related to the bridge deaths, initially, but her husband persuaded her to call the information line in case it was important."

"Only two women arguing?" DI Blackman queried.

"Yes, and the lower path runs here." DI Waters indicated on the map on the wall next to the incident board. "Her full statement is in the case file now. Unfortunately, because she couldn't see them, we can't identify who was arguing, but she was sure it was two females and a male, which fits."

Dove was trying to get her head around the significance of this as the DCI called around the room for an evening brief. Her mind was spinning at the sheer volume of information, the threads of three different lives that had come to light, that might or might not have bearing on the deaths.

DCI Franklin looked quickly around the room, before summarising, "Night shift will be pushing on with sifting through witness statements and the lab results. For now, we are focusing on Max Carter, whose whereabouts is still unknown, and the unidentified DNA found on the car involved in the incident."

"What about the three bridges crash link?" DS Wyndham asked. "Amber Dionysus had connections to a possible scam previously, so what if she was involved in fraud linked to the funding page for the families of the crash now? Suppose Max and Neil were in on it, plus one other, and Mark and Rebecca found out?" He leaned back in his chair. "Sorry, thinking out loud."

The DCI was nodding. "Speculation is great, but we need hard evidence, and we need to find Max Carter. I'll be here until ten, catching up on the paperwork. The rest of you, clear off home and get some rest."

"We need Mark Davies to wake up and tell us what the hell happened on Friday night," Lindsey said dryly.

CHAPTER TWENTY-FIVE

*Audio Transcript * * * * * * C188362*

Thank God I wasn't in the bloody car, was the first thing that I thought. After it happened, it didn't seem real. We were, all of us who were left, totally freaked out.

We were expecting the police at any moment, but we realized quite quickly we could get away with it. It wasn't my idea, but I wasn't going to hang around to do any explaining. Shit, I don't mean it like that, but it wasn't meant to happen. It wasn't planned, and it was another terrible accident. But I just ran.

Until I saw her lying in the road, I didn't realize how much I had cared, or how ironic the whole situation was. But what good would it have been to admit what had happened? It looked like an accident, for fuck's sake . . . Just an accident. But there was a chance it wasn't, and I wasn't putting myself on the line for the police to decide who was right and who was wrong.

I swear I pulled out my phone to call 999, but we agreed that would be stupid. I could see down into the darkness, hear vehicles stopping, people shouting, and I knew someone else would do that. I also knew it probably wouldn't do any good. Nobody could survive what had happened.

Do you understand that? We were all there for one thing, all her followers for different reasons, all wanting to believe in something. If one caved, the others were screwed. I was scared, but I was never going to be the one to grass. Like I said, it wouldn't bring anyone back from the dead, would it? It happened, and everyone involved had to deal with it and move on. And for a while we managed it . . . Then it was all blown wide open by people sticking their noses in, digging up the past when she should've just let it be.

CHAPTER TWENTY-SIX

On her way home, aware Quinn wouldn't be there, Dove stopped in at her sister's house. She knew she couldn't sleep, and the adrenaline from today's findings was still crackling around her veins. Her sister always created a calm and homely atmosphere, and her presence was a complete contrast to Dove's busy life-and-death job. Plus, she admitted to herself, as she parked outside Ren's house, having lost one sister, she was clinging to her other one.

On the outside, Ren seemed to be managing the latest trauma to hit her family. Her house, with its little garden and smell of baking in the kitchen, was the kind of cosy environment Dove knew she could never create, nor would she want to, but she liked to settle there sometimes, just to catch her breath and enjoy the respite, the normality.

When she was stressed, Ren cleaned, and as Dove opened the door, she caught a waft of disinfectant and nearly fell over a mop and metal bucket. Clearly today was one of those days.

"Ren? Ouch. Is that to catch burglars, or the girls when they've stayed out too late?" she asked her sister, as she rubbed her ankle where it had caught the bucket.

"Hi, love, I'm so glad you popped round. How's the investigation going?" Ren asked brightly. She paused with a cloth in her hand. Her eyes were shadowed, and for most people, a full schedule of cleaning after a long day in the coffee shop would have been unthinkable. "Hell, Dove, what happened to you? You look like you've been fighting!"

"I'm okay, and you should see the other bloke," Dove tried lamely. Her sister looked stern, but concern shone in her amber eyes.

"Don't bullshit me. I've got some arnica cream in the cupboard, and it's brilliant for bruising. Just let me finish this floor . . ." Ren reached up, then threw Dove a tube of ointment.

Dove understood that cleaning was her sister's way of calming herself down, of avoiding the panic attacks, so she tried to keep things light as she talked a bit about her day, asked about her nieces, made light of her beating and obediently applied the soothing cream to her more obvious bruises.

Finally, after ten minutes of frenzied activity, Ren looked around her spotless kitchen with apparent satisfaction, and joined Dove on the sofa. She brought a bottle from the fridge and poured a glass of wine, passing it to her sister.

"Aren't you having one?" Dove asked.

"No. I . . ." Ren took a breath, pushed a black curl behind her ear, and answered while avoiding Dove's gaze. "I started taking the anti-depressants again this week."

"But, Ren, there isn't anything wrong with that. Why would you worry about telling me? You need to do whatever makes you feel okay," Dove said, a rush of emotion choking her suddenly. She bit her lip.

"I don't know. I haven't taken them since Eden went missing, and Alex, well, you know . . ."

"I know, but accepting help, from whatever source, isn't ever something to be ashamed of. Honestly, you know how many times I've screwed things up and got messed up because I've kept it all in here." She tapped her head and picked up the glass of wine. Dove had learned the hard way how to look after herself, and she felt strongly about it. She also knew how hard it was for her sister to talk about the monster she had married; the man who'd been responsible for his own daughter's incarceration. Thank God Alex was behind bars. And Eden was safe.

Ren waved her hand, and changed the subject. "You know, I keep thinking about the lorry that hit Gaia, and still wondering . . . Still wondering if it really was an accident. She was mixed up in a lot of shady stuff, at one point. What if we all got it wrong and this was something else?"

Despite the fact, Dove had wondered the same initially, she had now made her peace with the fact it had been an accident, nothing more. She dealt with evidence and facts, and there was nothing to suggest anything suspicious about her sister's death. Thank God she hadn't told Ren about the weird card from the Retreat she had found amongst Gaia's possessions.

But she understood that Ren wanted something practical, some reason behind the death, instead of an apologetic lorry driver who hadn't seen Gaia pull out, the devastated elderly lady whose sightline around the hedge had been impeded, and the motorcyclist, whose evasive action and fast reflexes, had saved at least two other lives that evening. But not Gaia's.

"Ren, she was killed in an accident, you know that. It wasn't anybody's fault. It was misty and the roads were slippery . . ." Dove spoke gently. Since Gaia's death, she, Eden and Delta had been watching Ren like hawks, deeply concerned due to her history of mental health episodes. She was pleased her sister was taking medication.

Ren was quiet for a moment, before she picked up a glass of water and sipped, hardly swallowing before she put it back on the coaster on the coffee table in front of them. "You said that Gaia went to the Retreat for a weekend, but why would she go to a place like that and not tell us? I was thinking about it, and it's like a whole different side to her we didn't know."

Dove had deliberated whether to tell Ren that Gaia had been a guest at the Retreat in August last year, because she had access to records that were strictly private, but she'd been anxious to know if Gaia had shared another side of herself with Ren. It seemed she hadn't. "Because we would have laughed at her? Maybe it was a one-off thing, and she didn't really enjoy it, but thought it might be my kind of vibe? Hence the voucher."

It felt so odd discussing something that, if she considered it rationally, really wasn't important at all. Everyone was entitled to their own lives, their own secrets.

"No, she genuinely didn't like stuff like that. She said it reminded her of all the hippy stuff we were fed as kids in the commune," Ren asserted. "She always said it was brainwashing, and mindfulness was for people who didn't have anything else to fill their heads with." She gave a reluctant grin.

Dove smiled, too, but needed to change the subject. Ren hadn't known another side to Gaia, either. Whether it had been one of the many facets of her complex life she had kept hidden from her sisters, or a one-off gig, that was okay. The only thing that wasn't okay was the odd compliments card.

"So, Ren, have you decided what to do about the clubs?"

"No. I mean, she left them to Delta for a reason, but Delta doesn't want a couple of strip clubs, does she?" Ren fiddled with the silver tassels on a blue cushion cover, turning them over and over in restless fingers.

"I still think it's a good idea to promote Colin Creaver to overall manager, and let him run both clubs for her. We know him well, and we know he can be trusted. Gaia had an excellent team, and she seems to have left everything solid financially. Delta can take the profits and just let it all run," Dove suggested. "It's not like she's a kid anymore."

"I don't know . . . I never liked the clubs, even when Gaia had them. You know I'm not a prude, but these kinds of businesses do attract some very odd, and potentially dangerous people."

"Delta is street smart and pretty savvy for her age. Hell, she's far more worldly-wise than we were at her age," Dove told her. "Let her have a go, and if it doesn't work out, she can sell them and put some money into property or whatever she wants to do in the future." She and the rest of the family had known Gaia was wealthy, but had no idea just how much money she had during the course of her career.

Being Gaia, she had made a will, which detailed every last investment, and ensured her two nieces, and Eden's son, Elan, whom she'd adored, had a large nest egg each. She had also left money to the rest of her family, and a lot to various charities she had supported. All this careful thought and planning made Dove want to cry whenever she thought about it.

"That's what I keep telling her." Delta's voice broke through Dove's thoughts, as she appeared in the doorway with mugs of tea on a tray, short dark hair framing her pretty face. "Eden's going to close up at the shop tomorrow, and I'm picking Elan up from nursery, Mum," she added.

"So, how's it going, Dove? Have you got anything new on the bridge jumpers?" She looked properly at her aunt and her eyes went wide. "*Shiiiit*, what the hell happened to you?"

Dove sighed, explained, keeping it as short as she could, knowing she was up for at least a week of this. Bloody Max Carter. Dove's youngest niece was extremely clever.

Although her eyes were dark blue, there was something about the way she carried herself, and her expression, that harked back to her aunt Gaia. She had changed in her year away travelling, Dove thought. Hardened up, muscled up, and there was a new understanding and maturity in her face.

But the sharpness, the keen intelligence, was still there. Dove had always thought it might be a tough gift to handle, and Delta had been bullied at primary school for being streets ahead academically. Until she had learned how to use her brains, to fit in without ever really doing so.

Ren frowned at her daughter. "You know Dove can't tell us anything about a current case."

"Hmmm . . ." Delta sipped her mug of tea, as Eden came into the room, hand-in-hand with her son, Elan. A boisterous three-year-old, stocky, bright-eyed and amusing.

But Dove could still feel Delta's curious gaze even when she turned away to talk to Eden, and laugh at Elan, who wandered out the back door and started kicking a ball outside in the dusky garden.

"How was work?" Delta asked her sister. "Did that hot bloke come in for his fruitcake? Cute Matt with the hair like Joe Wicks."

"Shut up, Delta. He just likes the cake." Eden was blushing at her sister's teasing tone.

"He's cute, and he obviously likes you. I checked him out. He works at the garden centre in Mill Road. Not married and no kids. Single at the moment, too." Delta smiled sweetly at her elder sister.

"*Delta*! Have you been stalking the poor man?" Ren asked sharply.

Delta, unabashed, rolled her eyes. "No, Mum, of course not. I just checked out his Facebook profile, because I happened to see his driving licence when he opened his wallet to pay for the cake last week."

"Are you sure you don't want to join the police or secret service or something?" Dove was amused. Just for second, while they were all together, it was okay again, and everything was back in balance. But then she found she was waiting for a witty remark from Gaia, who usually took Delta's side, and the small room suddenly seemed half-empty.

CHAPTER TWENTY-SEVEN

Dove shivered, despite the warmth of the house, filled with people she loved, and despite her reassurance to everyone, her outward show of confidence, she still felt like she was bleeding inside every time Gaia's name was mentioned.

Ren lowered her voice as her daughters bickered. "Are you sure you're okay with being back at work, Dove? I wanted to ask you sooner, but then you were caught up in the whole thing, seeing it happen. It's so soon after . . . so soon after Gaia, I'm worried about you. There are days when I can just about get up and function like a normal human being, and days when I just want to stay in bed, but I have the girls and Elan in the house, so I have a degree of normality."

Dove shrugged, again weighing up her feelings. The DCI had made it clear if she needed to take time out, it would not affect her chances for promotion, but none of that mattered when compared against the investigation. "I feel the same. Some days are good, and some are bad, but my job keeps me going."

"And the wedding?" Her sister brightened. "It almost feels wrong to plan it without Gaia, but you know, I can feel her a lot of the time, like she's close to us, but not?"

"Me too," Dove smiled. "And she'll be with us on the day too, checking out the gown, which incidentally, is not going to be the puffball princess dress, you two thought it would be so hilarious to sign me up for at that bridal shop."

"We wanted to give you a choice, even though it was so obvious you had your heart set on that vintage one." Ren laughed as Dove reached out to smack her and went into the kitchen to take something out of the oven.

Eden removed Elan from the flowerbed and retrieved his ball from an apple tree. Dove watching from the window, relaxed at the activity around her, the ebb and flow of family life.

"Wake up, Dove," Delta said in her ear, as she slumped down next to her aunt.

"I am awake." She pushed her niece away, but Delta sat with her chin on Dove's shoulder, her hair tickling her face, one arm wrapped around her shoulders. Even as a child, she had been very physical with her affection.

"You know, I was saying about the bridge jumpers. Everyone thinks it might be a cult. You know, like someone controlling their minds, making them believe shit just so they jumped off the bridges. It's all about mind control, blind obedience. Look . . ." She shoved her phone under Dove's nose and scrolled down numerous open tabs.

Dove tried to force her tired eyes to focus. "Delta, this is not about a cult, or mind control."

"You think that now, but you should see what some people are saying online." Delta flicked over to TikTok and clicked on the profile of a man with a Sherlock Holmes avatar as his profile picture.

"No way." Dove closed her eyes briefly, partly from tiredness, partly to shut out another armchair detective. Detective work was easy and solving crimes was just putting puzzle pieces together, unless you were the one in the frontline.

"Come on, just take a look!"

She squinted reluctantly at 'The Real Sherlock Holmes', and read a couple of posts in his TikTok grid. "Delta, these case studies you have apparently researched are well-established cults, and none of them are in the UK. I see your point and it is an interesting idea, and a sickening one, that psychological control could persuade people to take their own lives, but the logistics are immense. And this is not relevant to my case."

"Not if you're online the logistics aren't immense. They are totally doable. I mean, you can run anything worldwide online, and reach as many people as you like. Maybe they had to pass some kind of test, or maybe they thought they would be able to fly or something."

Dove blinked at her in confusion. Her niece was clearly still pursuing her own theory. Delta drew slightly away, navy blue eyes locking onto hers, defensive.

"What? Some of these forums are just *insane*," Delta continued. "Listen to the definition of a cult. It's wild. 'A system of religious veneration and devotion directed towards a particular figure or object'." She frowned. "Or it could be 'A person or thing that is popular or fashionable among a particular group or section of society'."

"Okay, I'll bear it in mind." Dove made an effort to look back at the screen. It *was* interesting, she thought as she scanned Delta's bookmarks, but it didn't fit with a sprawling coastal town on the south coast, with the people she knew lived here, worked here. This case was not about crazy cults, coercion and mind control. It was more personal, more . . . physical. This was murder. She could feel it in her gut. Unfortunately, her job relied on actual physical evidence, not vague feelings in the abdominal region.

Also, the initial investigations hadn't red-flagged any dark web use, any dodgy forums or known activists from any of the tech seized from the victim's homes. The press loved the idea of a cult, a suicide pact, or anything that was clickbait online, but there was no evidence to suggest anything along those lines. As she had done with Ren earlier, she firmly changed the subject. "Anyway, Delta, you were saying last week about a career, now that you're home?"

"I'm not sure yet," Delta said carefully, reluctantly pushing Delta's phone away. "Maybe going back to college, or doing an online top-up thing so I can get into uni and study business. Lots of time to think about a career, and I might do lots of things at once. I was quite keen on studying for a law degree, but now . . . I'm just not sure if I want something big, and I can't quite commit yet. You know, I don't want to start something and not finish it."

Dove was about to make some comment about how Gaia's death had affected them all in different ways, and there was plenty of time to think out a career plan, but a footstep behind her made her pause.

"Or maybe just carry on being a hacker," Eden suggested innocently, her long dark hair swinging in a shiny curtain as she walked in with Elan. The little boy was carrying his football now, giving his family a cute gap-toothed grin.

Delta flashed her sister a glare, but Ren, coming back into the room, gave her younger daughter a look. "What did Eden mean? A hacker?"

Delta pursed her lips, moving a long lock of hair across her shoulder in a gesture of defiance. "I'm not a hacker . . . not exactly. Well . . . Do you remember Tough Love?"

"*Oh no.* Still?" Dove sighed. "Actually, I really do not want to hear this."

"I don't know why you have to be so down on anything like that," Delta complained. "It provides a public service. Anyway, I wouldn't tell you anything, so you don't have to worry about whether you need to rat on me."

Ren, her lips pursed with disapproval, was clearly about to deliver a lecture, and Delta was shooting dagger glares at her sister, when the doorbell rang. Without hesitation, Delta grabbed a black cardigan from the sofa and swung out into the tiny hallway. "That'll be for me. Gotta get my stuff!"

Dove stood up and glanced out of the window, seeing a slightly familiar boy waiting on the doorstep. He had a mass of curly blond hair and tattoo sleeves on both arms. Despite the coolness of the autumn evening, he was wearing surf shorts and flip-flops. Her memory clicked in, and she turned back to her sister. "Is that Bollo?"

Ren nodded, and Eden smiled. "The romance is back on."

"I'm not sure it was ever off," Ren said dryly. "He's living in his dad's annexe and working as a personal trainer now."

"And also working on Tough Love with Delta," Eden said, lips pressed together in a pout, her forehead wrinkled. "I wasn't just trying to stir things — well, not much — but I am genuinely concerned about her." A shadow crossed Eden's face, and she kept her gaze on her son as she spoke softly now. "I know how evil these people are. Delta sometimes forgets that nobody knows better than their victims what these people are capable of. It isn't as simple as just playing games with these people online, luring them in and exposing them. It's dangerous, and they can make anyone disappear if they need to."

"I know, and after what you went through, I agree with everything you say."

"Plus, I know Delta joined Tough Love, started being part of this crazy vigilante thing, because I was abducted." Eden's expression was far away, and the tightness of her lips and jaw made her look far older suddenly.

Dove looked at her, compassionately. She vividly remembered the years her niece had been away from her family, and the Glass Dolls case, which had led to her rescue. She was about to say something when Delta sang out from the hallway. "See you tomorrow, Mum. Dove, see you whenever!" She stepped back into the room to give her aunt a quick hug, before hoisting a bag on her back and heading outside.

Leaving the cosy family environment for her silent and dark house, Dove felt ridiculously at a loss. This had happened frequently since Gaia died. She had always been happy in her own company, but now found herself clinging to noise, to bustle and her family, as she never had before. Because quiet now meant time for her grief to intrude, and the pain would hit her like a punch in the gut.

CHAPTER TWENTY-EIGHT

By the time Dove arrived home, Quinn had texted to say the night shift was pretty quiet so far, and had sent her a few links to property for sale in Cornwall, which made her smile. He had also messaged to ask if she had spoken to Ren about the wedding. Bugger, she hadn't.

She dumped her bag just inside the front door and sat down on the stairs to answer him. They had talked about saving up enough to maybe buy somewhere down in Cornwall near the coast, even if it was just a beach hut, but in one of the less-sought-after, wilder areas. The wedding wasn't going to cost much, so they figured, why not have a permanent bolthole somewhere that they loved? It came with a promise to make the most of every moment, and to take more leave so they could enjoy the memories and 'the now', as Quinn put it.

Dove, comforted by Quinn's message and realising she was a bit shaky, and needed to eat something, put a microwave lasagne in to cook. For the healthy bit, she chucked some salad leaves from a bag onto her plate. She also had a cracking headache, so she swallowed a couple of painkillers with a glass of water, and wandered around the house, closing curtains and blinds.

Finally, her dinner steaming gently next to her, she took refuge in the home office. A photo of herself and her sisters on the beach was set firmly on the shelf above her computer, and she smiled at the memories of sandy toes and sunburnt faces.

She couldn't sleep just now, so why not work for a bit? Doodling on a pad with her Biro, she drew a spider diagram of the group. But with every linked arrow, she kept coming back to Amber. Just as the DCI had summarized earlier, Amber was the one who linked to Neil and Max, and also to Rebecca and Mark.

Yawning, Dove went back to sifting through Amber's social media photographs on Facebook, drawing blank after blank, despite thinking she vaguely recognized a few people. Did everyone who lived in Abberley and Lymington-on-Sea area have some kind of tenuous connection to everyone else? Some chance meeting, wrong number text, brushing past in the street, and the connection was made. It was an interesting thought. Everyone being intrinsically linked to everyone else just by geography. Or by the three bridges crash.

Dove was soon exhausted, but desperate to stay awake and avoid her nightmares, or, conversely, slump into bed, sure she was going to sleep, only to wind up lying awake almost crying with frustration.

The remains of the lasagne sat next to a purring Layla, who was watching Dove through slitted green and gold eyes. She tapped the remaining cold pasta idly with her fork as continued the scroll.

"What are we missing?" she asked the cat. She reflected, as she had many times before, that it was an extremely good thing the MCT worked so well together. This was always highlighted with a complex case with multiple victims, and this particular case was one of the most convoluted she had ever worked on. Whoever had killed Neil, had done so because he had known something, or presumably witnessed what happened on Friday night. If the perpetrator was *not* Max, then who?

Before Layla moved in, Dove had always cringed when people said they talked to their pets. Now she had daily conversations with her cat and was convinced Layla understood her. How times had changed. She half-smiled as she remembered Gaia as a teenager, adopting two snakes and a tank for them to live in. To her parents' credit, they had allowed the new pets, on condition Gaia looked after them.

She was just about to give up for the night, scoop up the purring cat and curl up on the sofa for a while, trying to shut down her busy brain, when she saw it.

A photograph from Amber's Facebook page from way back. In the foreground a middle-aged man, beaming at the camera, holding a plastic glass of lager. Peering over his shoulder, clutching a red balloon each, were two teenage girls. Young teens, with long curly dark hair and big brown eyes. With the distinctive cheekbones already emerging, and matching red lipsticked pouts, one was Amber, and the other . . . the other girl was identical in looks. It was like looking at a mirror image. *Wait.* Dove leaned forward until her nose almost touched the screen. Amber had *what? A twin sister?*

She grabbed her phone, still taking in the photo. A party, a celebration. The caption underneath read *'Big Dave's Birthday'*.

"DC Milson, do you even know what time it is?"

But she didn't feel guilty. DI Blackman never seemed to sleep either, and it was well known among the team that he lived alone and was happy to be contacted twenty-four seven, if there was a case running.

She didn't bother with pleasantries. "Amber had, or *has,* a twin sister. I've got a photo of them right here. Looks like it was one she posted on her Facebook page right back when she joined the site in 2016. I suppose she did what everyone does and uploaded a whole load of old photos. Anyway, it's a party, and they might be around fifteen or sixteen at a guess. I'll send it over."

"Okay." She could almost hear him processing this. "An identical twin, you said?"

145

"Yes. I thought I was looking at a filter, or it had been edited in a weird way, but I think it's genuine. Apart from that picture, nobody has ever mentioned Amber has a sister. No neighbours, not the best friend, Elise, not even her mother, or Bernie would have told us." Dove's mind flipped back to Bernie's last update. "Actually, Amber's mum still won't talk to us, but she is also still insisting her daughter was murdered. Maybe she won't talk to us because this is something to do with the sister?"

"Or the sister may have passed away?"

There was a pause. She could tell what he was thinking but stayed silent.

DI Blackman continued, "It would explain why she hasn't come forward after Amber's death, and also why the mother didn't mention her. This twin sister wasn't one of the three bridge crash victims, I suppose?"

"I was just thinking the same thing. We don't know what her name is, and if she married and changed her name, she could well have been on the crash list and we would never have made the connection," Dove said. "Neil Barnes's girlfriend, Tanya, identified Amber from the photographs of the victims from Saddle Bridge, and Tanya also said Max's girlfriend was called Kerrie or Karon. What if it wasn't *Amber*, but her sister Tanya had seen?"

"Hang on. Max Carter confirmed it was Amber, though, didn't he? Odd he wouldn't mention it if he had been dating her sister instead, or even mention she had a sister. No caption to go with the photo, I assume?" the DI asked.

"Nothing that names the two sisters. It just says, '*Big Dave's Birthday*'."

"First thing tomorrow, you and Steve can find Big Dave," DI Blackman said. "And if Amber's sister is still alive, I certainly want to know why she hasn't been mentioned. Or, more to the point, come forward, once she heard her sister was deceased. Bernie said there were no other family members."

Dove agreed. "If she hasn't made an appearance, not even now she knows Amber is dead, she might be with Max. Which doesn't add up to anything very pretty, does it?"

146

CHAPTER TWENTY-NINE

Quinn arrived home from work just as Dove was leaving, and apart from a quick hello and goodbye, there was no time to talk properly. She was already looking forward to this run of night shifts being over. To avoid the awkwardness, she had been sure to text a few photos of her battered face and make light of her beating.

As she had expected, as soon as he could, Quinn was on the phone, his voice quick with concern. She had managed to reassure him, and today, had plastered on a tinted moisturiser to hide the damage as best she could.

Now, he stopped her, put the tips of his fingers to her chin and tilted her head. "Still hurting?"

"Yes, but I'm honestly okay, Quinn," she said, hoping she was projecting confidence into her voice.

He nodded slowly, before he released her. "Oh, Dove?"

She had turned on the doorstep, bag in her hand.

"Did you speak to Ren about the wedding?"

Guilt made her fudge it. "We're talking properly today, before we book the hotel?"

He yawned, and ran a hand through his hair. "Okay, just make sure you do, or we might not get the date, and we don't need any extra stress. It's supposed to be fun."

She was buzzing with energy as she drove to the station, still on a high after finding the photo last night. A bit of preliminary work on tracking down Big Dave had been surprisingly easy, and she had surprised herself by managing five hours of restful sleep, without waking from nightmares or struggling with insomnia.

The rain had stopped, and weak rays of sunlight lit her way across the car park to the door. She ran upstairs and checked her watch. It was 06.25. The morning brief would summarize the findings so far, but everyone was now tentatively working on the premise that this might be a potential murder case of three victims, and attempted murder of Mark Davies. The search for Max Carter had cranked up, and Dove's discovery of Amber's twin sister was also added to the case file.

Scrolling through the latest results from the lab, with a coffee in one hand and her iPad in the other, Dove could see evidence placed Mark, Amber, Rebecca, Neil and also Max Carter at the scene. Despite the wet weather, analysis of the tyre marks and the road showed the car had appeared to accelerate from a standstill towards the railings where the fatal incident had occurred.

She made some toast and escaped from the crowded kitchen, ready to continue reading through her notes ahead of the morning brief. The forensic findings also showed the car had stopped just as suddenly as it had started. An accident or a deliberate act?

While she waited for her bread to pop up, she gazed out of the rather grubby window. The view of the town was half-obscured by a broken yellow blind, but she could see the traffic milling around the traffic lights. A beautiful vintage car, decorated with a swathe of ribbon and roses on the bonnet, made her jolt back to real life.

Quickly, before she forgot, she texted her sister the new details. The reply came back as she was spreading marmite on her toast.

So happy for you both & of course will help. Hotel said they would let you move the dates, didn't they? Just book the date before you lose it. Xxx

Dove felt a slight surge of panic. Book the hotel, talk to them about food . . . She was sure they would just go with what had already been planned and postponed, she told herself firmly. *Later.* She would ring later, so she could text Quinn, say it was confirmed.

The open-plan office space was soon full of officers, and the briefing was swift, before the teams headed out to concentrate on their allotted angles.

"So quite a party on top of the bridge on Friday night, then?" DS Wyndham said, thoughtfully, as he walked next to Dove towards the desks. "I wonder if Max Carter is still alive?"

"Who knows, but it's got to be someone with a pretty big motivation for all these deaths," Dove said.

"I heard it was you who found Amber's sister," he added.

"Lucky guess."

"You do seem to get lucky a lot. That'll be good for promotion," he told her, with a slight sneer.

She nodded vaguely and went into the kitchen to ditch her plate. Pete Wyndham was just one of those people, and her way of dealing with thinly hidden slights was to ignore them.

* * *

Dove paused to grab a snack from the vending machine on the way out to the car, and turned to Steve. "You can have shortbread or M&Ms. What a choice!"

"Didn't you just have toast?"

"I'm still hungry, and anyway who knows if we'll even get a lunch break. It's called being prepared," she told him.

"Right, Mum." He grinned and shook his head, then turned away as his phone rang. Dove found some loose change, thumped the button, and picked up a packet of shortbread. She turned towards the stairs as her partner ended a phone call.

"That was Bernie. Martha Dionysus wants to see us today. She's working this morning, but will see us at 12.30 p.m."

"*Okaaay* . . . Nice that she's finally ready to talk." Dove held the door open for Steve and the cool air rushed inside. "Kind of weird that she seems to be scheduling an appointment, but I can't judge. Grief does funny things to people, doesn't it?"

"I haven't asked, because I don't want to pry, but are *you* still okay with everything?" Steve turned to her as they got into the car. His expression was genuine, eyes concerned, and she knew if she answered in the negative, he would move heaven and earth to try and find a way to help.

Dove took a deep breath and looked out at the sunshine over the sea, the glitter of gold over the Downs in the distance, and the busy, dirty streets surrounding the police station. "Yes, I'm doing okay." She started the car and pulled out into the traffic. "And I would tell you if I wasn't."

Big Dave, or Dave Attwood, who Dove had quickly traced through Amber's Facebook page, conversely turned out to be exceptionally hard to track down in person. Eventually, Steve and Dove ran him to ground on a building site in the village of Turner's Lee, just north of Abberley.

The building site was a chunk of new housing eating into the green Downs beyond, taking a great mouthful of the countryside, leaving a slashing livid scar of white chalk and mud. It was noisy with machinery and workers, but Dove located the site manager's office, and he directed them towards a new block of flats, reaching completion.

"I heard about Amber. Tragic. She was a great girl." Having descended from some scaffolding to talk to them, Dave seemed amicable enough.

He was a giant of a man, with huge shoulders and a square face framed with a bristly beard. His hazel eyes were faded and bloodshot, and his tangled blond hair hung down his back in a long ponytail.

"Had you seen Amber recently?" Dove asked. From last night's research, she knew he had previously had a relationship with Martha Dionysus, but they had split six years ago, when she'd taken his name off the mortgage deeds on her house.

150

"No, not for a few years. Just kept up on Facebook, really, after she left school."

"What about her sister? Did you know Amber's sister?"

His expression dimmed further, and he licked his lips before answering nervously, "She didn't have a sister."

"Come on, Dave." Dove pushed her iPad over to him. The photo had been cleaned up and enlarged as much as possible. It was grainy and pixelated, but it was impossible to miss the two smiling girls in the background or ignore their likeness to each other.

"I've never seen this picture. She didn't have a sister." But his voice was uncertain now, and he darted his gaze between the two officers. "Her mum will have told you that. I suppose you've spoken to her. It's nothing to do with me."

"Dave, we can see that she did have a sister. Amber is dead, and we are trying to find out what happened to her. Anything you can say to shed a bit of light on that would be very helpful. We can do this down at the police station, if you prefer," Steve said.

"Amber was a lovely girl," the big man hedged cautiously.

"So we've heard. What was her sister's name?"

He scowled at them, rolling his cigarette between his fingers, leaning back against a tree. "This has nothing to do with what happened to Amber, or her death, okay? It's old ground. Bad blood or whatever you want to call it, but it's history."

Dove waited, sensing Steve beside her, waiting and also silent.

Big Dave cracked in a matter of minutes. "Cora. Okay? She was called Cora, and she was a fucking bitch. Amber hasn't had anything to do with that little witch for years, and I'm surprised she had that picture of the two of them still up on her Facebook, if I'm completely honest with you. I thought she got rid of all the photos of her."

"It was an old one, and she probably just missed it," Dove pointed out. "But perhaps you could tell us why she would have essentially erased her sister. We aren't trying to

151

pry into painful family history, we just need to know what happened on Friday night. The chances are, this may have no bearing on Amber's death, but just in case it has, we are following every single lead that comes up."

They waited, as he became increasingly uncomfortable, before he said, "I get it, and I'll tell you for Amber's sake. I can't see how it would link in but whatever." He paused to take a drag of his cigarette. "They were so different, even as little kids. Martha, that's their mum, she did her best after Donnie passed, but Cora was always wild. She used to fight with the other kids at school, once pushed a kid off the climbing frame at school because she got into a rage, and the kid needed stitches. She almost got kicked out for that."

"Where does Cora live?" Steve asked.

"Now, I don't know, but she used to date a bloke who worked down at Benson's — you know, the garage? Amber tried to help her, always she tried to help her sister, getting her out of scrapes, taking the blame for things Cora had screwed up. And that was easy, because physically, they were absolutely identical. Even their mum had trouble telling them apart as kids. I'm telling you, it was freaky."

He scuffed the toe of his dirty boot against a pile of stones, kicking them gently as he spoke. "But I like kids, and those two, whatever Cora turned out like, they were special."

Dove gazed unseeingly at the roofers on the block of flats as she spoke. "The charity scam? That wasn't Amber at all, was it?" It was more than a guess.

"No, of course not. That was Cora. I told Amber, and Martha told her, to just let Cora take the rap. But Cora told everyone she had just been accepted onto this art course and they wouldn't give her the funding to do it if she had a conviction. She was very convincing, but it was always bullshit. She'd end up spending the whole lot on drugs or clothes if she ever had any money. Or even cars."

"Did Cora own a car?" Steve asked.

He finished with the pile of stones and leaned back against the wall of the brand-new block of flats. "Cora liked to borrow cars off her boyfriends. Before she disappeared, she was tearing around in a white Ford Escort, with a big spoiler and stickers all over the back windscreen." Dave snorted in disgust. "It was retro even then, but she liked the attention."

"Where is she now?" Dove could feel the case swing from twisted and tangled straight into clarity, and she could tell from Steve's expression he had also picked it up: the three bridges crash video that Amber, Mark and Rebecca had been repeatedly watching, the white Ford Escort that had been instrumental in the chain of events leading up to the tragedy.

"Dunno. I mean it, okay? After the charity thing, Amber finally wised up and cut her off. She hasn't been in contact with her for years now. Talk to Martha. Cora had another boyfriend who treated her like dirt, but that was before the funding scam, I think. Amber tried so hard to help that girl, even putting her own career on the line . . . But Cora wasn't worth the effort. Amber always said she felt responsible for her somehow, like her life could have been Cora's and vice versa." He dashed a brisk hand across his suddenly wet eyes. "Doesn't matter now, does it? Always the good ones that get taken."

Dove nodded in sympathy and empathy. "Did Amber date Max Carter or Neil Barnes?"

"Max! *Cora* dated Max. He's the bloke from the garage. But Neil? Name doesn't ring a bell, so I don't know. I just sort of kept Martha company after their dad passed, so I was there right from when they were five years old, until they were about sixteen. Those two girls were magic when they were younger, and I loved them to bits." He sighed. "But when me and Martha spilt, I didn't see the girls as much. Amber kept in touch, but they were all grown up by then, and didn't need me anymore."

"One last thing . . . did Cora ever get married or change her name, that you know of?" Steve asked carefully.

"No. But I haven't seen her since around 2018, so anything could have happened since then."

CHAPTER THIRTY

Back in the car, Steve updated the DI while Dove drove towards Amber's mum's house. She had pulled into the MacDonald's drive-thru by the time he was off the phone.

"Coffee and veggie flatbread for me, ta," Steve said. "I'm substituting meat for plants one day every week, now."

Dove gave him a look and ordered her usual cheese-burger and fries. They pulled into the lay-by to eat their greasy meals.

"Why does fast food always taste nicer before you eat it?" Steve muttered, picking bits of limp shredded lettuce from his meal with distaste and leaving them on the side of the wrapper. Without waiting for an answer, he continued, "What do you reckon about Cora?"

"She might have got back in contact with Amber, might even be blackmailing her in some way. She sounds a nasty piece of work. Certainly, the kind of person to chuck her sister off a bridge. I reckon that gives us the motive," Dove said. "Amber found out Cora was in the car that caused the three bridges crash, and maybe she was blackmailing her, or she wanted her to tell us what happened." She paused to consider. "And if Amber told Mark and Rebecca what she suspected, it gives a good motive for murder, but if anything,

I would have thought Cora would be the one in trouble up on the bridge. I do keep coming back to this: why the hell didn't any of them just go to the police?"

"Maybe they weren't that concerned about justice at this point, and perhaps they just wanted answers."

"I can understand that I suppose," Dove said, and caught Steve's sidelong glance.

"And Cora brought along her ex-boyfriends perhaps, as back-up, or insurance?" Steve suggested. "If Cora was driving the car in the video, maybe she had passengers. Say Max and Neil, who she would be able to drag into this kind of scenario, because she had the crash hanging over them."

"Perhaps it was Amber who started this. She somehow twigged her sister was driving the car, got in contact with her and kick-started this chain of events?"

"Even if it was, driving at three people and sending them over a motorway bridge is a very long stretch from pushing a kid off a climbing frame, and scamming a charity." Steve took a sip of coffee, and scrunched his food wrapper into a ball.

Dove stared out of the window, watching an elderly lady cycling briskly through the traffic, weaving between two lorries stuck at the traffic lights. "Not if there's money involved. Or blackmail. I'd say Cora sounds just the type of person who might be preying on vulnerable people, or even passing herself off as Amber. It might have been someone using Amber's profile making comments on the three bridges crash Facebook page, but Cora could have hacked her page easily enough." She started the car again and indicated left towards the port. "Maybe Cora is somehow scamming the three bridges crash donations page, and Amber found out? I don't know. This case just seems to get more tangled every time we think we're getting somewhere."

Dove drove to a row of cottages opposite the busy port. The soot and dirt from the road had coated what must once have been a line of pastel fishermen's cottages, in a layer of grime.

Rain was now falling steadily from a sulky grey sky, and Dove splashed her feet into a puddle as she got out of the car. Cursing, she pulled on her jacket, tucking her long ponytail inside and yanking the hood up. She had been right not to want a wedding out of season, but hell, if it poured all day, she would just wear wellie boots and go swimming in her wedding dress. The thought made the corners of her lips curl up. A welcome respite.

Martha Dionysus greeted them sulkily and showed them into the dusty lounge area of her little cottage. She didn't offer them drinks, and her defensive expression and nervous chain-smoking seemed to indicate Big Dave had tipped her off to their imminent visit.

Dove took a quick look around the room, noting photographs of Amber lining a wooden sideboard, and also noting dust-free spaces where perhaps other frames had sat. Pictures of Cora, perhaps? But the spaces would have been made recently, so why would their mother only now hide away photos of her twins?

"We are so sorry for your loss, Mrs Dionysus," Steve said gently. "Just to be clear, we are not trying to dig up any hurtful family history, we are trying to find out what happened on Friday night."

"Make it Martha," the woman said, as she stared defensively at them, but her interest was clearly caught. She sat heavily on the pink-striped sofa. Her dark hair was caught up in a pink plastic clip, and streaks of grey highlighted the curls. Her brown eyes, so like her daughters', were bloodshot, and her skin sallow. "I was going to tell you today, anyway, even before Dave called to say you already knew. We dated for a long time when the girls were little."

Suddenly she looked more accommodating, and Dove decided the apparent sullenness could be a coping mechanism, keeping everything locked inside. Was that why she had felt unable to speak to other members of the investigating team? Or was it because of Cora?

"Dave was concerned, and I can understand why he rang you. But we want to find out what happened to Amber, and anything you can remember, even if it doesn't seem relevant, might help us to put the pieces together," Steve suggested kindly. "Martha, does Cora have anything to do with Amber's death that you know of?"

Martha shook her head, sadness and anger in her face as her eyes strayed to the photographs of Amber. "Cora hasn't been in touch with any of us for years, and I haven't seen her since the summer of 2019. Amber kept taking the fall for her, with her money-making schemes and her drugs, but after the charity thing, when Amber lost her job, she grew the balls to cut her off. You know, despite being constantly on the edge, Cora never had any police charges. She always got away with it, whatever she did."

"Do you think Cora had something to do with Amber's death?" Steve gently repeated the question. "Could they have been in touch again recently?"

Martha's head jerked up, but this time she shrugged. "I've been over and over it in my head, and I can't think of any other reason Amber would have been up on the bridge, other than Cora was back on the scene. Her job was going well, she had her own place, and she was excited for the future. With Cora, things were always unpredictable. When Amber was sucked into one of her schemes, they would turn up in all sorts of places, getting into trouble with the boys, going off to all-night parties."

"Do you know where Cora was living the last time you were in touch?" Dove asked, making a few notes on her iPad.

"No idea. Four years ago, it was with a friend who was working with a car dealer, I think . . ." Martha took out a carton of cigarettes and offered them around. She took one herself, and the flame from the lighter illuminated her grief-stricken face. "Benson's Garage, that was it. The bloke was Max Carter. Cora told Amber she was going to move on, get a fresh start, but Amber didn't believe her until she vanished."

Dove shot Steve a quick look. "Were you worried when Cora disappeared?"

"No, she sent Amber a couple of texts . . . It's on her old phone. I've got it in a box somewhere. It was more a relief I didn't have to worry the police would turn up, or Cora would be trying to get money off me."

"What about Max Carter? Did he know where Cora had gone?"

"He only came round here a few times, when they were dating, but I never saw him after she left, so I suppose he knew where she went. They lived in the flat above the garage. To be honest, I hope I never see her again, if this has anything to do with Cora." Dark eyes filled with tears. "If anyone should have died, it should have been her. My Amber was a lovely girl. She was always so generous, and everyone loved her. There was something strange about Cora, always, even when she was a baby. Physically, you couldn't tell them apart, but personality-wise, Amber was an angel. Cora, she had the devil in her!"

Dove raised her eyebrows at this emphatic statement. "Was Amber depressed or unhappy, or did she mention anything that was bothering her? Like her sister getting in touch again recently?"

"No. Your colleague, Bernie, already asked me that. Not really . . . With her, it was always Cora. That was the only reason she would be stressed. She felt . . . *responsible* for her, I think. They always had a weird bond as kids, even for identical twins." She paused, and the cigarette smoke drifted in the sunlight between them. "Amber once said she felt like Cora was her other half, and each of them the person the other one might have been. She felt like one wrong decision, and she could be Cora."

She got up and moved to the cupboard, taking out half a dozen framed photographs. "Here, I still had these up before Amber died, and then I couldn't bear to see Cora's face anywhere, knowing she's still alive somewhere, probably still scheming and screwing good people over, while my baby is dead." Her face pinched in anger. "If I thought for one minute Cora was still in town, or I had one shred of evidence, I wouldn't hesitate to suggest she was responsible for Amber's murder, or for those other poor people's deaths."

Dove nodded along, silently encouraging the woman to continue, even while thinking that if her own mother thought that, there was every possibility that either Cora could have been pulling all the strings in this case, like some crazed and expert puppeteer, or that the poor girl had every reason to be screwed up.

The bond Dove had with her own sisters was extremely close, but she never considered she might be that similar, to an extent of following a different path in another set of circumstances. It was almost disturbing, looking at the photo gallery Martha produced. The two faces an exact match. physically identical as far as she could see. The picture gallery stopped abruptly in their mid- to late teens. There were no photos of Cora on her own.

Martha picked up one of the photographs and stared blankly at it. It showed the girls ready for a night out, full make-up and black velvet crop tops. "That was when Cora and Amber were fifteen. Cora had another boyfriend, and he used to encourage her wild side. Neil, he was called. Nothing wrong with that, but Amber found out he was using her to deal too, and she was furious. They had a massive row."

"Neil Barnes?" Steve queried.

"Umm . . . I had a photo somewhere." She got up and rummaged in the sideboard, eventually producing a couple of loose photos of the teenage twins at a party.

The sisters were pouting for the camera, one either side of a charming-looking boy. He had tousled blond hair, big brown eyes, and the kind of shiny, happy smile that would have drawn people in. Ducking in front of the camera, waving two fingers, was another boy, also with blond hair, but with a round cheeky face. Next to him was another girl, her pink hair pulled into two bunches, laughing at the camera.

"Look on the back."

Dove flipped the photo over. In a scrawl of green biro someone had written:

Max, Neil & us (2016)

"Yes, that was Max Carter." Martha jabbed a finger at the picture. "Neil Barnes is the other boy, and the other girl was Holly or something. She was more Cora's friend, but they all seemed to lose touch in their late teens."

"What kind of car did Cora drive?" Steve asked.

"All sorts. Those boys would lend her whatever she wanted. She had a white one for a bit, but never one of her own. They were always borrowed."

Martha delved further into the back of the cupboard and dragged out a cardboard box full of electrical wires, chargers and batteries. She rooted through the dross and triumphantly brought out an old Nokia mobile phone. "I should have thought of this before, even though it isn't anything to do with her death. Amber's old phone. I can give you the password. It will show you the kind of person Cora was." Tears filled her eyes again. "And the kind of person Amber was."

She scribbled the password on a bit of paper and handed the phone over. "I know what's on it, because Amber showed me. There are the last messages from Cora, and a strange one from Neil. He said she should keep her mouth shut or he could make her lose everything she had. Such a vile thing to say. I remember it clearly." Martha picked up her empty mug and lifted it to her lips, apparently deep in thought. "I told Amber she should have gone to the police about that one, but she wouldn't. She said it didn't make any difference now Cora was gone, and she just got a new number. She said she would be safer without any contact with her sister or those boys."

"She used the word 'safer'?" Steve queried. "Martha, was Amber afraid of her sister? Or perhaps of Max and Neil?"

Martha nodded. "I think she was in the end, and that's what really made her cut the ties. She finally saw them for the kind of people they really were, and she saw she was risking being dragged down with them. So yes, she was scared, really scared."

CHAPTER THIRTY-ONE

Dove took the driver's seat as they headed back to the station, while Steve examined the phone, experimenting with his own charging lead. "Doesn't fit, but tech will have one that does. I'm not convinced this is going to help, but it would be good to eliminate Cora from our inquiries, if we can find her."

"Somehow this does all link together, and the more I hear, the more I think Mark and Rebecca were only involved incidentally," Dove said. "Unless we get a load more background and links at the briefing, or someone uploads a major lead to the case file, this is becoming all about Amber, Cora and the boys."

He was silent for a moment before he answered. Steve liked to weigh everything up in his mind before making decisions. "It's obvious from what Dave said, that Amber was the absolute apple of her mum's eye, as they say. But whether Cora is as bad as he says, or she was just a misunderstood kid, there is still the question of where the hell is she? It's like she dropped off the face of the earth in 2019, and if she is back in this area, why hasn't someone else seen her? Her name doesn't come up on any official searches."

"Which makes sense if she was driving the car that caused the three bridges crash. She ran away, escaped any investigation, after she realized what she'd done, and started afresh somewhere new," Dove suggested.

Steve was stretching his injured knee as best he could in the seat well of the passenger side. "But she did get away with it, because they weren't ever able to trace the vehicle or driver, so why has this all surfaced now?"

"We need to get this phone over to the lab, but if we get it charged and check the texts first, it might give us a clue as to where Cora might be right now," Dove pointed out.

Steve nodded. "Out of all the garages in this area, Amber took her car to the one Max Carter worked at, and ditto car rental, but she rented a vehicle from Neil Barnes. She was making contact. If Cora is still around, I reckon she would have been on Amber's list, too. They were a trio, and if Amber somehow worked out that it was Cora's car in the crash, it would be a way of checking in with the old crowd."

"But if Amber was needling Max, Neil and her sister, what did she actually want? Say she arranged this meeting in the woods at Saddle Bridge with Mark and Rebecca, too. Why? If she suspected the car in the video was her sister's, why not just come to the police, and let us investigate?" Dove pushed her hair back behind her ears, trying to clear her head. With three victims, a fourth in hospital, and multiple threads, this case was one of the most complex she had ever worked on. "I don't get the sudden interest. Surely, because they were all local and it was all over the news, Amber must have seen the video before?"

"And if Amber only recently discovered her sister was involved in the crash, that doesn't explain her cutting off contact just after it happened," Steve agreed wearily. "I'm getting a headache just trying to put it all together."

Steve's phone rang, and he put DI Blackman on speakerphone. "Updates from the lab confirming Amber was in regular contact with both Rebecca and Mark. She was also calling and receiving calls from the same unknown number as the other two victims."

Steve quickly updated him on Cora and explained they were bringing Amber's old phone in.

"Okay, keep going, and we'll see if we can join the dots. We've got a lot of officers on Max Carter, and a possible sighting in Ashford. If he's gone on the run with Cora Dionysus, two are easier to track down than one, but we need to get the specifics."

"Any news on Mark Davies?" Dove asked quickly.

"Hanging in there, but still unconscious."

Steve ended the call, and Dove pulled into the heavy traffic at the bottom of North Shore Road. The rain, which had been easing off as they left Martha Dionysus' house, was now torrential, blotting out the busy road, blurring red tail-lights and neon signs, thundering on the window. To their left, the sea churned and boiled, throwing white froth up onto the promenade area. The pier was deserted, and the pavements scattered with scurrying pedestrians huddled under umbrellas.

"It's like a bloody monsoon," Steve complained, as the wipers, despite being on max, had little effect on the torrential downpour. "So much for the Indian Summer."

"According to the report, it was this kind of weather the time of the three bridges crash," Dove said thoughtfully. "A hot day and then sea fog coming in, followed by a downpour, according to the reports. '*A perfect storm*', the coroner called it at the inquest, and not because of the weather. Every little thing that happened on the road at that time and place that evening could just as easily have not happened. Wrong place, wrong time for the victims."

Steve shot her a concerned glance. "Is that your current bedtime reading? The Three Bridges report?"

She said nothing, but instead gripped the steering wheel more tightly, seeing her knuckles whiten as she slowed down for the pedestrian crossing opposite the pier. Steve knew she wasn't sleeping, and this was the closest he would come to checking in on her. She didn't want to admit she was struggling, because she honestly believed she had it under control.

Her partner nodded as though she'd replied, clearly drawing his own conclusions, and changed the subject. "Do you think it might have been Max Carter who got them all up on the bridge on Friday night? If he was spooked by Amber, by her threats or even just what she knew, perhaps he asked for a meeting?"

"Maybe." She stopped at the traffic lights again, eyes on the road, mind replaying the scene from Friday night, the fingers of her right hand tapping the wheel. "And maybe Neil got cold feet, or perhaps wanted to do something different. I do find it strange Cora has vanished, but I suppose if she and Max planned this whole thing, it makes sense. After whatever happened on the bridge, they killed Neil and legged it."

Steve agreed. "Quite extreme for covering up what would hardly be a life sentence. But who knows how the CPS would react if it was proven beyond reasonable doubt that Cora was responsible for setting those wheels in motion? I can make an educated guess, but the press and public opinion would be what really crucified her."

"Understandably. If I was the families, I would be howling for justice," Dove said thoughtfully. "Especially if she was driving under the influence."

Steve frowned. "I was thinking, too, if the unknown DNA from Amber's clothes and the car *was* Cora's, it would be a near match to her own, wouldn't it?"

"Shit, you're right." Dove drove in silence for a while, mentally kicking herself for not considering this vital point. So many little things she would have done automatically before Gaia's death, and she should have ticked this box, but although she seemed to be functioning okay, there were still times where her mind and heart seemed to freeze. *I'm okay, really,* she told herself.

She glanced at Steve, hoping she hadn't spoken out loud, but he was evidently humming along to a tune inside his head, chewing gum, scrolling down his iPad, tapping in names, checking databases. Serene and dependable as usual. She felt a wave of affection for him, pleased she had at least done one thing right: staying on this case, to stay with her partner.

By the time they pulled into the car park, he had the results. "No hits for Cora Dionysus after September 2019 on any searches, official or unofficial. Wherever she went, she went completely off grid, and chances are she's heading back to wherever she's been hiding out, with Max Carter in tow."

"It is odd we haven't been able to find a more recent photo of her. If she's not on the socials, not with her real name anyway, and Amber had nothing relating to her sister at her house, either."

Steve was starting the manoeuvre out of the car, wincing as his knee straightened and he put weight on his foot. "You know, we could be reading this all wrong. Cora could be just as much of a victim as anyone else. Perhaps she's been subject to cohesion and manipulation from her boyfriend, our Max Carter, say. Maybe she wasn't driving at all the night of the three bridges crash. Maybe Max or Neil were."

The rain was still hammering down, but from her vantage point outside the police station, Dove could see a thread of gold through the gloom, high over the Downs above the town. The gold seemed to glow right around the Retreat. She ducked in through the swing doors, raincoat hood pulled right up.

Pausing briefly, she held a door open for her partner, before they made their way towards the lift. She knew Steve could take the stairs now his knee was so much better, but if she happened to go for the lift, he didn't complain.

She took a breath, voicing the idea that had been buzzing around her head, "Or, maybe Cora vanished because she had taken Amber's identity."

Steve hit the button on the lift. "So if Cora became Amber, catfished her, using her social media, maybe using her contacts, who else might have known about it?"

Dove shook her long hair back, combing out the raindrops with her hand, pulling it into a high ponytail. "Exactly. Shit, this case just gets even more twisted every day."

She always found it horrifying how easy it was for people to just vanish. A gradual slide you have more chance of a trace back, especially if there's a history littered with mental illness or addiction and abuse, but so many people just disappeared

165

from society and never came back. Steve was right: they had just assumed Cora was running and hiding with Max, but what if she had come to harm as well? What if taking on her twin's identity was an effort to escape from someone or something in her past?

CHAPTER THIRTY-TWO

After the incident in my early teens, I continued working on my mask, my disguise that made me just like everyone else. There were no witnesses, and it could easily have been an accident. That was the whole point, and the biggest mistake people like me make. They get too confident and egotistical, and then they get caught.

Before that day, I was drifting, not sure of my way in life. I could also tell I was getting far too dependent on my little chemical pick-me-ups. They made me lose control, become whiny and demanding.

I couldn't keep my mask properly in place if I was under the influence, and I certainly shouldn't have been driving after the amount of shit I put in my body that afternoon.

I remember the hot, stormy day, my unusually clear head that morning, which led me to make plans for the evening. But there was also the nagging need to prove I was still as much fun as I'd ever been. I was planning to leave, take the car and drive right away.

It had been a shock running into Neil once more, because I kept quiet after I previously slept with him. I never wanted a relationship. He was just hanging out at the bar, looking for the same thing I was. To be fair to me, I didn't realize he was in a relationship until he suddenly got a guilt trip the morning after and told me he had a girlfriend. A loser, but I had a fun night, so I kicked him out, sent him on his way with promises our paths would never cross again, and carried on with my life.

Except I saw him that day of the crash, and he was with his mates in a pub at lunchtime. A couple of them laughed at me. I can't even remember why, and I suppose I just snapped. That familiar blinding flash of anger that takes over my brain. I didn't show it, but I waited for Neil to go to the toilets, followed him in and seduced him in the ladies.

He didn't put up any resistance, and for a second, I felt I'd made myself feel better. I still had it. But as I slipped out of the pub, and looked back, I could see him at the back door, looking after me. There was pity, compassion in his eyes.

Apart from the odd slip-up since then, I've been good, because I've had to be. I assumed I would carry on moving from place to place, doing exactly what I wanted when I wanted, keeping my true self hidden. But that all changed after the text message. Suddenly my past was in danger of dragging me away from my perfect life. I had already run away once, and it worked. I found I didn't want to do it again. There had to be another way of keeping the secrets, of keeping everyone together. The teachings at the Retreat, the immersive experience it provided, acted like a magnet for a certain type of person. It was fascinating.

My whole life imploded in that one evening, and it made me stop and think, change what I was doing to a certain extent, but it also reinforced what I had previously learned: it always needs to look like an accident.

Even when it isn't.

CHAPTER THIRTY-THREE

DI Blackman listened in silence to Steve's theory about Cora Dionysus while they waited for Amber's old phone to finish charging.

"The phone was last used in early 2020, according to Martha Dionysus," Dove added. "We also wondered about her actual relationship with Max Carter. Is Cora a victim, rather than the aggressor?"

"Max's laptop went to the labs, but there isn't anything back yet," DI Blackman pointed out. "I don't think we should discount the possibility of them working together, but, as you say, we should keep an open mind as to the context of their relationship. He's been visible, and present in town, at work as usual, post the three bridges accident. That would give him the perfect opportunity to put up a legitimate front, if one was needed."

Steve leaned forward. "It has occurred to me that Cora might not have disappeared at all. She might be using another identity. In which case, she could even be linked to the Retreat. They told us they have loads of freelancers."

"Okay, I'll nudge the lab on the tech, but I'm liking the Cora idea." The DI added, "Although reservations about the new identity, Steve, because she could hardly stick around her old hometown, in case someone recognized her." His grey eyes narrowed. "Unless that's exactly what happened."

Amber's old Nokia pinged to indicate the phone was charged, and Steve picked it up.

"I've got the password Martha wrote down." Dove passed him the scrap of paper.

"I'm in!" There was silence as Steve navigated his way to the messaging. "Shit, look at these."

Dove and DI Blackman were both leaning over his shoulder, reading the texts, and Dove felt a flash of excitement. Cora's texts were angry, demanding, filled with expletives, just as Martha had said.

"This is Max Carter's number," the DI, having taken the phone from Steve, was checking through the contacts list. "His last text to Amber was dated October 2019 . . ."

Just keep your mouth shut. You won't get away with anything if you start digging around. Stick with the plan. If you don't, you know what I'll do.

Amber's reply was a shrugging emoji.

The last text from Cora was the same one Martha had received:

I'm going away now. I've caused so much shit to happen and I want a fresh start. Sorry. I'm going abroad and then who knows? I won't contact you again, but I am sorry. I'm getting a new phone number, a new life and I'm going to try again. C x

"Let's get it over to the lab and we can dredge up all the deleted stuff," DI Blackman said, heading for his office. "I'll fast-track it and see if we can get any clues as to where Max and Cora might be now. Neil Barnes' PM results are due back later, too."

Five minutes later, as Dove was finishing the paperwork on Max Carter, he stuck his head out of the office. "Two of the freelance instructors who missed the initial interviews, because they weren't around, are at the Retreat now and want to give statements. They were both working at the retreat Mark, Amber and Rebecca attended."

"Yes, boss," Steve said.

"Louise knows you are coming and is very happy to facilitate in any way she can."

"She's almost a bit too helpful?" Steve queried idly, picking up his bag.

"You're just used to the haters, DS Parker." Dove could hear amusement in the DI's voice. "Louise's partner is a DI on TFU." TFU was the Tactical Firearms Unit. "I realized a few days ago, we did some training together way back. Oh, and while you're there, do some more digging on these bloody cards that keep cropping up. Take ten minutes for a lunch break on the way."

Dove had the greatest respect for the TFU, but she still agreed with Steve. She also viewed anyone who was super helpful with suspicion, and the reason in this case might not be just because of her personal connection with the police.

* * *

They stopped at the BP garage on the Coast Road and sat in the car with coffees and rolls, while Dove attempted to scroll through the Retreat website without getting mayonnaise drips on her iPad screen. "You are a genius, DS Parker," she told him.

"I know that already, but why in particular this time?" He grinned through a mouthful of crisps.

"You know you mentioned Cora changing her identity." She swigged some coffee, jamming the cardboard cup awkwardly back into the cupholder in the centre of the car.

"So?"

"*Soooooo* . . . The Retreat uses a load of freelancers, lots of whom are listed and photographed for their website, but not all of them are up here. What if Cora went off abroad,

171

reinvented herself as a yoga teacher or something, and came back to her hometown?"

"You mean she starts making contact with, perhaps, her old boyfriends? But not her mum and sister yet, because she's unsure of her reception." Steve nodded.

"She did say in the text she was sorry and was going to start again, so perhaps she really did. But then she's teaching at the Retreat and her sister is a guest."

"Hang on, though, even if she dyed her hair, wore coloured contacts and got loads of piercings and tattoos or something, the physical likeness between Cora and Amber would have been noted. You can't change your height, and your essential physical appearance, without doing something drastic. Somebody would have mentioned it, surely?"

"Not necessarily. If the guests were all busy with their own reasons for being there, maybe nobody did notice," Dove argued, as she drove carefully over the speed bumps and pulled up on the gravel in front of the farmhouse. "And didn't Kirstie mention Louise had a converted barn or something that freelancers could stay in? If Cora came back a changed woman, maybe wanting to live close to her childhood hometown, it would have been a big risk, but she may have thought it was worth it."

"Let's go and have a look," Steve agreed. "Who knows, we might even find Max Carter hiding under the bed."

She rolled her eyes, grinning despite herself. "Yeah, hilarious."

Kirstie, the Pilates instructor, greeted them cheerfully as they got out of the car. "Hello again. Are you here to talk to Louise?" She was carrying a bag of yoga mats and a water bottle.

"If you could let Louise know we're here, that would be great," Steve said.

"Sure. Same room as before. Louise has got a migraine today, but she's been struggling on." Concern touched her face. "She's devastated about what happened. We all are."

Louise did indeed look rough, but she was as efficient and calm as ever and pointed them towards a shelter in the sunny garden. "That's a kind of writing retreat for journaling and keeping records. It's more private than the house, and I've told Meredith and Tina to meet you there, with a fifteen-minute interval."

"Thanks for setting that up at short notice, Louise." Dove smiled at her. "Kirstie mentioned you weren't feeling great."

The other woman gave a dismissive wave of her hand. "Just a migraine. I've had them all my life, so I know how to handle them. The one thing that would really make me feel better would be to clear mine and the Retreat's name. I've been losing bookings, and we are getting a lot of accusations and hate on social media."

"Why?" Steve asked.

"Everyone seems to know all three victims were guests here, and thanks to press speculation and our social media detectives, it appears we are running everything here from a satanic cult to a drugs ring. Jeez!" She winced and put a hand to her forehead. "Go on, I'm okay. I just need some water."

Dove found the kitchen and brought a glass of water to where Louise sat. The other woman thanked her.

"We'll crack on with the interviews, but if we could have a chat afterwards?" Dove said.

"Has something else happened?" Louise's voice was sharp. She took a gulp of water, closed her eyes briefly.

"We just want to clarify a few points, and talk to you about your freelance instructors," Steve reassured her.

Louise opened her eyes. "Everyone here, they are more than employees and guests — they are family." Her expression was suddenly intense, fierce, and Dove felt a twinge of unease.

They headed out into the sunlight and walked down towards one of the many converted outbuildings. Dove could see the first person already waiting for them, seated on a wooden bench inside with a mug in her hand.

Tina was twenty-two, tall and wiry, with short dark hair and a sharp expression that soon softened as she talked about her guests, or her *people* as she kept calling them.

173

"I found my place here. It sounds trite, but I like helping, being part of someone's life in a good way. I wish them nothing but positivity. This is a peaceful tribe, not somewhere for negative energy." She fiddled with the beads around her wrist, before she added, "I was so shocked to come back from holiday and find out what had happened. And devastated, of course."

"You told Louise you remember Amber in particular, but you had both Mark and Rebecca in your classes, too," Steve clarified.

Apparently genuine grief crossed her face, like a shadow flickering over water. "I was down for the weekend, because I'd just qualified on a Level Three course, and I needed the hours to complete my studies. We talked a lot, me and Amber. We just clicked. We kept in touch a bit. Look, sometimes it happens, and you meet people who are just meant to be in your life."

CHAPTER THIRTY-FOUR

"What did she talk about?" Dove asked gently.

Tina ignored the question, but seemed eager to put her views forward. "First up, I don't believe she would have killed herself. I don't believe either Mark or Rebecca would have, either. We see a lot of people on edge coming here, who need nurturing to find their inner peace and centre again. From what I remember, they were all in a good place, and they spent a lot of time together. The energy was *very* positive, and the teachings are geared towards encouraging that."

She was so earnest and enthusiastic it was hard not to like her, Dove thought. She could feel Steve cringing at the use of certain phrases, though. If there was anything guaranteed to bring her partner out in a rash, it was yoga, healthy eating and talk of negative or positive energy. In a place where all these terms and more were readily used, he was clearly uncomfortable.

"Amber talked about her sister," Tina said suddenly. "She did say she was carrying a lot of grief and guilt that she hadn't been able to help her. Amber said she was her twin, and when Cora was in pain or whatever, she felt it messed with her head, too."

"Did she mention having been in touch with Cora recently?" Dove asked. If Cora had definitely come back into

Amber's life, from what they had learned already, that could only be a bad thing.

"I got the impression they had been estranged for a long time." Tina considered, plucking and turning a piece of grass over her hands, so the seeds sprinkled out over the matting on the wooden floorboards. "No, she didn't say so. I think it was more that it was something in her past, and she was coming to terms with the toxic relationship. She didn't say any more about Cora the next day, but I got that perhaps she hadn't had an easy life. As I say, she seemed positive, and very focused when she left the last time."

"And you kept in contact for how long?"

"Until the beginning of this month, and then she suddenly ghosted me. I was surprised and a bit worried, but I thought maybe she had stuff going on, so I only sent one more text. Then she turned up after one of my classes, just before I went on holiday. She was very agitated, and I was worried about her." Tina's green eyes were wide with concern. "This is the main reason I wanted to give a statement today. Something was badly wrong, and she didn't seem like herself at all. But she was angry, not depressed."

"Did she say what was wrong? Was it maybe to do with Cora?" Dove asked.

"She wouldn't say. It was like she wanted to, but maybe she bottled it at the last minute. It was all about how she was putting people in danger, and it wasn't right, that she had lost control of what was happening, but she couldn't put the brakes on whatever was planned." Tina considered. "She kept saying it was too late to stop the secrets coming out."

"Any names, dates or places?"

"No. You can have my phone if you like, to see what she said on the texts." Tina's eyes were wide and distressed as she offered the device. "But there was never anything serious or concrete, just that it wasn't her planning to kill herself, it was something she was maybe investigating."

"Did she mention Max Carter or Neil Barnes?" Dove asked, taking the phone.

"No. She told me she was finally going to put something right, like the universe had been off kilter for her for so long, and now that she knew why, she was going to rebalance everything."

"Which, translated, means?" Steve asked, with a slight note of exasperation in his voice.

"I don't know, but it didn't mean she was going to kill herself!" Her expression was intense. "I don't know what happened with her, Mark and Rebecca, but I got the impression they were the ones she felt she was putting in danger. Every time I asked her a straight question, like was she in danger, or should she think of going to the police even, she brushed me off."

Steve frowned. "Is there anything else you can think of that she said? Any clue at all as to what she was planning?"

Tina frowned, head slightly tilted, eyes narrowed. "Amber got a text, just as she was leaving. It was around 9 p.m., and she was walking back to her car. Oh, she said she was taking her car into the garage for repairs, but I don't think that's important, is it? Just trivia."

"Did she tell you who the text was from?" Dove asked, leaning against the wooden wall of the barn, trying to make sense of Amber's behaviour. *Cora*. If Amber felt she had to get her sister to confess to being involved in the 2019 crash, she would have conflicting feelings of guilt and compassion.

She tried to imagine her own sisters being involved in something like this. Gaia had been in trouble for years, often dipping onto the wrong side of the law as she established her place in her own business world. Running lap-dancing clubs brought her into contact with the criminal fraternity on a regular basis. Dove, working on the other side of the law, had often felt torn.

According to their search histories, Mark and Rebecca had both been investigating the crash since it happened, desperate for justice, so somehow all three made a discovery at the retreat in August. And what if that discovery had been the driver who caused the crash? The long-lost sister Amber thought she had finally seen the back of in 2019?

She dragged her thoughts back to Tina.

"She never said who the text was from, but it seemed to worry her, and I told her to drive safely and call me if she needed help." Tina was drumming her fingers on the table, face scrunched, eyes distant, in her efforts to remember. "She made a call when she got into her car. She had the windows open, and it was hands-free, so I heard her greet the person on the other end, and then she told them this was their last chance."

Dove glanced at Steve. "Do you know any of these people?" Steve showed the screen on his iPad to Tina, with photographs of Max Carter and Neil Barnes.

"No. Sorry, I have no idea who they are," Tina said without hesitation, as she looked at the faces.

"One last question. Did Amber ever mention a road crash to you? Specifically, the three bridges crash in 2019?"

"The one where loads of people died? No, never." Attention caught, her dark eyes flickered from one officer to the other. "What's that got to do with this?"

Satisfied that Tina had nothing further to add, Dove thanked the woman and she and Steve waited for their next interviewee, Meredith.

"We've got unknown DNA and an unlisted number, and Amber arguing with someone earlier in the week. It would fit with her pushing Cora to come clean. If she did meet her sister here at the Retreat by chance, surely, she would have shown some shock, maybe been upset, and Tina didn't mention any of that at all," Dove said thoughtfully.

"But would they have killed to stop her telling her secret? And how did Mark and Rebecca fit in with all that? I was thinking, though, that we have our victims, and we also have Cora, Max, and Neil as three possible suspects," Steve pointed out. "Somehow, Neil fucked up enough to get himself killed. Or maybe he was always just the spare part?"

They stared at each other, and Dove could feel her heart pounding as her idea finally clicked into place. "I was thinking about the text messages, and why they don't appear to have all been in contact. What if they all had different agendas, and none of the group knew exactly who was going to be in the woods that night? They pitched up expecting one person, only to find 'X' instead . . ."

Steve nodded slowly. "But someone still had to mastermind the whole thing, even if just that one person was the only one who knew what was going on."

CHAPTER THIRTY-FIVE

Meredith was definitely not Cora either, Dove realized reluctantly, as she came into the barn. Of course, that would have been far too easy, but occasionally miracles did happen to bring a case to an unexpectedly sweet close.

Meredith was around the same age, but there was no chance that this was Amber's twin. She was small and sweet, with a soothing voice and long curly red hair. With her pale skin, sprinkled freckles and button nose, she looked a lot like a little doll.

But as she reached out to shake hands, Dove could see her biceps pop out and muscles ripple under her tight sleeveless top. Less of a doll, and more like one of those tiny but incredibly powerful Olympic gymnasts, she thought, taking the cool hand that squeezed her own gently in greeting.

She and Steve ran through the same questions, showed the same photos, but Meredith had nothing groundbreaking to add. She recognized Amber, Rebecca and Mark, of course, but, like Tina, denied knowing the two boys.

"I've been teaching in a retreat down in Dorset for the weekend, but I wanted to talk to you, just in case anything I remember might be important. It's been worrying me ever since I heard the news. Louise phoned us all individually and told us what had happened." Her eyes were shiny with emotion. "It was a hell of a shock."

"When did she call you?"

"What? Oh . . ." Meredith bit her lip, and pulled out her phone. "Saturday afternoon. I suppose the names had been released by then and she made the connection." She looked up and her pale blue eyes filled with tears. "It really is awful, and I can't understand why it would have happened. They were all three such normal, lovely people." She wiped her eyes and blew her nose loudly. "Sorry, I'm such an idiot getting worked up, but still . . . It isn't fair, is it?"

"Do you stay on-site when you're here?" Steve asked.

"Yes. I left for Devon around lunchtime on Friday." She considered. "There weren't that many guests booked in here for the weekend, and Kirstie. Louise, of course, lives in the other wing of the farmhouse with her partner."

"Can you tell us about Mark, Amber and Rebecca?" Dove suggested.

"Mark was such a sweet boy, and he seemed to be doing so well." She sighed. "It just goes to show, you never can tell, can you? I remember all of them very clearly. Amber and Rebecca both swam down in the lake beyond the trees. Over there." She gestured vaguely downhill. "And they attended all the classes. I don't think I was here on Amber's first visit, because I was away teaching at another retreat. I do remember all three of them getting on well, but that happens here." She smiled. "It's that kind of place where you just seem to make friends." She slapped a palm on the table and laughed. "God, how corny do I sound? Seriously . . ." A shadow passed across her face. She shook her head. "I still can't believe this is real."

"Did Amber ever mention the name Cora to you?"

Meredith narrowed her eyes. "I don't think so . . . Mark was the one I got to know the best. He had lost someone in that terrible road crash, you know, under the three bridges. He said she had been like a mother to him. It affected him deeply, even now, years later."

"Did you have any contact with any of the three guests after they left the retreat?" Steve asked.

"No, Louise doesn't encourage that at all," Meredith told them. "I help run the WhatsApp group, but she is really strict about personal stuff like exchanging numbers."

Steve had jotted down both Meredith and Tina's phone numbers, and after they thanked and dismissed Meredith, Dove was keen to cross-check them with the unlisted and unknown number connected to the case.

"Let's walk down and take a look at the bunkhouse while we do that," Steve suggested.

It was peaceful, the skies stretching and darkening towards evening, the trees rustling gently in the breeze further down the hillside towards the lake.

Dove completed her search within minutes, and she shook her head in answer to Steve's raised eyebrows. "No matches."

* * *

The 'bunkhouse' was a homely, converted barn, with five bedrooms, a communal kitchen and two bathrooms. Dove called out as they knocked on the door, and Kirstie appeared from the garden area, flip-flops crunching on the gravel path as she approached.

"Do you want to see inside?" Kirstie offered. "It's pretty basic, but nice."

"You were staying here on Friday night, weren't you?" Dove asked, as they walked in the door.

"Yes. I was helping Louise with the weekend guests." She scooped a pair of trainers up from the floor and slotted them neatly into a shoe-rack in the hallway. "Sorry, I'm the neat freak of the house and Meredith is the untidy one." She smiled, and ran a hand through her shiny ponytail. "They're all used to me tidying up by now. It's a bit of a joke."

"My partner is pretty untidy at home, too," Dove sympathised. "Did you have dinner down here on Friday night?"

Kirstie shook her head. "No, we ate with Louise at the farmhouse. She went to bed early because she was a bit under the weather." She frowned, "In fact, she told me that she had to take the car out to the petrol station on the roundabout after dinner on Friday, because she'd run out of painkillers. It's the one with the Tesco Express attached, you know? She's been overdoing it recently, running this place, training for the marathon with Meredith . . . and, I shouldn't say anything, but she gave us the impression her partner might be quitting his job."

"Did you hear her car going out on the Friday night?" Steve asked idly. His laid-back tone and deceptively relaxed approach worked well for a certain type of person. Even Dove, who knew him so well, sometimes had to bite back a grin as her partner coaxed information so subtly the interviewee hardly realized what was happening. "What time was this, Kirstie?"

"Yes. Well, I heard *a* car going out, and I mentioned it the next morning. That was when she told me about the painkillers," Kirstie confided. "I think around nine, or even a bit earlier. Do you want a drink or anything?" Her smile was gentle, and her eyes rested on Steve's face.

They politely declined, and Dove led the way back to the car. As she began the drive back to the station, she paused suddenly at the roundabout, and indicated right. "Pit stop on the way back to the station?"

Steve shrugged. "If you like. I'm still mulling over Louise going out Friday night for painkillers. And Kirstie, I can't quite get a handle on her. Is she playing a role, or is she genuine?"

"Mmm . . . I reckon Kirstie is sharper than she lets on. And with the painkillers, you would think they should have a plentiful supply," Dove agreed. "But I honestly can't think what kind of motive Louise might have for meeting our victims on the bridge and subsequently murdering Neil Barnes. She certainly isn't Cora Dionysus."

She pulled into the car park for the woodland walks on the west side of Saddle Bridge. "It's getting late-ish, and I wanted to just take a look and see who's around at this time."

"For what?" Steve glanced at his watch and shot her a baffled stare.

"I don't know yet, but the search team has moved down to where Neil Barnes was found, so this area is clear now. Ten minutes max, I promise." She got out of the car and shoved her phone into her pocket.

"I think I'll stay here, if you don't mind?" Steve called. "In fact, I'll do the paperwork, and check-in Tina's phone. She's another one I'm not sure about. Although I do admit the whole place gives me the creeps. I think it must be all that positive energy and yoga."

Dove made a rude gesture with her middle finger, and he laughed.

"No, it's fine, you stay where you are." She jogged up from the car park on her own in the semi-darkness.

CHAPTER THIRTY-SIX

The paths were wide, bordered by wooden railway sleepers, and partially covered with fallen leaves. The mud squelched beneath her feet, but she persevered until she reached the wide-open clearing on the bottom path.

At this time, early evening, it was still fairly busy with runners, dog walkers, a few couples. There was a mobile coffee van packing up for the day, and she walked over for a chat.

"I've just turned off the electrics, sorry," the man said, clearly assuming she was after a drink.

"Don't worry, I'm good," she said. "I hear this path has only just opened again."

"Yeah, this is my first day back here."

"Were you here Friday night?"

"Are you a journalist?" His eyes narrowed with suspicion.

"No, police officer."

"I did speak to one of your lot, because my regular customers said if anyone would have seen anything, it would be me." He grinned, his round face, shaggy hair and bright eyes making Dove think of a cheerful teddy bear. "Makes me sound like a right nosy parker, doesn't it?"

Dove knew if he had witnessed something it would have been flagged, but she just wanted to walk the scene, to think, before the evening briefing. "No, I imagine you see a lot."

He rolled up a tarpaulin and stowed it carefully. "It's my spot, and I'm here most days. I didn't see any of those poor people who topped themselves, though."

"It must be a bit of a pain driving into here with all this mud," Dove said, as she started to turn away.

He laughed. "Funny you should say that, because the council, who are normally as useful as a chocolate tea set, have just laid a proper gravel track out to the road." He indicated off to his right, and Dove could see fresh workings.

All this would have been checked, she thought, but still the evening shadows and the calmness held her under the trees.

"In fact, the same lot who laid the track did the new railings on the bridge," the chatty coffee seller told her. "Smartening it up down here at last. Although I don't think much of the firm they used." He frowned. "They have a reputation for leaving jobs half finished, or taking the cash and not doing them at all."

Interesting, Dove thought. If that were so, perhaps there'd been no sabotage to the railing. Just sloppy workmanship. She pulled out her phone. "I'm sure you've already been asked this, but do you recognize any of these people?" She tapped her screen to bring up the photograph gallery.

He studied the pictures, head tilted slightly, a frown creasing his forehead. "I did get asked, and I thought not . . . But seeing you standing there with your dark hair kind of makes me think . . ."

Dove waited, holding her breath. A few leaves drifted gently down past her nose, adding to the wet carpet at her feet.

He jabbed the picture of Rebecca, and then tapped the headshot of Mark. "I think these two were here on the Friday night, but that could just be because I've seen them in the news now. Is the boy going to be okay? I heard he was still alive."

"Fingers crossed," Dove told him. "Are you sure enough to make another statement?"

He shook his head and took out his keys. "No, sorry. But if it was them, they bought drinks at around six. It was before seven, because I pack up then. I like to just catch all those afterwork fitness freaks and dog walkers."

"Do you remember how they seemed? Which direction they went in?" Dove pressed.

"Nah, but if it was them, they were on their own. That other woman who died, she wasn't with them," he said.

Dove handed him her card and thanked him. She watched as the small mobile van drove carefully out of the woods, the driver waving cheerfully.

If Rebecca and Mark had been on their own, and already in the woods an hour and a half before they plunged off the bridge, what did they do during that time? She was also thinking that, in the evening shadows, with the weather still warm, the paths were busy. There were even a few lights attached to the trees bordering the path in this clearing, and she could clearly see the floodlit narrow road up to Saddle Bridge to her left.

She jogged back to Steve and the car.

* * *

The evening briefing was a chance to summarize the day's evidence, and it met with mixed reactions from an exhausted team.

DI Blackman was just starting when DI Waters came into the room, her face alight with excitement and purpose. "Mark Davies has recovered consciousness. His medical team has okayed some questions. DS Allerton and DC Conrad, can you get over to the hospital?"

Lindsey and Josh headed straight for the door, and the buzz of excitement and anticipation at busting the complex case wide open seemed to revive everyone.

"Okay, everyone," DI Blackman called over the conversation. "Updates. Rebecca Hale's PM showed she was crushed by a vehicle. That vehicle is now confirmed as the rental car from Pink Lady Cars. Neil Barnes was discovered inside with a fatal head injury. Mortuary is backed up, and they busted a gut to bump Rebecca for us, so we can't expect another miracle." He held up a hand. "However, our CSM is fairly confident on Barnes's cause of death and time of death, which was Friday night. He was hit hard on the back of the head. The possible murder weapon is a lump of flint the search team discovered in the trees near the car.

"Therefore, just before we arrived on scene, someone or multiple persons were very busy on Saddle Bridge, and in the surrounding woods. The road from the bridge leads straight past the old quarry, so Neil must have been killed and dumped in fairly quick succession to ensure our perpetrator managed to get away."

DI Lincoln entered the room, an iced cake in one hand and a cup of tea in the other, and added, "This means, we are looking for another vehicle used by our perpetrator, probably Max Carter, as a getaway."

DI Blackman took over again. "Communication between our three victims: it was constant, and although they seem to have been careful what they say in the text messages, with no names mentioned, it is obvious they were all three investigating the three bridges crash. Further, it seems that they thought they could identify the driver of the white Ford Escort."

"I don't understand why they wouldn't just come straight to us if they figured it out," DS Allerton said.

"If Amber did recognize her sister at the Retreat, she wasn't one of the instructors," Dove said. "Steve and I went through all of them. Which could mean she was one of the guests, using a different name, or even that she wasn't there at all."

DI Blackman continued: "As you can see from the audio and digital files uploaded to the case files, the mobile phone conversations were highly relevant. This was their last conversation." He clicked on a slide and the screen behind him lit up:

Rebecca: Are you sure you still want to do this?
Mark: Yes. What did she say?

Rebecca: I didn't tell her.
Mark: WTF! That's the whole point!
Rebecca: No it isn't. I want to see what she says in person,
so no lies.

DI Blackman turned back to the room. "If we are looking at blackmail that went wrong, then exactly who were they blackmailing, and why?"

DS Amin said, "I mean, we haven't found any evidence of Cora, even though I agree her involvement fits, and Max Carter is still on the run."

"If Mark is awake and talking, maybe he can shed some light on this whole thing. He could also be in danger, if he is coherent, because if we are thinking murder, so is the person who instigated all this," DI Waters suggested, glancing down at her phone. "I'll let the hospital know. Just a thought, but this could be worth leaking, to see if we can get a hold of Max Carter? It might flush him out, if he thinks he's about to be exposed."

DI Blackman agreed. "But it could go one of two ways. Hell, we're running out of options, and this case is like a tangled ball of wool at the moment."

Dove repeated her conversation with the coffee seller, but reiterated he wasn't one hundred per cent sure, and Steve added nuggets they had gleaned from their time at the Retreat.

"We can add to Amber's timeline for the week," DI Blackman said, "Shame Tina didn't hear who she was talking to."

Dove was still mulling over the many text conversations between Rebecca, Mark, and Amber which had been uploaded to the case file. She could feel an idea lurking somewhere in her exhausted brain, but it wasn't fully formed yet, so she said nothing more, and tried to stifle a yawn as the DI dismissed the day team, promising to update if Mark was able to provide any answers.

CHAPTER THIRTY-SEVEN

It was quite dark by the time she got home, and the wind had a slight chill. Dove, desperate to escape the hamster treadmill in her mind, pulled her wetsuit on and took her board out. One of the reasons she had bought her house was the proximity to the sea. It was a short drive to some of the best wild beaches on the coast, or a quick walk to the main shoreline. She preferred to head further out for solitude.

There was nobody else around, and, concentrating on her own safety, enjoying the feeling of the light rain on her face, the swell of the waves, she could switch off from work, from grief. The sea was always her peaceful place. Alone with the gulls soaring overhead, her senses filled with the salt, the water and the freedom they gave her.

Sometimes she would look at the skyline, idly watching the wind turbines, narrowing her eyes to catch a glimpse of the dark mass of land far away. The ever-changing light danced on the waves, creating a net for dreams.

The sea was a good place to cry, to scream and shout. Only if it was on a more remote beach late at night or early in the morning, and there was nobody else around. It was the reason she favoured Claw Beach over the more heavily populated tourist areas, even though she could walk to those from her house.

Although she was alone, she kept an eye on her new fitness watch. It was an expensive investment, made a couple of months ago, with an eye to her safety as well as well-being. As well as tracking her health, it tracked her physically, downloaded activities to her laptop and had an emergency function, should she ever need help.

Tonight, she had the paddle board, and as she stood up, dipping the paddle to one side, then the other, the rhythm soothed her, and she headed out to sea on the calm waters.

After an hour, restored to some kind of equilibrium, she headed home. The drive only took fifteen minutes, and this end of town was quiet. She parked in a space next to the post box, a few hundred metres from her house. Just for a moment, as she stepped out of the car, she experienced a frisson of fear, a moment of unwelcome memory, as she half-saw a movement on the footpath leading in from the next street.

As she turned, keys clenched in her fist, heart racing, one hand still on the car door, she saw a striped cat jump down from the fence and run lightly across the road. *Idiot*, she told herself, feeling her heart rate slow, her body relax.

Back at home, she wiped and dried her board in the new garage area, locked the door and went into the house to have a shower. The bathroom was above the kitchen, where the fire had started, and had been completely gutted and refitted. It would never be big, but it was bright and clean with its tiled floor, and had space for Dove to put her candles on the window ledge.

The hot water gushed over her head, and she closed her eyes, enjoying the beat of drops on her head, warming her frozen flesh. She towelled off and dragged on sweatpants and an old, soft hoodie.

Layla fed, she wandered into the office, scanning her messages, going over the case in her head. *Cora? Max? Neil?* Perhaps Cora had never been recognized, spotted at the Retreat or anywhere else, but had approached her sister, asked for help, relying on Amber's previous subservience and willingness to prop her up. But perhaps this time Amber had said no, had told her friends from the Retreat, maybe.

Something was niggling her about the movements at the Retreat on Friday night. Why would Kirstie mention Louise going to get painkillers, and confide that her partner was leaving his job? Did she think it might have relevance to the case? Kirstie came across as ditzy but straightforward and earnest, without anything to hide.

Dove glanced at the office clock. Quinn was doing a short shift to cover someone else tonight and would be home by 2 a.m. She would stay awake for another couple of hours to avoid the nightmares. It did feel ridiculous being dependent on having him home, but she sure as hell wasn't going to say anything. It would pass, this insomnia, the painful nightmares. At least after the fresh air and exercise, her body felt blissfully tired and relaxed.

Her mind drifted back to the case. Cora, Max and Neil had been drug users, according to various intel. Where would they have got their supplies?

The place Mark was currently living in, along with his boyfriend, housed many using the place as a kind of half-way house. The council waiting lists for help and housing were long, and the population of a place like Roedean House was transient. Neil's girlfriend, Tanya, had mentioned she thought Cora, who she had probably wrongly identified as Amber, was a drug user.

She bit her thumbnail, thinking hard. The threads that connected all three victims seemed fairly random, but one or more was going to be key in unlocking the why of this investigation. Something had come to a head on Friday night, but who had pushed too hard?

Where did it start for all three of them? The answer, in the darkness of late evening, seemed obvious.

She pulled up all the traffic cam footage from the 2019 crash records and case file once again. There had been an inquest, of course. Hundreds of witness statements, lots of reasons that could have contributed to the final carnage. A blown tyre, a piece of wood that slipped from a builder's van, a lorry with flapping canvases not securely tightened, obscuring a view at that vital moment. All creating a perfect storm that September evening.

But there was that vital unanswered question, a witness who had never come forward. The driver of the white Ford Escort. Someone who was crucial to that perfect storm, someone whom the police had failed to trace. Someone who had united Mark and Rebecca in their efforts to bring them to justice.

Dove squinted at the screen, her eyes tired and gritty, trying to see if she could pick out a passenger in the vehicle, knowing it was useless, and this had already been viewed by people far more qualified than her.

This was the best footage they had come up with, and she watched it again and again. A dirty white Ford Escort, the registration indistinguishable from the dirt, the driver hidden by the poor-quality footage and distance from the cameras. The vehicle had been sitting behind the lorry with the flapping canvas.

Just ahead of the first bridge, the Ford Escort driver changed lanes twice, weaving in and out past two motorcyclists and a builder's van. As it changed lanes for the third time, it pulled out right into the path of a red Mini, which braked sharply, starting to skid. In response, the driver of the builder's van also braked, slewed sideways, and a small piece of wood slipped under the tarpaulin, onto the road, right into the path of the first motorcyclist.

The Ford Escort was long gone by the time the crash closed the road, but there was no question that the driver had contributed significantly — if not caused the accident.

There was a lot of speculation in the statements about the car. Had the driver been under the influence of drink or drugs, or simply impatient and driving badly? Numerous sightings of the car were listed as reported, but traffic cam showed it turned off at the exit to Lymington-on-Sea, took a route down past the Cloud pub, and then vanished.

A lot of time and effort had been devoted to trying to track down the driver and car, but to no avail. Dove leaned back, closed her eyes and yawned. It was horrific, that a few things like wet weather, a careless driver, a van load not properly secured, could cause the deaths of eighteen people. Her heart hurt for those victims and their families.

Somehow the three bridges tragedy seemed to have spawned another trio of fatalities. Was it really down to Cora and Max?

Pausing only to head to the kitchen for a mug of tea, Dove sank back onto her chair, logged in and scrolled through the HOLMES directory, trying various matches. It was a standing joke amongst her colleagues now that Dove got more work done at home in the evenings than in the office. But that was how her brain worked. She often struggled with the noise, the intensity of her working environment, even though, at the same time, she enjoyed it.

DI Blackman told her he didn't care how her brain worked best, but to carry on with what made her feel comfortable. And this was it, in the hours of darkness, with the sounds of the night trickling softly through the open window into her peaceful house. This was when she could access all the niggling ideas and subjects she had stacked up during the day.

Finally, she pulled up all the incidents logged in the twenty-four hours before and after the 2019 crash. By circling back to the older incident, she felt there might be a chance of finding something she had missed.

One stood out so strongly, she wondered why nobody else had made the connection. The same night, there had been a hit-and-run on Clover Street. The witness reported a dirty grey, or maybe green, car. He couldn't remember what make, but said the plates had been so dirty he couldn't have read them anyway.

Heart beating fast, she pulled up the witness statement, which was from a man who lived on Clover Street and had been disturbed by sounds of an argument outside in the street. Two women had been arguing on the pavement, he said. The argument was heated, but he couldn't hear what was said, as they were a small distance from his house.

One of the women was clearly being aggressive and pushed the other in the chest. She staggered into the road, the other woman following threateningly, just as the car appeared round the blind corner, "going too fast," the witness said.

The car hit the women in the road head on, and the driver stopped a little further down the street. The witness reported that he began to run downstairs, fumbling for his phone, tripping over his dog in panic and haste. He placed the 999 call, which was logged at 11.45 p.m. By the time he was at his front door, which he estimated probably took at least ten minutes, both the car and one of the women had vanished. But the first woman lay dying in the road.

CHAPTER THIRTY-EIGHT

The witness, clutching his phone, followed the instructions of the 999 call handler, did what he could for the victim, which wasn't much given her traumatic injuries, and waited for the ambulance.

Dove could feel tears running down her face as she read the last part of his statement: "I couldn't do anything else for her, and it was obvious she was in a really bad way, but she was still breathing, very slowly and softly, so I held her hand. I got down on my knees next to her, which was hard because of my arthritis, but I told her I was there and who I was, because they say hearing is the last thing to go, and I didn't want her to be alone when she went."

More tears. For the victim, for the witness, and for Gaia, until she was dimly aware of Quinn arriving home, calling her name and finding her sobbing.

"Hey, babe, come here." He held her tightly until she started to calm down. "What's going on?" He glanced at her screen and understood instantly. Reaching over, he saved the document and led her back to the sofa.

Dove, her cold hand in his, allowed him to pull her close, wrap a blanket round them both, and put the TV on.

She stared blankly at a replay of a football game with sore eyes and an aching heart. Eventually, she blew her nose noisily and smiled at her fiancé. "Sorry. I lost it for a bit. It's this case, and then reading that witness statement. I hope Gaia really did die instantly, because if not, there was nobody holding her hand under that lorry."

Quinn pulled her closer. "Don't be sorry. I haven't seen you cry properly since she died. It's not good to keep it all inside. And you know I'm speaking from experience, right? Therapy is great, and however you want to carry on, you do that."

"You know what really gets to me? All these four steps or stages of grieving, that suddenly seem to be everywhere. Why should there just be four steps? Maybe I need more, or maybe they aren't steps at all. And the 'dealing with' or 'coping' are not the best words to use when someone has just died." She could hear her own voice as though it was echoing pettishly inside her head, disliking the anger she was directing in the wrong place.

"True, but it can be hard for people to know what to say, especially when they maybe haven't experienced a loss like you have. Don't push people away, even if they are struggling to comfort you, because I bet most of them mean well, and would be mortified if they had said the wrong thing." Quinn's expression was gentle, and he was still holding her hand.

"I know. It's more the assumption that you must feel this and that. You don't deal with grief and then it vanishes, do you?" Dove said, her head on his shoulder.

Quinn had lost both his parents within a year of each other as a teenager, and she felt completely comfortable discussing grief with him. He was never awkward about it, never stepped around the subject. His natural instinct to honesty, now coupled with his training, made him the only person she could properly talk to.

"No, it doesn't go. It kind of changes form. But it is different for everyone, and you're right, I don't like the idea of some generic process either. It seems insensitive to some, but it probably helps others."

"I guess." Someone scored a goal on the TV and Quinn beamed. "Nailed that one!"

"Is that a technical football term?"

He grinned at her, wiping her eyes with his fingers, very gently.

She smiled back. "I keep forgetting to tell you. I rebooked the hotel for October twenty-second."

He nodded thoughtfully, a smile lifting the corners of his mouth. "You, me, Ren and the girls and Elan as ring bearer?"

"Ren's told me I'm incapable of wedding organisation, and she's taken over, so we're sorted." Feeling slightly warmer, she snuggled up and gazed unseeingly at the match, exhausted by the storm of grief. But also, now, excited by her find relating to the case. "Unless Layla wants to get in the act, too."

The cat was lying along the back of the sofa, her tail flicking, eyes half-closed as she appeared to follow their conversation.

Quinn levered himself off the sofa. "Are you okay if I take a shower? And then it might be a good idea to get some sleep." He winked at her, and she felt the corners of her mouth curve upwards, even though her body was cold without his presence.

She heard Quinn grab a glass of water from the kitchen, make his way upstairs, and, crisis passing, she started to think properly about what she had just discovered.

Dove wrapped a blanket over her shoulders and went back to the file. The woman from the hit-and-run had been pronounced dead at the scene, as the witness had described. She had never been identified. The report suggested from the autopsy she might have been homeless, and nobody had reported her missing, and she had no ID on her, not even a phone or wallet. No DNA matches. A Jane Doe.

And the other woman, who according to the witness had also been hit, had just disappeared, despite an appeal for any witnesses to the incident. The car and driver had also vanished.

Dove skimmed the PM on the hit-and-run victim. She had been around twenty-five, well-nourished and healthy apart from her massive injuries. No distinguishing marks, nothing to suggest any kind of abuse. But she did have dark brown hair and brown eyes, and the PM noted an old fracture, probably from a childhood injury, in her left wrist. So where had she come from, and what had she done, that nobody reported her missing?

CHAPTER THIRTY-NINE

"The good news is, Mark Davies looks like he's going to pull through. The bad news is, right now, he can't remember anything about Friday night," Lindsey reported at the morning brief, to groans from the whole team. "His consultant said it is very possible the memories will come back, but just now the last thing he remembers is going to the Retreat in August, so he's basically lost a load of information from his memory bank. Until the news was broken to him, he'd thought Amber and Rebecca were both alive and well."

It was a massive disappointment for the whole team, and Dove could feel weariness creeping back in, despite her discovery regarding the hit-and-run. She had booked an evening at the Retreat to recentre herself after the wedding, and she was wondering if it was such a good idea after all. Would it help or would it just remind her of her loss?

Josh continued, "So Mark basically has pretty important information missing from his memories, which is inconvenient, poor bloke. He has given us a statement based on what he can remember, which is that he got on well with everyone at the Retreat, but he doesn't recall they discussed anything in particular. He does admit to having been trying a bit of detective work after the three bridges crash, but doesn't recall this came up in conversation with Rebecca or Amber."

"Do you think he sounds genuine?" DCI Franklin asked.

Lindsey and Josh exchanged glances before Lindsey answered, "Hard to tell, but he seems so. I mean, he ended up in the road, so I'm thinking that wasn't planned."

"He seemed to be quite calm, and if anything, only got agitated when he couldn't remember," Josh said. "Of course, he was devastated to hear Rebecca and Amber were dead, and his reaction did seem very genuine."

Dove glanced down at her phone calendar. The thought of Gaia's six-month anniversary and her own impending wedding drove her on through the exhaustion. She needed to be with her sister and find out what Gaia had found in the peaceful woods and downland. Plus, she genuinely found yoga and meditation a healing and restorative process. It was just typical the very place she needed to go was somewhere the three victims seemed to find inspiration, too.

The fizz of excitement at the discovery and storm of grief last night had left her feeling empty and exhausted this morning, and the hit-and-run, if it was the same driver, only served to confuse the issue further, and throw in another body.

"But we did talk to Mark's boyfriend, Lee, again, and he mentioned Mark had been very interested in the three bridges crash since he came back from the Retreat," Lindsey continued. "Lee didn't think it was healthy for Mark to be raking back over old ground, and told him so. He thinks Mark must have simply continued his research when Lee wasn't around, rather than shelving it."

DI Blackman glanced around the room. "More on our phone conversations from the lab. The unknown number is another burner phone, but judging by the record of chat conversations between Mark and Rebecca, the person or persons on the unknown number lured them to the bridge on Friday night with a promise of answers to their questions. I'll make sure the files are all loaded to the main case file, but essentially, they were promised answers if they didn't go to the police. We also have the 2019 Jane Doe hit-and-run, an unsolved cold case, which was uploaded this morning."

"Which makes this even more complex, because if the same car, possibly driven by Cora Dionysus, was involved in the three bridges crash, and then carried on into town to be involved in a hit-and-run, we have another victim, or two victims, to consider," DS Amin suggested wearily. She rubbed her forehead and slipped her glasses over tired eyes.

Dove took a gulp of coffee, grateful she had arrived early, picking up a decent coffee from Starbucks on the way. She had wanted to get straight in and tell DI Blackman about her discovery.

DI Waters was studying the incident boards, which now numbered five enormous whiteboards, covered with arrows and coloured writing. "It seems clear that we are looking at someone who was about to have their secrets busted wide open by Rebecca and Mark, with their amateur detective work. Evidence is all pointing at Cora Dionysus and Max Carter." She tapped Max and Cora's photos on the incident board. "If those two were in the car that night, Cora probably driving, as she was the one who then disappeared . . . They could be responsible for not only inadvertent involvement in the three bridges crash, but also hit-and-run. A hit-and-run where, according to the witness, the car stopped afterwards, momentarily. They knew they had hit someone, and they stopped to see two bodies in the mirror, and then drove off."

"Shit." Lindsey blew out a breath through pursed lips. "And they got away with the whole bloody lot until now . . . October 2019 was about the time her ex-boyfriend and her mum said Cora had dropped off the radar, wasn't it? She sent the messages saying she was sorry and going to make a fresh start."

DI Waters nodded. "If Amber somehow found out her sister was responsible, and let slip to Rebecca and Mark what she had discovered, might they have tried to blackmail Cora? But instead, they maybe put the wind up her, to the extent she realized she needed to put a stop to their detective work before she was caught."

"Max Carter is still missing," DC Josh Conrad put in. "And wherever he has run to or is hiding out, he didn't take his car. I checked with the neighbours and the garage owner, and it's always parked in the same spot under the CCTV. It's been checked and it's clean. I also looked at the CCTV on the Friday night, and unfortunately there are no cameras near the flat, only on the cars."

"What about the back of the garage?" Dove asked, picturing the huge expanse, crowded with vehicles.

"Only close to the building. You said he took off on a motorbike, but he's not registered with the DVLA as having a bike licence," Josh added, with a shrug.

DS Wyndham was staring at the screen, now on the freeze frame of the white Ford Escort on the motorway. "So possibly Max Carter and Cora Dionysus are the only ones left alive in this particular party, and the only ones, barring Mark Davies recovering his memories, who can tell us what the hell this thing is really about."

The whole team was buzzing, absorbing this new knowledge, making connections, dismissing old theories, but Dove felt only emptiness and exhaustion. This was bad. She needed to pull her weight, needed to be part of the conclusion. *Come on, you got this*, she told herself.

DI Blackman began to say something else, but his phone buzzed, and he left the room briefly to take the call, and returned with a grim expression. "On-call team, head down to the Retreat at Saddleworth Farm. Someone has just been dragged out of the lake."

* * *

Steve and Dove, as part of the on-call team, joined their colleagues at the Retreat. Dove winced at the sight of the victim lying on the bank, the woodland shadows shrouding her body.

The ambulance crews, three teams plus a Critical Care Paramedic in a rapid response vehicle, had attended. She didn't recognize them, but in the handover, they stated the victim had a rope around her neck and pronounced bruising around the neck and face.

Other members of the Retreat, guests and staff, were being kept away behind a cordon. The shadows from the trees danced crazily across the lake in the wind, their darkness sketched on the deeper blackness of the still waters. Despite it being daylight, the storm clouds covering the sky made it seem like early evening.

The victim was a young woman, maybe early twenties, and as she went closer, Dove could clearly see the marks on her skin. The realisation hit her in the gut and she heard Steve, who was right behind her, make some noise of frustration.

DI Blackman walked down to the body and stood with Dove and Steve. "First responders say they also noticed a phone fall out of her pocket as she was dragged out of the water. After they clocked the suspicious circumstances, they left it in situ."

"The victim is Tina Martin," Dove told him. "We interviewed her yesterday. She's one of the freelance instructors, and she gave us the information on Amber. Shit! How could this happen? I thought we'd moved right away from the Retreat with the investigation."

The DI met her gaze. "Maybe our killer also thought that, and wanted to bring us back."

"Or our perpetrator discovered Tina knew something else, something she might well have remembered after our conversation?"

He nodded. "Possibly. Look, Jess is just arriving, and I want you and Steve to start talking to the staff. Lindsey?"

"Boss?" Lindsey looked over from her position at the lakeside.

"You and Josh start talking to the guests."

"Dove, start with Louise . . . And check that barn where all the instructors sleep. You said you were in there yesterday?"

"Yes, boss." Dove beckoned to Steve, ducked under the cordon and approached the group slumped on various wooden benches and logs. Someone had brought a few blankets, which were draped over shoulders and across laps. Two women were holding each other, crying, but most looked blankly, silently, at the scene, shock evident in their faces.

"Can you put your phone away, please," Steve said sharply to an older man, who sat alone on a tree stump. "This is a crime scene, and you filming it isn't going to help anyone."

He had the grace to look slightly shamefaced and shrugged, but shoved his phone into his pocket.

Lindsey, who had also witnessed the filming, immediately suggested the man be the first to come over 'for a chat'.

Louise was sat slumped on a log, being comforted by various members of her community. Dove recognized Kirstie, Meredith and two others she couldn't name, but remembered from the photos as catering staff.

As Steve began to talk to Louise and the staff, explaining what they needed from them, Dove watched their faces intently. There was no escaping the fact that this wasn't necessarily a Max-Carter-shaped phantom from the woods who had killed Tina. There could easily be a murderer sitting in the group.

She jumped as Josh tapped her on the shoulder and pulled her aside.

"Did you and Steve interview Louise initially?"

"Not properly, because she didn't have any useful information, but she gave a statement about the victims regarding the August retreat." She glanced in the woman's direction. "Why?"

"I just ran a check, and the blue VW Golf parked up by the house is hers . . . I thought I'd seen the registration somewhere before . . ."

"And?" The wind was cold, blowing her hair across her face. She pushed it away impatiently, all thoughts of exhaustion forgotten.

He showed her his phone screen. "It was on the traffic cam nearest the old quarry on Friday night, just off the roundabout with the BP garage. Time was 07.16 p.m."

Dove digested this. "Tina said she went out on Friday night for painkillers, because she had run out. But Josh, her other half is TFU, for Christ's sake. She's not going to be part of this mess, is she?"

"You're ruling her out because her husband is on the force?" His eyes were hard.

"No, of course not! Well, I'm not sure." She was trying to remember everything about the interview. Had she missed something? Been distracted with her own grief and been misled? But no, Steve had been there too, and he was a good copper.

There was a BP service station with a Tesco Express grocery store attached off the roundabout, nearest to the motorway slip road. Heading over the first bridge, you went straight into Abberley town, or you took the turning to Pengrove Road and the old quarry. The road then wound up past the woodland walks to Saddle Bridge.

"Talk to her first," Josh said. "We could have been reading this whole thing wrong from the start."

Leaving Josh to corroborate his find, she went over to where Steve was calmly organising the small group of staff, along with uniform colleagues, to walk the short distance to the farmhouse.

She could see him walking alongside Louise, asking her something as she shook her head, shoulders drooping, her steps slow and heavy. Dove took a last quick look at Tina's body lying on the wet grass and followed.

CHAPTER FORTY

"I honestly don't think I can tell you anything useful," Louise said. She was now sitting on the sofa in the farmhouse, hands wrapped around a mug of green tea.

In various other rooms, Dove could hear her colleagues supervising guests and staff. Everyone on site was a suspect. Everything would have to be bagged and tagged as evidence. Another job for Jess's team, and another life taken. It was sickening.

"Just run through the last time you saw Tina, your evening, anything out of the ordinary," Steve suggested.

Louise ran a hand over her short hair. Her eyes were shadowed and red-rimmed, but she managed to put together a coherent account of Tina's last movements, as she was aware of them.

"Thanks, we do appreciate this is tough," Dove told her. "Can I also just ask if Tina usually went back out, maybe down to the barns to get ready for the next day's sessions?"

Louise smiled wanly. "No, she liked to get to bed early, and she liked her routine. I got the impression she was devastated when Amber died, because they had made a connection, and she was clinging to her routine."

Steve nodded. "And going back to Friday night, do you remember anything else that might be useful, in light of what has just happened?"

"Not really. I had . . ." She paused. "My partner and I have had some financial trouble, and it has been causing a great deal of concern. Confidentially, he is also thinking of a career change, so our attention has probably not been a hundred per cent on the Retreat and our family here."

"Did you go out on Friday night?"

"No." She shook her head, speaking slowly, softly. "I'm not sure if one of the instructors or guests did, because I heard a car around nine, but I didn't take much notice. This is a retreat, not a prison."

Steve glanced at Dove across Louise's bowed head, and she acknowledged his thought with a tiny nod. Kirstie had said Louise left to get painkillers, and had spoken to her the next day about it.

Finishing with Louise, they quickly ran through the logistics, and afterwards, summarized the findings. Steve was tapping notes into his iPad and Dove was collating information. This would be compared with the other statements from everyone currently on site, and also against Josh and Lindsey's findings from the guest statements. Finally, it would be matched against the physical evidence collected.

"At approximately 8.15 p.m. last night, Tina had dinner with Louise and the other two staff members, the cook and the general assistant, at the farmhouse. Meredith went out for a run on the Downs, so missed dinner," Steve began.

Dove nodded. "Meredith got back to the bunkhouse at 9 p.m. She showered and made a sandwich, by which time Tina, who was the only other person staying in the bunkhouse, had returned. They worked independently on their laptops, got ready for the sessions tomorrow, and then Meredith says Tina mentioned she had forgotten to ask Louise something, and went out to the farmhouse."

"The other two staff members were still helping clear up at the farmhouse, but they didn't see Tina. They both mentioned Louise was working in her office on schedules and bookings the whole time, but neither of them actually went into the office until they were ready to go home at 10.15 p.m." Steve frowned. "So according to our timeline, apparently nobody saw Tina for a good hour, and the last person to see her alive was Meredith."

"Or the last person who admits seeing her alive," Dove pointed out. "And it was the cook, Alexa, who raised the alarm, as she started her drive home, her headlights picked out what she thought was someone swimming in the lake. She was concerned enough to take a second look, as guests are supposed to swim in pairs or with an instructor, for safety."

"She found Tina," Steve finished. "Fished her out and called 999."

"Let's check out the bunkhouse." Dove snapped her iPad shut and stood up.

The converted barn space was quiet, with just a few lamps lit. The smell of food drifted from the kitchen, where Meredith had stated she ate after her run.

"CCTV is only up at the farmhouse," Dove said, glancing into the eaves of the barn.

"Hello?" A voice from outside. It was Meredith.

"Can you stay at the farmhouse with others, please?" Dove told her. "It's for your safety."

"I'm going right back, but I left my watch and phone on my bed." She looked distraught, red hair tangled from the wind, cheeks streaked with tears. "I just wanted to get them."

"We'll bring them up for you when we come," Dove reassured her.

Steve smiled at Meredith. "It's okay. I'll walk you back to the farmhouse."

When their footsteps had crunched away on the gravel, Dove had a quick sweep of the building. No sign of anything out of order, and no signs of a struggle. Two rooms were set up for occupants, and she identified Meredith's by the phone and watch on her bed.

With gloves on, she picked up the devices and the screens glowed. Meredith must have been downloading her run. The phone was paired with the watch, tracking activity, heart rate and distance. She had a similar one herself.

The phone screen was locked, but the watch was easy to access. Idly, she checked the last activity. Meredith had said she finished her run at 9 p.m. A circular route across the Downs. Puzzled, she reset the watch, her heart beating fast. According to the tracker on her watch, Meredith had finished her run half an hour earlier than she stated.

The watch had stored activity for the month, and Dove quickly checked back to Friday. She told herself it was just curiosity, and Meredith was a significant witness, not a person of interest, but the woman's insistence she needed to get her phone and watch had made an impression.

Tina's room was tidy, and her laptop was open on the bedside table. She had been planning her yoga sessions, and a quick glance at her emails showed no red flags. Dove continued downstairs. This was only a preliminary search, and Jess's team would do a thorough inspection.

The back door was locked, and she met Steve at the front door. His expression was quizzical. "What's up?"

"I just checked the history on Meredith's watch. It's the same brand as mine, so it tracks activity." She found her breath was coming faster, body tensing with the discovery. "Guess where Meredith was on Friday night?"

He shook his head. "*Shiiiiit.* And she just told me, *in confidence*, that she thinks Louise has been acting strangely ever since the bridge incident, and she and Tina were talking about it tonight. She's worried Tina went off to confront Louise, not to talk about schedules."

"That's a bit far out, isn't it?" Dove said, "And she never mentioned that in her statement."

"I already told her she would have to come in for an interview tomorrow morning, as a sig wit," Steve said. "Bearing in mind we have evidence she lied about where she was twice now, let's keep that as it is, and not scare her off."

"There is just one thing," Dove pointed out. "Maybe Meredith wasn't the one wearing the watch?"

Steve slapped his forehead and didn't bother to answer, as Dove ensured the incriminating items were bagged, tagged and ready for the evidence log.

By 1 a.m., the MCT on-call team were ready to quit, leaving Jess and her dedicated search teams on scene.

"Nice one with the watch, you two," DI Blackman told them. "We've had another possible sighting of Max Carter." He paused to take a drink from his mug of tea before continuing. "The Coast Road traffic cam at the pedestrian crossing caught a motorbike speeding, and the PNC check shows it registered to a Cameron Carter."

"He has other family, then? Why hasn't that come up before?" Josh queried.

"No idea, but the coincidence is pretty unlikely, so I'm hoping we manage to snag him, now we've got the registration." The DI sounded weary. "Although I honestly can't wait to hear what Meredith Brown has to say in her interview tomorrow, because where the hell does *she* fit in with Max Carter?"

"If she fits in with him at all," Dove said, staring out over the Downs, the solid mass of ancient dark shapes of hills rolling away from the sea. A huge expanse compared to their floodlit crime scene, the torch-lit dots of teams in the surrounding woods, and the slow methodical drone of the police helicopter overhead, as it too, joined in the search for the murderer.

CHAPTER FORTY-ONE

After the late night, Dove managed to grab a couple of hours' sleep, before driving quickly into work. Her sadness over Tina, coupled with the anticipation that the case was about to break wide open, effectively pushed away any tiredness. The perpetrator (could it really be Meredith?) had been pushed into killing Tina, then had done a lousy job of covering their tracks, which meant they must be feeling the pressure.

Something or someone had tipped the killer over the edge, and once the first mistakes were made, it was the beginning of the end. Tina's phone, along with Meredith's watch and phone, had been rushed to the lab, and it would hopefully provide extra evidence, as would the motorbike capture on the traffic cam. They were so close. She could feel it.

The morning brief was filled with rather more people than usual. Another murder meant extra additions to the team to help with the caseload. Many more had been drafted in for house-to-house searches in the rural area around Saddleworth Farm, to check CCTV and traffic cameras, and to investigate Tina herself, and ensure her family was being kept up to date.

The DCI gave the bare bones before dividing up the teams and adding, "Tina Martin's murder takes our body count up to four on this case, and as you are all aware, Max Carter and Cora Dionysus are still unaccounted for. We need to get this solved, people."

"Nice one on the watch. The local news and the socials are saying there's a serial killer in the area," Josh muttered to Dove, as they left the room.

"Shit, I haven't looked at the socials deliberately, because all this armchair detective stuff really pisses me off," Steve said, overhearing. "I'm surprised all those keyboard warriors haven't solved our case already. They probably have more time and expertise," he added sarcastically.

"They probably think they're safe as long as they stay behind their screens," Dove suggested. "Louise has come in and wants to give a statement with her solicitor present, but as the DI's taking that one, I reckon that must be about the supposed outing on Friday night. Meredith is coming in for half twelve."

"We need to do a deep dive on her background, and find out where the hell she might fit in to all this," Steve told her. "Most importantly, we need bacon sandwiches. If you get breakfast, I'll make a start."

Dove was standing in line at the catering van in the car park, waiting for her order, when her phone rang. "Hi, Ren, how's it going?"

"Okay, love. I saw on the news that they found a body at the Retreat."

"And you want to make sure I cancelled my booking?"

"What do you think?" Ren's voice was anxious.

"Yes, I did. I emailed this morning," Dove told her, feeling bad for lying to her sister. With the case on her mind, the discovery last night, she hadn't even considered her own booking at the Retreat.

"I think Gaia would have understood. I . . . I was look-ing at photos of us as kids last night, and Delta's made me a video of all the clips she could find . . ." She could tell Ren was smiling. "Do you remember when you and Gaia swapped places with that boy she was dating?"

Dove did, forcing her mind off Tina's death and onto chatting to her sister. "I had to put up with his crappy conversation just so she could go to the funfair with someone else. She only paid me five pounds!"

"Your fault for looking so alike, and for letting Gaia get you involved in her scams," Ren said, laughing. "When you were that age, you could almost have passed for twins."

The clear autumn day, the busy car park, the thronging crowd around the catering van, and the smell of bacon and coffee threading through her senses, all seemed to spin. Dove put a hand on a bollard to steady herself. It was blindingly obvious. Everything else, including Tina, must be a distraction.

"Ren, can I call you back?"

"Sure. It's not important. Just come around any evening Quinn isn't there," her sister said. "Love you!"

"Me too," Dove told her. Quickly, she found Martha Dionysus's number, keeping her fingers crossed she would pick up.

She did.

"It's DC Milson. I was wondering: after 29 September 2019, do you remember if you saw Amber a lot during that month or the next?" She was almost holding her breath.

The other woman was silent, apparently thinking. "It was a few years ago, so I would need to check, but I think that might have been when her friend died in the 2019 crash. Amber took two months' leave from her job to do some travelling abroad."

"Do you know the name of the friend who died in the crash?" Dove asked.

"No, sorry, she just texted me to say she needed some time out. I've got to admit I was worried Cora had got her spikes into Amber, and persuaded her to go with her, but Amber was in contact almost every day while she was away. I think it was a friend's house in Kent. Have you found out who killed Amber?" Her voice was sharp with hope. "Because I saw another girl died at the Retreat last night."

"We are following up all our leads at the moment," Dove said, feeling bad for the cliché response, but she couldn't possibly tell the woman what she was really thinking.

"One last thing, and I know this seems very random, but did Amber or Cora break her wrist when she was younger?"

"I . . . Yes, Amber did. When she was twelve, she fell out of the tree she was climbing. Why?"

CHAPTER FORTY-TWO

She finished her call, found she was still clinging to the bollard, and took a deep breath.

Steve was sitting at his desk, working on his iPad, and he looked up as she balanced the coffees and bacon sandwiches. "Long queue?"

She shook her head, sat down and tried to process her thoughts. "Steve, what if we've been looking at this all wrong?" She told him what she had discovered. "The hit-and-run after the crash. Two women, and neither ever identified."

Steve's face registered shock. "You mean it was Amber who died in the hit-and-run?"

Dove licked brown sauce off her fingers and nodded. "What if Cora wasn't the hit-and-run driver, but instead, she and her sister were the victims?"

He nodded, thoughtfully. "I wonder if that's where Meredith fits into the puzzle."

Dove continued, slowly. "It would mean the sisters were the two women our witness saw arguing in the street, and it would also mean, somehow, and for whatever reason, Cora saw her sister was dead, and saw it as an opportunity to change places with her."

"You said Martha told you she went away to get over her friend dying in the 2019 crash, so I suppose that would have been enough time to insinuate herself into Amber's life. Do you think she had help?"

"Neil and Max. They all had history." Dove was tapping her pen on the table in front of her. "I haven't had a chance to check, but I do remember Amber changed schools a couple of times with her job. As a teaching assistant, with all the background checks already covered by Amber, Cora would be free to assume a brand-new life. Her sister's life."

"But what about her mum? What about her friends? You would think someone would notice." Steve was already scrolling through his iPad. "I suppose if she explained any odd behaviour as grief for the friend who had died, maybe — but shit, the balls of it!"

"Amber was a teaching assistant, which Cora, if she was smart, could pick it up. It wouldn't have worked if Amber had a degree or something, because you can't replicate that amount of knowledge, can you? But if she put some work in during the time that she took away . . . She had Amber's laptop, her phone, and if she was in contact with Amber before her death, she would have known what was happening in her life."

"What about the school where she worked? Worth a quick shot, just in case it is linked to Meredith. You know what it's like, once you get one piece that fits, all the others fall into place. We've got time if we're quick," Steve suggested.

* * *

The headteacher of St Stephen's, Mrs Tulley, was petite and grey-haired, and her green eyes were sharp with intelligence.

"I checked the files after your call, and I have some paperwork for you. Copies." She walked briskly towards the office and Dove, always uncomfortable in any kind of academic situation, even this friendly, brightly painted primary school, felt like she was heading for a detention. When she had been at school, she had worked hard, so she knew this feeling was completely irrational.

"These are Amber's files." Mrs Tulley pushed the paperwork towards them. "Tea?"

"Thank you, that's very kind." Steve accepted the paperwork.

"Amber has only been with us for eighteen months, but she has been excellent. She works with Mr Coleman in Year Three. He's on his honeymoon just now, but I know he will be devastated when he hears what happened to Amber." She paused. "Let me just chase up some tea."

The headteacher walked briskly out of the door, and Dove could hear the tap of her heels as she progressed down the corridor.

She looked around the bright, tidy office, noting framed photographs of the year groups, solo photographs of children who had achieved greatness, names on trophies and cups in a long glass cabinet.

"Nothing much in here." Steve closed the files. "She's great at her job, helped them sail through Ofsted. Lots of emails from grateful parents." He was staring at the photo neatly clipped to the file. "I wonder if they were really so alike."

Dove was peering inside the trophy cabinet when a name caught her eye. It was a swimming gala trophy, large and silver-coloured, and it was the last name on the plaque attached to the base that had caught her eye. Next to the trophy was a small, framed photograph of a red-headed girl with a fistful of medals beaming at the camera.

Meredith Brown 2008.

"Steve?"

He looked up and she indicated the trophy. "Meredith Brown."

Mrs Tulley returned, bearing mugs on a tray. "Sorry I was so long. Everyone is busy, and my wonderful PA is off sick. I thought I would make refreshments myself."

Dove thanked her and asked about Meredith Brown.

"Oh, I thought you wanted to talk about Amber?" the woman said, her forehead creasing as she picked up a large pair of glasses and peered through them. "That's better. It's hell getting old," she added with a spark of wry amusement.

"We can start with Amber. Is there anything you wanted to add to your statement regarding Amber?" Steve asked, looking at his watch. "Apologies for the rush."

"No. I wish I could have been more helpful." The sparkle vanished, and her expression darkened. "She seemed very happy here, and never gave me any cause to think she was at all depressed or anything like that."

"Did she ever mention her family, a sister, maybe?"

"I think she was an only child. She didn't really say, that was just the impression I got. Her mother, poor woman, is down as next of kin, and she never mentioned anyone else."

Dove indicated the swimming gala trophy. "I realize it was a while ago now, but did you teach Meredith Brown?"

"Meredith?" Again, the change of expression, and this time Dove could have sworn she looked wary. Mrs Tulley sighed. "Did she have something to do with Amber's death?"

"Why would you think that?" Steve queried.

"Well, you are investigating the death of Amber Dionysus, and now you're asking about Meredith," the headteacher told him.

"Sorry, her name has just come up in connection with the case, but she is in no way a suspect. I just caught sight of the trophy and wondered if she had any kind of connection to Amber?" Dove explained.

Mrs Tulley regarded them for a moment and then appeared to reach a decision. She stood up and rummaged in the filing cabinet behind her, before pulling out a brown folder. "We've gone digital, but these four cabinets are the last ones to go to the archive storage, so you're lucky I have them to hand."

Dove leaned forward and studied the brown file she placed onto the desk in front of them. There was a photograph of a little girl at the top of the first page.

"Report cards, progress reports, everything is in there. As I say, it's all digital now, but we still keep hard copies of anything up to twenty years ago."

"Did you teach Meredith personally?"

"I did. I try to have a presence in every year group, but I teach Years 5 and 6 as a rule. Merry was certainly someone I had my eye on. Generally, this would be because I want to catch any early signs of learning difficulty, but with Merry it was because she seemed to have trouble making friends, trouble communicating with the other children."

"Was there a reason for this?" Dove asked.

"There didn't seem to be. We eliminated most possibilities, then suddenly, in Year 4, she seemed to have a group of friends and to be one of the most popular in her class. That was when she started competitive swimming, and she was so focused, almost obsessed, with the sport." The headmistress frowned. "She was a very clever child academically, too, very astute, but there were still differences. When she fell over in the playground one day and needed stitches, while I waited with her for her dad, she never cried. In fact, she seemed to retreat into herself."

"Shock?"

"That's what I surmised, but when I thought about it later, I realized I had never seen her cry. She got angry when she was younger, and quite violent even, but as she grew older, she showed less and less real emotion."

"And in Year 4?"

"It sounds ridiculous now, but it felt like she had read a book, or watched a film on how a popular nine-year-old should act, and that she was now confident in playing the role. She had a lot of friends."

"Meredith was expelled before she finished Year 6?" Steve was reading the reports.

"Yes, it's all in the report. She locked another child in the sports equipment shed during Bonfire Night: Holly Adams. All the parents were here, the children were running round in big groups, but safety is always a priority. Holly wasn't in the shed for more than an hour or so, but she was claustro-phobic, and the event triggered an asthma attack. She didn't have her inhaler. Or rather, she thought she had put it in her pocket, but it was found in the bushes the next morning." The headteacher sighed. "I remember she couldn't think who might have locked her in, and was very loud and clear it must have been some kind of accident."

Dove nodded. "But you know differently?"

"I'm afraid so."

"What do you think really happened?" Steve was still scanning the incident report.

"I think Merry lured her into the shed and locked her in on purpose, because she told her she was afraid of the dark." She took a deep breath. "I would also consider whether Holly's inhaler accidentally fell from her pocket, or if Merry stole it as she pushed her into the shed."

"That's a big step from a silly dare game going wrong."

Mrs Tulley frowned, a sudden flash of anger in her eyes. "Merry admitted it. Only to me, and she continued to lie to everyone else, but when we were alone in this office, as I opened the door for her, she suddenly leaned close and said, 'Miss, it wasn't an accident.'"

CHAPTER FORTY-THREE

Mrs Tulley sighed. "I was deeply shocked, but I asked her what she would have done if Holly had suffered an asthma attack, but she just shrugged and said nothing more. Afterwards, her mum came in, and she started crying, but gave me one more little look from under her lashes. It was not a look you expect to see from a child. It was unsettling, hard and . . . yes, triumphant. I had no choice but to expel her."

Steve was making hasty notes on his iPad, his cup of tea forgotten. "Even though, officially, it was an accident?"

"Yes. I didn't know what she might do, and I felt the overwhelming need to protect the other children from her. Her parents were horrified, of course. It's hard to admit failure with a child."

"What happened to her parents? Do you remember where they went?" Dove was seeing those puzzle pieces fall into place, even as she took in the office walls, bright with artwork and class schedules. The smell of school mingled with the smell of tea. She could remember it vividly from her own younger days.

"I have the vague memory Merry's family may have moved abroad. The father was in the armed forces, I think." She took off her glasses and wiped them on her shirt sleeve. "I do hope Merry *isn't* in any trouble. Even after she was gone, I would think of her occasionally and hope she had settled down, found other things to occupy her mind. I still feel I failed her somehow."

* * *

Snagging another coffee and a packet of shortbread on their way back into the office, Dove sat down at her desk. She could see Steve in the DI's office, updating him. Keeping an eye on the clock, she dove into researching anything she could find on Meredith Brown. With surprising results.

On the surface, Meredith was a model citizen, without even a parking ticket to her name. She had a basic Facebook page, focusing on her yoga and Pilates teaching. After a cursory glance, Dove ran the deeper checks, scribbling notes, putting together a timeline of Meredith's life as much as she could.

"Look at this!" she called to Steve as he came back into the room. On her screen was a newspaper article:

> *A 15-year-old boy has received 'non-life threatening' injuries following an incident involving an alleged 'unsafe barrier' at the top of major tourist attraction Newton Lighthouse. According to Abberley Police, the incident took place on Wednesday this week, when the boy and his 13-year-old friend visited the attraction. The Police said the two teenagers climbed to the top and were leaning against the balcony taking photographs when allegedly the barrier broke, leaving the 15-year-old with a broken wrist.*
>
> *Mr and Mrs Brown, whose daughter, Merry, was involved in the incident, have called for better safety measures to be put into place. Mrs Brown (pictured with Merry) stated, "Newton Lighthouse is not only a tourist attraction, but also a place local teenagers like to gather. My daughter could have been seriously injured, or worse."*
>
> *The owners, Karen Whitley and Andy Holburn, who also run the popular Lighthouse Cafe, have stated they*

Steve unwrapped a sandwich, and peered at the contents unenthusiastically, before starting to eat. "Nice. Lab results are in on the watch and phone, but apart from the watch activity tracker, there isn't anything incriminating. I would suggest she communicated with Amber — or maybe it's Cora, jeez — via a burner phone. She's not stupid."

"The family did move away, to France, but I can't find the parents now." Dove was scanning searches on the screen. "Meredith is very careful what she puts on her Facebook page, but I suppose that's hardly a crime. She does say in her blog she has travelled a lot, but that Abberley is her hometown, and she grew up here."

"The DI said run with it, and we've got enough to ask for a DNA sample, which will either eliminate or incriminate," Steve said between bites. He screwed up the sandwich wrapper and hurled it across the room to the bin, where it landed with a dull thud.

* * *

"So, she likes heights, maybe, but it's quite a jump to throwing people off tall buildings and bridges. But there is nothing on her since the lighthouse incident, so perhaps the hit-and-run, coupled with the 2019 crash, scared her onto a new path . . . Until someone tried to bring her past back into focus," Dove said, thoughtfully, as Steve opened a bag of doughnuts and passed her one. "Thanks!"

Steve shook his head. "There is one thing, though. If Cora did recognize Meredith at the Retreat, did Meredith recognize her?"

"No idea, but it makes sense if she did recognize Cora she would have kept quiet. It's not in Meredith's interests to out herself, but from what we've heard, Cora was obsessed with trying to make things right, as she saw it." Dove suggested, picking sugar off her shirt. "Come on, we know it only has to make sense to the perp half the time. As long as we get the result, I don't care why or how."

"That's not like you," Steve told her.

Dove couldn't explain it, so she just shook her head, but felt she needed to wrap this up, move on. This case had become tied in her mind to her grief over her sister. She wanted it done now, justice served for the families, and then they could all move on.

Steve picked up his phone as it buzzed. He read the message and said, "Meredith is waiting downstairs. Let's crack on with her interview, and then circle back to the Amber-slash-Cora thing. Go and talk to the DI before he goes down to interview Louise, and let him know the latest, can you?"

"Done. I'll meet you downstairs," Dove agreed.

Meredith, her red hair pulled back, and face very pale, sat with her solicitor as Dove, the formal introductions and the legals ticked off, explained anything she remembered could help to bring Tina's killer to justice.

"Sorry, I hope I can help, but my head is all over the place," Meredith said. She rubbed her nose with her cuff and smiled. Her eyes were bloodshot, and she kept biting her lip as though to stop herself crying. "Tina and I were good friends. We all were."

"Can you tell us your movements that day . . . Anything unusual? Any guests behaving differently?" Steve started with the easy questions.

"It was a normal day. I taught my classes as usual, swapped with Tina at lunchtime . . . Louise took over for the late afternoon session." Meredith was frowning. "Tina was great with the guests and always so friendly. In fact, she swapped numbers with Amber on the August retreat."

"Did she tell you about Amber?" Dove asked.

"What about her?"

Interesting, Dove thought. Was that a little bit of tension breaking through? "Amber came to see her earlier this month."

"She never mentioned it."

Definitely tension. Dove said nothing, sensing Steve sitting next to her, playing the same game. What did Meredith know?

"Did you keep in touch with any of the guests after they left their retreats?"

"No . . . Well, actually, I was admin on the WhatsApp group, so does that count?" Meredith glanced at her solicitor "In fact, I think maybe Amber did call me after the August retreat . . . I'd forgotten. She had some query about a sports injury, I think." She smiled. "Yes, that was it."

"And when was the call?"

"I don't know . . . Maybe two weeks after the retreat?"

Steve took her back to the night of Tina's murder. "What time did you get back from your run?"

"It must have been about nine," Meredith said.

Dove checked her notes. "Can you recall your conversation with Tina before she went out?"

"Well, as I said before, she wanted to see Louise about something. I didn't interrogate her. The retreat was a safe place, and I can't imagine what happened to her." Meredith's eyes shone with tears again, and her face clouded. "If I had any idea at all, I would tell you. The only thing I can think of was that Tina was somehow mixed up in the Saddle Bridge deaths. Because nobody would have hurt her, otherwise."

Steve moved on to the activity tracker on her watch, and Dove watched Meredith's facade crumble and fear show through. And anger. But she was still fighting, and she was clever enough not to be antagonistic.

Dove ran through the dates of the 2019 crash and the bridge deaths incident, but nothing could dent her. She circled back to the activity on Friday evening.

"I was at the Retreat last Friday teaching until 6 p.m., as I already mentioned in my statement." She smiled at Steve.

"After that, I tidied up and treated myself to some solo meditation down by the lake. There is a little lodge we often use, and I listened to the rain and stayed down there for around an hour. I guess I must have left my watch in the farmhouse or the bunkhouse."

"Were you aware of anything unusual happening at the Retreat on Friday night?" Dove asked, as though she was falling for this bullshit.

"Well, I did notice Louise's car was gone when I walked back up from the lake about eight-ish, and I was surprised, because she hadn't mentioned going out. We, the instructors and other staff, normally all ate together around ten, after we had packed up for the day and got ready for the weekend guests."

"And did you see Louise that night?"

"She came into dinner with soaking hair and all flustered." Meredith shrugged. "She said she had been trying to sort out the main yurt, which had come down."

"Which could have been true," Steve pointed out.

"Maybe. I don't like to grass, and I like Louise, which is why I didn't mention this earlier. I just didn't see how she could possibly have had anything to do with the deaths of Amber, Mark and Rebecca." She sighed prettily, looking up with wide eyes, shaking her head, as though forced to grass up a friend. "But now, I don't know."

"Did you not think that by withholding information, you could be putting someone else at risk?" Dove played along. "Tina was murdered last night, and still you said nothing?"

"My client has admitted she regrets not speaking out earlier, and she wishes she had," the solicitor said.

Dove nodded politely, catching another overpowering wave of aftershave as the man shifted in his seat. The whole room smelled like a perfume counter.

"On 29 September 2019, a Ford Escort was instrumental in causing the three bridges crash. Barely half an hour later, the same night, a hit-and-run was reported on Clover

Street. It was witnessed by a resident who stated two women were knocked down by a vehicle. One of these women, Cora Dionysus, survived the incident and that was the woman you met at the Retreat. You would know her as Amber Dionysus."

A whole range of emotions crossed Meredith's face. "How could one woman be the other? I'm afraid I have no idea what I was doing in 2019. It was a long time ago, and I was travelling a lot. Look, I can't believe this! I came here voluntarily to try and help, and now you're trying to tell me I'm involved." Her blue eyes filled with tears, and she turned to her solicitor. "I need a break."

After a fifteen-minute break, Dove took her place at the table once more, as Steve explained about the DNA swab.

Meredith exchanged glances with her solicitor and agreed to the swab. She was the picture of a victim now, her hair falling over her shoulders, muttering *no comment* to every question and turning big, bewildered eyes to her solicitor a few times.

Frustratingly, they needed more, and by the end of the interview, Meredith's solicitor smiled at them. "My client has been extremely helpful. As she has stated, she has no idea why her watch tracker registered the activity it did, but suggests someone else may have borrowed the watch on Friday 29 September. As for last night, it is a matter of half an hour, and given the stress my client has been under, following the violent death of a close friend, you have no option but to let her go home."

Dove thought he could have been reciting the lines of a solicitor in a TV crime drama, while Meredith was still portraying the grieving friend. But he was right. They didn't have enough to charge her. Steve excused himself for a moment, and she knew he was going to check if anything had come through from the lab.

Half an hour later, they were sitting upstairs in the office commiserating. Meredith had walked out, and was no doubt laughing at them, believing she had got away with it.

CHAPTER FORTY-FOUR

I'd like to say it doesn't haunt me, that I didn't care, or even dismiss the whole thing as a hallucination.

But that wouldn't be true. If my memory strays back to 2019, all I can see in my head is the blood on the road.

The day, the evening had been hot, and the night wrapped a stifling blanket over the Downs. I had my windows down, and I was singing along to the radio, flying along, careless of my speed. Careless of the other traffic.

Would I have been any less careless if I hadn't just drunk the best part of a bottle of wine? Undoubtedly. But I had my bags packed in the car boot, had cut my ties with any casual acquaintances, and I was heading south-west for a new start.

By midnight, I had killed people. I waited for them to arrest me, I waited for that knock on the door. I honestly couldn't work out how cameras hadn't caught my number plate. I got rid of the car the next day. Luckily it was an old banger, and I sold it to the scrap-metal woman as soon as I reached Plymouth. No questions asked, no explanations volunteered, and I watched from the other side of the wall as the crusher removed the evidence.

Finally, after many months, a year, I realized I had probably got away with it. Got away with everything. It was a sign to turn my life around, that night, and I did. Nobody knew me in the vast sprawling city of Plymouth, and when I ventured into Cornwall, crossing the river by bus the first time, I found plenty of casual work, plenty of people who took my charm at face value.

I couldn't resist occasional little cruelties, the times when my blood seemed to heat in my veins and pound in my head. But I kept it small, and nobody would have known it was me.

I knew I had killed people, but it didn't seem real, and because it had been out of my control, unplanned and unaccounted for, I allowed the memories to fade and complacency to set in.

Eventually, I found myself drawn back into the south-east, almost daring myself to tread my old paths. I was older, although only by a few years, and nobody looked past my profession. In fact, they trusted me because of it.

And so when I saw her sitting, laughing, with the fragile boy and the other woman, I had no inkling of who she was. She was tanned, happy, her hair glossy and her posture strong and confident. Yes, I caught her stares, but I was busy, and used to crushes. I began to feel uneasy as she continued to watch me, but I still didn't get it, didn't understand.

That night, I really only glimpsed one figure in the seconds after I stopped the car, got out to see if I had really had two bodies fly across the bonnet. Her long curly hair had been spread across the wet tarmac. The other body lay in the shadows, and I could only see black boots and blood.

Later, the day she left, as she sat in front of me, with that long dark hair curling over her shoulders, the sunlight on her face and her brown eyes serious, and she told me who she was. She told me why, and she told me what she wanted me to do.

CHAPTER FORTY-FIVE

After Dove watched Meredith walk right out of the police station with her solicitor, the DCI called a quick briefing. "I want her back in. Her smart-arse, sweet-smelling solicitor might have gotten her out, but we are pretty sure we have our perpetrator. We're waiting on the DNA confirmation from the lab. There was a minor fire there last night — luckily, no damage to our case exhibits — but it's caused a pile-up while they sort themselves out."

Lindsey ticked off points on her fingers: "Meredith has no alibi for either crime scene. She was not anywhere near Dorset when she said she was. She also slipped up on when she said she last saw Cora — who has been impersonating her dead sister, Amber since 2019 — in August."

Josh was reading notes from his iPad, and added, "I made a quick dash to the hospital because Mark has recovered some of his memories. He is now adamant he and Rebecca were meeting Meredith and Amber on Saddle Bridge, that Amber was the only one to contact Meredith, and he was surprised to see two other men along for the ride. He said they weren't introduced, but of course we know those were Neil and Max."

"Cora recognized Meredith as the woman who killed her sister in the hit-and-run, but because she also had something to lose, perhaps she wouldn't have pursued it, if she hadn't then met two people whom the three bridges crash had hurt so badly."

Dove joined in, as the whole team began to focus on the evidence. "Cora recognized and became obsessed with Meredith, and befriending Rebecca and Mark changed her goals once again. The only explanation is that she was fighting for justice and the truth, not only for her sister, but for her friends, too. Rebecca and Mark both lost loved ones in the 2019 crash, and if Cora discovered the truth, that Meredith was involved in both the crash and the hit-and-run, it meant she was perhaps doubly guilty in Cora's eyes?"

"And Meredith promised to tell them the truth that night. Mark says he remembers that she confessed, told them all about the night of the motorway crash, but insisted she was only responsible for the hit-and-run." Josh tapped his screen. "Mark's given us an updated statement, so I would say we've got more than enough to bring her back in until we get the DNA from the lab."

DI Blackman nodded, but the DCI raised a hand. "Before we bring her back in, I want a watertight case. We've been ridiculed in the press this week. I've got management breathing down my neck, and if we arrest Meredith Brown pending charging her, we can't afford to screw it up. Go and get everything you can, and I want her brought back in tonight. No mistakes."

"What happened with Louise, boss?" Dove asked.

"She's in the clear. She did go out for painkillers. But later, she panicked when she realized that she was out during the critical time frame, and didn't say anything." He smiled. "Since Kirstie neatly dropped her in it, she confessed, and I've checked the cameras, plus the BP service station CCTV. It checks out. She was close, and the right timing when it was all kicking off, but she wasn't involved."

Wearily, the team began to sift through the case file once more. Dove lingered on the witness statement from the hit-and-run, willing the lab to call.

CHAPTER FORTY-SIX

Amber spoke about her sister in our sharing circle at the Retreat, and her sparkle faded as she spoke. She never mentioned the accident, just said she had lost her sister and was trying to move forward, slowly and painfully, in the wake of this.

She reminded me a little of another woman earlier in the year, one who had concerned me enough to send one of my little cards, just as a reminder who had the upper hand. Gaia was smart, and funny. And strong. And I couldn't get inside her head. I wouldn't have wanted to, if she hadn't seen me talking to one of the other guests. I was feeling cruel, and this guest, I can't even remember her name, was so pathetic.

Gaia came in as I was talking, summed up the situation and gave me a cold stare. I was only talking, but not in a way I would speak to guests in public, grinding away their self-esteem. It was a momentary loss of control, my other self, fighting to escape, and I regret it. Later, I considered how to play it. Gaia never said a word to Louise, but she did take me aside and let me know she considered my bullying unacceptable.

I sweated it out once she had left, sent the card just . . . well, just because I wanted to. I think Gaia had secrets, too, and her strength bothered me. But she never came again and never made any complaint, so I was free. Until the August retreat, when it all fell apart. Was Gaia herself a warning shot?

233

"I don't think so. Maybe I just look like someone you know. They say everyone has a double somewhere, don't they?" I laughed, but even to my own ears, it sounded high and nervous.

We were alone by the lake that evening, when she finally told me. She tapped a finger on her lips, eyes narrowed, sun bouncing off her hair. "I know where we've met. It's come back to me. Normally, I have a really good memory." Her smile was sweet, reflective. "You were driving the car that night, weren't you? You were driving the car and you killed all those people, and then you killed my sister. That's a lot of people dying because you were stupid, isn't it? What do you think we should do about it?"

I think I recognized something in her eyes then, not because I had seen her before for that brief moment, but something deeper. She was like me, and for the first time, I felt a chill of fear dancing across my body, making my stomach clench and my breathing fast. She was like me, and I have always done whatever I want to get what I want.

CHAPTER FORTY-SEVEN

While they waited, DI Blackman pulled Dove aside. "Are you okay?"

"Fine, just pissed off with waiting," she told him. The tension in the room was palpable.

He changed the subject, speaking quietly. "The promotion we talked about a few months ago is a good idea, Dove. Don't stop being ambitious and doing what you are good at. Your sister was an astute businesswoman, wasn't she? Forgive me if I'm speaking out of turn, but from what you have told me, she lived a very full life. You should, too." He smiled, grey eyes soft, concerned.

Dove felt a flicker of surprise, which she tried to keep hidden. It wasn't like him to give personal advice. She had always thought there was a lot about her boss he kept hidden. The sadness, the privacy, the apparent lack of partner or friends, the obsession with pushing his body to the limit in his ultra-marathons. "Okay," she said softly, as her phone buzzed in her pocket.

She excused herself, moving away to answer the call, slipping out into the corridor, away from the mass of bodies waiting for the lab results. The smell of sweat and coffee was making her feel sick.

"Do you know what?" Delta's confident, clear voice.

"Not until you tell me. How's Ren?"

"Yeah, she's okay. Going through Gaia's things seemed to help a bit. And she said you were right, about not having to throw anything out."

"And you?"

"Fine. I'm fine. Although . . ."

"What?" Dove tried to focus on her niece, but she was watching the activity back in the office, straining to hear the conversation. Was there a quick burst of activity?

"I know it's crazy, but I keep worrying that Dad . . . *Alex* might get in touch if he saw the news about Gaia. Like, would they have told him? He might have read about the accident online, or the prison guards might have told him. Mum wouldn't be able to cope."

"He isn't allowed to get in touch after last time. He might have read about it, but there is no reason why he should." She would personally make it her mission to get the appropriate authorities to come down on him like a landslide, if he tried any contact after what happened last time.

"I suppose."

"Why are you suddenly thinking about this now, anyway? What's happened?" Dove asked gently.

"Nothing really . . . It's just, you know six months since she died and, I just miss her, Dove, I really do. I don't know why I'm freaking out now."

Dove heard the break in her niece's voice and thought this was less about Alex, more about Gaia. "We all do, and it's totally okay to freak out, however it happens. Cry, throw stuff, scream, whatever makes it hurt a little bit less."

Delta was sniffing a bit, but her tone lightened. "Yeah, you're right. See you tomorrow." A hesitation. "Love you!"

"Love you too."

She went back in, expectant, but there was still no news. "Steve, I'm going to get some fresh air. Do you want anything from the van?"

"I'm good, thanks. I'll wait it out," he told her, face strained and arms folded as he leaned against the wall.

As Dove walked out the door, taking a deep breath of the autumn air, feeling the warmth of the sun, she forced herself to relax a little. The DNA would be a match, she was sure of it. And her brother-in-law was in prison, and he would stay there, serving out his sentence. He couldn't get in touch with his family. She had seen to that already.

She was debating whether to grab some food from the van, when she saw a familiar face hovering near the station entrance. The woman had long platinum blonde hair, which floated in the breeze.

"Tanya?" Dove called, making her way across the car park towards Neil Barnes' girlfriend.

"DC Milson." Tanya half-smiled in recognition. She seemed nervous, and she was twisting the strap of her handbag around and around her fingers.

"I'm so sorry for your loss. How are you?" Dove asked gently.

"I . . . Pretty crap if I'm honest," Tanya admitted, and now Dove was closer, she could see the heavy make-up couldn't disguise her grief-stricken face. She stood staring, silent and ill at ease.

"Is there something I can help you with?" Dove suggested.

Tanya blinked hard and squared her shoulders. She slipped a hand into her bag and pulled out an envelope. "This came in the post this morning. It's from Max Carter." A tear escaped, and she brushed it roughly away, smudging her eyeliner. "He wanted me to give it to the police, so you would know what really happened on the bridge, and from before."

CHAPTER FORTY-EIGHT

Ten minutes later, with a cup of hot sweet tea on the table in front of her, Tanya was sitting opposite Dove and Steve. She had been adamant she wanted to sit with them while they listened to the audio files on the memory stick, which had been delivered to her home.

"This note came in the envelope, too." She pushed a small piece of paper across the table. "I already listened to some of it, but I couldn't keep going . . . He wanted you to have it, so I got my sister to watch the kids while I brought it down."

Steve inserted the memory stick into his laptop, while Dove reread the note:

> *Tanya,*
> *Sorry. Listen to what's on the stick, then take it to the police.*
> *Don't tell anyone else you've got it.*
> *Max*

They waited for DI Blackman to join them before Steve pressed play on the audio files. Dove looked at Tanya, who nodded. "It's okay." She pulled out a tissue and blew her nose hard.

A voice Dove recognized immediately as Max Carter's started to speak:

"This is Max Carter, and this is what really happened on 19 September 2022, up on the bridge. Don't bother trying to find me, because you won't. I'm only doing this because I saw in the news Neil is dead, and I don't want Tan and the kids to think he was anything but a good bloke trying to help out his mates. Tan, I can only imagine how upset you are, but give this to the police after you've listened to it and know that Neil loved you and the kids more than anything. He tried really hard to turn his life around for you, but he made mistakes like we all do."

Tanya was crying properly now, but every time one of the police officers suggested she sit out, or call someone to be with her, she was fiercely insistent they would continue. With some difficulty, Dove turned her attention away from the woman's distress, and back to what Max's recorded voice was saying.

"I'm not a bloody saint, but me and Neil would never have been part of this if it wasn't for Cora. It seemed to make sense at the time, but after a few weeks, months, I began to think, hang on, me and Neil didn't do anything wrong. We could have just gone to the police and blown her cover, but we didn't.

"But she seemed to be doing the right thing, and hell, it didn't hurt anyone. She also seemed to need us, the only friends she had from the crowd we used to hang out with. She said more than once that me and Neil were the only people she could truly trust. That was why we agreed to back her up on the bridge. I do remember Neil was a bit funny about it to start with, but he came good.

"Why the bridge? Because Cora thought it was important to lay the ghosts to rest. Now she had put it all together, past and present, met Rebecca and Mark, she saw this as a kind of retribution maybe. Cora drove up in the car she rented off Neil. I did ask her why she was at that shitty pub, and she just shrugged it off and said she needed to keep everything separate from her daily life. That was weird though, wasn't it? But it made sense in her head. I mean, her car needed fixing, so she came to me; she needed a rental car, so she went to Neil. All the players in the game.

"At that point, as her face got tight and her fists clenched, I did start to wonder about her mental state. Was this the end game or the start of something else? She had left the driver's side car door open, and she was standing opposite Meredith now.

"No, I wouldn't say what happened next was premeditated in any way at all. I said to Neil beforehand that Cora was really brave to risk everything, but she had become so fixated on it, like she owed it to Amber, like it would make everything right. She had become obsessed with getting justice, and went on about karma and positive energy and stuff.

"I don't know who made the first move. We were all edgy, and you could feel that much emotion in the air. Neil to Cora to get back in and we should just go home, that she'd got what she came for. She ignored him and he just went right over and got into the passenger seat, shut the door and got him phone out, like he was taking himself out of the game. He was right in a way. What were we achieving?

"So, they were still talking it out, tears and apologies, until the point Cora asked Meredith about Amber, about the hit-and-run, and I saw Mark and Rebecca just stand with their mouths open. It got me then that she hadn't told them. They were there for closure about the 2019 motorway crash, and I do genuinely think Cora wanted to help them, to get them to move on with their own lives, I guess. But really, Cora was focused on the hit-and-run after the crash, and that was when things turned nasty. Meredith, shit her face . . . She was angry, so crazy angry, and there something else in her eyes, like she was truly losing it. She was standing with one hand on her hip, the other on the open car door.

"Suddenly we were all scuffling like kids, shouting. We were close to the edge, and I had my back against the railings, was aware of traffic on the road below. The railings aren't high in that place, on that bridge, just about my shoulder height really, enough so you would have a tough time climbing over. It's not like anyone was thrown over, we were all just arguing, and somehow, they were just in the wrong place . . .

"That was when I realized: Cora was shouting something about the car, pushing the others away, and it seemed to happen in slow motion. The car shot forward with a jerk, a real bunny hop, revving, pinning one of the women, and the others were trying to help her.

"*I could see Neil's face behind the windscreen on one side, Meredith's on the driver's side. The passenger door was open now and I was shouting at him to do something to stop it, when the top rail suddenly gave way behind us, and they just fell. I nearly went with them, but I managed to fling myself sideways at the last minute.*

"*Hell, nobody pushed them, they just fell. I don't think Meredith could have ever planned it, and the more I replay the events in my head, the more I think she was maybe trying to drive away, but something went wrong. Or perhaps not. The jerk when the car moved; maybe she stalled it? Or was just so angry she wasn't thinking straight at all. Had she taken something before we met up? It would make sense.*

"*Anyway, I was on the end of the group, next to Mark, and I grabbed onto the next section of fencing to save myself as the top rail on the next section just broke away. I couldn't believe it. It came loose like it wasn't fixed in place. Someone screamed, it was a woman, and I don't know what happened next, but the car stopped rolling, although the engine was still running, it was dead quiet and they were gone.*

"*I looked into Meredith's eyes, as she sat behind the wheel, and I just turned and ran. I'm not proud of myself at all, but I just ran so fucking fast. Straight through the woods and into town by the back roads. It was really important to get out of there straight away, because with my record, I knew I would have been blamed. And they were dead.*

"*I was sure they must be dead. As I got to the end of the bridge I heard the car engine noise change and I knew Meredith was following me.*

God, Dove thought. What a terrible mess, all growing out of the need for justice, for accountability, for closure. Mark and Rebecca were the truly innocent victims, but Cora, Max and Neil had also, however flawed they were as people, apparently been trying to do the right thing for people they loved. Only one person on that bridge had been a truly malevolent person. The damage Meredith Brown had done to people's lives was almost incalculable, and what may have started as an accident, a genuine, thoughtless accident all those years ago, had led to murder and devastation.

The audio files ended with a chilling final word from Max, his voice rough with emotion, repeating his earlier words:

"I don't know where Meredith is now, but I do know she's twisted enough to put the blame on me. I've got a record, haven't I? But I promise when I went to the bridge, I was just supporting a mate, helping Cora to get the justice she needed. I hope you get Meredith and put her away for life, because Neil was alive in the car with her when they drove away from the bridge."

Back in the office, Dove and Steve walked into a buzz of activity and high-fives.

"We've got three DNA matches to Meredith!" Lindsey told them, face red with triumph. "Bloody hell, we've got her."

"Let me see the report." Dove scrabbled to find the case file, and opened the latest email from the lab. "Shit, a match to both scenes, and with Max Carter's testimony, plus the watch, Meredith Brown is going down. The CPS are going to love that one, it's practically cut and dried."

"We'll send a car down to pick her up," DI Blackman said, satisfaction evident in his voice.

The buzz of a job well done made the office noisier than usual. Other cases were still in progress, and officers seconded onto this one would be hastily redeployed, but just now, Dove stood with Steve, enjoying the moment.

"Good thing your bruises have gone down, or it would have looked a bit odd in the wedding photos." Steve grinned at her.

Lindsey slapped Dove on the back. "Get the hell out of here and get ready for the party, girl. We'll see you at the bar!"

Dove moved slowly away from them, heading for the door, smiling, shaking her head. A tiny part of her wanted to be here when the call came in to say Meredith had been picked up, but most of her heart and mind were already focusing on celebrating something very different. She could almost feel Gaia watching her, giving her a wink. *"Leave the bloody job behind for once."*

"You're one to talk," she whispered back, as she let the door bang shut behind her, and started down the stairs. All the way home, her sister stayed, bright and warm, an image in her head, in her heart.

CHAPTER FORTY-NINE

This is it. My flight to Sydney via Singapore booked, and I have spent the last few hours tying up loose ends while the police try and find other things to charge me with.

It's pretty unfortunate that the police have been so tenacious, but my solicitor assures me they need more evidence, or the CPS won't even bother, and it is all hearsay and fairy tales. Coincidences can be explained away. Accidents, always accidents, but some people are just unlucky.

I slipped up with my watch, but they can't prove I was wearing it.

I've bagged a tourist visa, and a good job at a city-centre wellness retreat. Time to shed another skin. It was easy to get a fake passport, a new identity, off the internet, and I'm going via France by ferry, then to Paris by train, and finally I'll catch my flight from Paris.

I'm going before the police can get it together, because in this case, I have a bad feeling they will. Getting a fake ID back in 2019 and trawling through the dark web probably wasn't strictly necessary, but I was on the brink of running away then. I realized I didn't need to, but everything stayed in place, ready to put into action at a moment's notice.

I enjoyed it, my walk on the dark side. The prickle of danger, the sickness and darkness of some peoples' fantasies was interesting, and made me feel less alone. It was expensive, too, the ID, but I've worn this version of myself out, and it's time to be someone brand new. Merry turned into Meredith, and now it's time to leave her behind completely. I know I'll be tempted to visit the dark web again. I'm . . . intrigued. And I need that buzz.

The sun is shining through the barn windows, making the dust dance and highlighting the dirty plates in the sink. A parting gift for my sanctimonious housemates, whenever they return. One will never return, but I don't regret killing her. I do regret I had to do it in such a hurry, and ultimately screw up. But as soon as the words were out of her mouth, I knew I had to stop her talking.

"Hey Meredith, why did you come back on the Friday night?"

"What do you mean?"

"I heard you come in and I saw you in the kitchen. I'd just come out of the shower, and I thought we had intruders."

"Oh, I forgot my bag."

The look, as it clicked slowly into place. "I saw you right after Kirstie said Louise's car came back. But Louise said she never went to get any painkillers, and I wondered why Kirstie was lying. I bet the police did too. Then I figured maybe they were both concerned it made her look guilty. But she isn't, is she? Did you take her car, Meredith?"

"Why would I take her car? I have my own."

"Maybe you drove over to Saddle Bridge." Her eyes were hard, almost fearful. "Did you go to Saddle Bridge? Were you there when those three guests were killed?"

We stared at one another, her halfway out of the door, me near enough to touch her, holding tightly with both hands to the rope I used to tie my yoga mat together.

"I found your other phone, so I know you were planning to meet them. We've been friends, and I didn't want to believe it . . . Why, Meredith? Just why?"

I killed her quickly and took her to the lake. She was tiny and it was dark. Not so very difficult. I was in full control of the situation and after my fuck-up on the bridge, it felt good to be back on top.

I banish Tina's ghost to the shadows, pull a rucksack over my shoulders and walk out of the door, excited for my new life.

On the curb, two police cars wait to receive me.

EPILOGUE

Delta was finishing her document with a flurry of fingers on keyboard. Her long hair was twisted into a knot on the top of her head, and she wore a white crop top and red leggings. Her long legs were curled awkwardly underneath her on the sofa.

Dove smiled fondly at her. "Did you decide about the clubs? Is that what you're doing?"

"Yes. You and Mum are right; I need to learn business before I run one. The managers are going to run them. Mum and I spoke to the accountant and there's plenty of money coming in. In fact, both clubs make such a good profit, I've decided to invest some in a flat down the coast. Bollo's dad is a property developer, and he's made a killing."

Dove laughed, genuinely laughed, and enjoyed Delta's surprise. "You are so like Gaia. She would have been proud." The pain was still there, the loss, the memories, but slowly, Dove was beginning to see that her sister was still with them in so many ways.

"Do you think so?" A shadow of sadness crossed Delta's face, but her smile of pleasure lit up the darkness.

"I'm sure of it. Even with your illegal internet scam, which I do *not* want to hear anything more about, please . . . but seriously, Delta, she's given you a gift. Use it well."

Later, when Delta had departed to meet Bollo and Eden was out with a friend, little Elan asleep upstairs, they sat in silence for a long time.

"Do you remember how Gaia would never sit with us on the sofa?" Dove said suddenly, as she looked at the empty armchairs flanking the fireplace.

"Yes. She was always happiest on her own, keeping her distance," Ren agreed.

"I miss her so much."

"Me too, but I see Delta and Eden, and even Elan, and I see Gaia in them, and I see her in you, and in my own reflection when I look in the mirror in the morning."

Ren said nothing more, simply leaned her head against Dove's shoulder, as they sat together in the tidy room, her breath warm on her sister's bare arm, her dark curly hair mingling with her sister's long coarse mane. Warm and alive. Dove shut her eyes and held her close.

Eventually Ren lifted her head, kissed her cheek, and smiled. "We'd better go to sleep. You're getting married tomorrow!"

* * *

Dove had never wanted a wedding, had never dreamed of white dresses and diamond rings, even as a kid. But somehow, the long lacy charity shop discovery in vintage cream and gold, a bunch of marigolds and the burnt orange ferns from Ren's autumn garden, plus her family and friends, made her feel like a wedding was what she had wanted all along.

Quinn was in a dark suit, hair a little messy as though he had been running his hands through it. His green eyes sparkled, mouth curving into a soft smile as she slipped the ring on his finger.

A quick service in Abberley church, and then they walked across the road to the modern boutique hotel. A new opening for the area, its stark architecture in dark wood and glass shaped like an upturned fishing boat.

Dove and her husband led the wedding party through the building, and out onto the terrace area. This was why she had chosen the venue, Dove thought, as the cold sea breeze caught her dress, her hair, making her gasp.

The huge glass wall accessing the beach had doors which were slid partially open, to allow the indoor setting to reach outside. As the buffet was being set up, and the BBQ on the decking outside started to smoke, she and Quinn walked out barefoot onto the beach.

The storm clouds had been gathering over the sea since early morning and as they walked hand-in-hand, the rain started. It was still unusually warm and muggy for October, and as the light rain soaked her dress, her hair, Dove grabbed Quinn's hand and pulled him down to the sea.

"You're crazy!" her husband said, but he was laughing.

They stood knee-deep in the sea, gasping at the chill of the swirling indigo waters, and Dove pulled a single orange flower from her bouquet and threw it out as far as she could. It landed in a sunbeam, and as suddenly as it had begun, the rain stopped. Far above them the clouds started to break apart, letting the light back in. The storm danced overhead, growling and threatening, before moving further inland. Dove trailed a hand in the water as the sea swirled and glittered around them.

She didn't need to explain to Quinn that the flower was for Gaia, just as she didn't need to explain the reason her face was soaked with tears as well as the rain, and that was one of the reasons she loved him.

They clung together for a long moment, before moving back towards the music and the laughter, tracking a path up the stony beach, hands clasped, bare feet cold on the pebbles.

Delta was popping corks, Ren and Eden fussing over the cake, topped with marigolds and sugar craft surfboards. Further over, on the next beach, an old man, sitting next to his shopping trolley, onto which he had piled all his belongings, turned and winked at her, before pulling out his instrument and starting to play some jazz. Her mum and dad were playing with Elan.

Dove took one last look back, the music floating on the sea breeze around her as she narrowed her eyes to catch a last glimpse of Gaia's flower floating gently away with the ebb and flow of the tide.

THE END

ACKNOWLEDGEMENTS

I can't believe Dove has finished her fifth outing. Thank you so much to everyone who has supported me throughout this series, and my others. This is book nineteen! How did that happen?

Massive thanks as always to the readers, the book bloggers, the bookstores and the libraries. Without you my books would never fly so far or reach so many readers across the world. I have been lucky enough to meet so many of you in person this year at events including CrimeFest, which remains one of my favourite weekends of the crime calendar.

Thank you to my wonderful agent, Kate Nash at the Kate Nash Literary Agency for supporting me when things are tough and celebrating with me when we get a little win!

Big thanks to Joffe Books for publishing the Detective Dove Milson series and the Ruby Baker series. I learn something new with each book I write and am fortunate to have the most incredible editors.

Thank you also to cover designer, Nebojša Zorić, who has done the most amazing job of creating the beautiful covers for the entire series.

Thank you to the experts who help with each book, especially Eric Storey, who never fails to answer my police procedural questions, my paramedic friends, and all who have contributed to this series. I must point out that any errors in these areas are entirely down to me twisting the plot to meet the fictional needs of my characters, and not to my professionals. Big thanks also to Graham Bartlett for his invaluable recent advice on police procedural!

A note for my readers on geography, because I know many of you ask where the Detective Dove Milson books are set: Abberley, Lymington-on-Sea, the roads and surrounding areas are all fictional, but loosely based on the south coast UK, where I now live.

Thank you to Sue Mills, for telling me about her cult experience.

To my fellow authors, thank you so much for your friendship and support — when times are tough it is so amazing to know we can share both good and bad times! Special mention to my writing buddy and Blue Pier Creative retreats and workshops co-host, Lisa Brace for being just amazing and always on our WA chat for some criminal planning.

Thank you to my wonderful family, who have supported me throughout my writing journey — and who keep asking if Dove Milson will be on TV lol. I hope one day, the answer might be yes, but in the meantime, thanks for keeping my dreams alive!

To everyone in the day job, the greens and the reds, you are all amazing, and although the shifts are long, we have the best times, and I learn so much every day.

Finally, I do hope you will enjoy this Dove Milson book, and the four preceding it. It has been a lot of fun, and a lot of hard graft to get the series down. It's tough to write when things are not going well, but we struggle onwards, and your reviews, comments and encouragement keep me going.

I invite you to continue this journey with me and connect on the socials (I'm always up for a chat). I am also unbelievably excited to be bringing you two new psychological thrillers in 2024, plus the third book in the Bermuda Mysteries, and lots more TikTok book hauls.

To stay up to date with all my latest news and be the first to know about new releases, please hit the follow button on Amazon, and BookBub!

With thanks and gratitude for all you do,

D.E. White x

www.dewhiteauthor.com

TikTok: tiktok.com/@d.e.whiteauthor
Facebook: facebook.com/DaisyWhiteAuthor/
Instagram: instagram.com/d.e._white_author/

THE JOFFE BOOKS STORY

We began in 2014 when Jasper agreed to publish his mum's much-rejected romance novel and it became a bestseller.

Since then we've grown into the largest independent publisher in the UK. We're extremely proud to publish some of the very best writers in the world, including Joy Ellis, Faith Martin, Caro Ramsay, Helen Forrester, Simon Brett and Robert Goddard. Everyone at Joffe Books loves reading and we never forget that it all begins with the magic of an author telling a story.

We are proud to publish talented first-time authors, as well as established writers whose books we love introducing to a new generation of readers.

We have been shortlisted for Independent Publisher of the Year at the British Book Awards three times, in 2020, 2021 and 2022, and for the Diversity and Inclusivity Award at the Independent Publishing Awards in 2022. We won Trade Publisher of the Year Award at the Independent Publishing Awards 2023 and were shortlisted for Publisher of the Year at the RNA Industry Awards in 2023.

We built this company with your help, and we love to hear from you, so please email us about absolutely anything bookish at feedback@joffebooks.com

If you want to receive free books every Friday and hear about all our new releases, join our mailing list: www.joffebooks.com/contact

And when you tell your friends about us, just remember: it's pronounced Joffe as in coffee or toffee!

ALSO BY D.E. WHITE

DETECTIVE DOVE MILSON MYSTERIES
Book 1: GLASS DOLLS
Book 2: THE ICE DAUGHTERS
Book 3: THE ABBERLEY BEACH MURDERS
Book 4: STONE COLD KILLING
Book 5: THE FALL

RUBY BAKER MYSTERIES
written as Daisy White
Book 1: BEFORE I LEFT
Book 2: BEFORE I FOUND YOU
Book 3: BEFORE I TRUST YOU